The Glass Dolphin

ROMANTIC WOMEN'S FRIENDSHIP FICTION

FIVE ISLAND COVE
BOOK NINE

JESSIE NEWTON

feel good fiction
ELANA JOHNSON

ISBN-13: 978-1-63876-253-9

Chapter One

Julia Harper couldn't keep herself from glancing over to Liam Coldwater every few seconds. She told herself to stop at least a dozen times before Laurel leaned over and whispered, "What is with you and him?"

Julia couldn't answer, so she stuffed another piece of bruschetta into her mouth. She'd eat the whole platter if she had to. She wasn't going to answer any questions about Liam tonight. It would be great if she could stop looking at him.

She focused on a conversation Alice was having with Kristen, but she knew few of the players in the conversation, and it didn't hold her interest. She felt the weight of a gaze on her face, and she once again looked across the living room, past the dining room table, and into the kitchen, where Liam stood.

He'd been talking to Arthur Rice and Duke Grover, but they'd both dispersed. Liam stood there alone, and their eyes met. The entire Appetizer Hour fell away, and while Julia felt certain someone very nearby was talking to her, she couldn't hear them. She couldn't look away from the handsome Liam Coldwater.

At the same time, shame burned through her chest, and the embarrassment of their encounter late last week forced her to drop her head and break the connection.

The conversations surrounding her continued, and she looked up as Alice's son joined the table. They all started adjusting to make room for the extra chair, and Julia smiled at the young man. He was a good-looking kid, and he reminded Julia so much of her own sons.

"May I speak to you for a moment?" The man's voice in her ear hummed, lighting Julia with a fire that burst into a white-hot inferno. She didn't have to turn to see who it was, but her chin dropped in Liam's direction. The scent of his breath—like raspberry jam and mint—and the warmth of his skin filled her from head to toe in a single inhale.

She took the napkin from her lap and put it on her plate, though she'd only eaten half of her food. "I'll be right back," she managed to say.

"I'll save your spot," Laurel said. Julia bore the weight of several pairs of eyes as she faced first the kitchen. Liam stood in the direction of the front door, and he made the choice for them by taking her hand and tugging her in that direction.

She sucked in a breath at the electricity flowing from his arm and into hers, and she wasn't sure if she wanted him to feel that too or not. Her track record with dating the past couple of years hadn't been good, and she'd come to terms with healing herself before bringing someone new into her life. If she ever did.

Liam said nothing, and the party continued behind them as they went outside. It had been raining when Julia had arrived with Tessa and Maddy, and a steady drizzle still covered Five Island Cove.

He released her hand as the door closed behind them, and Julia wrapped her arms around herself. She wanted him to speak first, because he needed to explain why she'd caught him in a lie.

Liam continued down the four steps to the sidewalk, but Julia stayed on the porch, under the eaves and out of the rain. He paced to the end of the sidewalk before he turned back to her. "I'm sorry," he called across the distance to her.

Part of her wanted him to lower his voice. Alice's neighbors would surely come investigate the source of the thing disturbing their holiday dinners. She glanced around, a sense of romanticism entering her bloodstream. What woman didn't want a man to proclaim his love for her to the world?

He's not doing that, she told herself. They'd been on one date—a fantastic, amazing date. Julia had even given herself permission to kiss him should he make the move when he dropped her off.

He hadn't, but they'd had another evening planned for a few days later.

"He's my son," Liam yelled now. "His name is Ian, and he's the best thing in my life. I don't tell women about him until things are more serious, because it's a lot." He threw his arms out to the side. "*I'm* a lot for them to take in. The job. The badge. The insane hours!" He yelled into the storm now, his head tipped back to the angry, gray sky.

Julia found him downright adorable. Strong, tall, sexy, and utterly charming. All adjectives she'd use for Liam Coldwater.

He looked at her, the ends of his longer, curly, blond hair dripping with the drizzle now. He looked absolutely tormented, and Julia wanted to erase all of that for him.

"So I didn't say anything. When you ran into us in the market, I froze. I didn't mean to lie, and I've hated myself every hour since." His arms dropped to his side, and that was almost the permission Julia needed to move. Like he was an air traffic controller, holding her at bay with his arms up, and now that they'd gone down, she could go to him.

She went down the steps deliberately, not looking at

them. Only him. She walked toward him slowly, the way she'd approach a scared dog she desperately wanted to get closer to. He let her come all the way to him, the silence between them only punctuated by rain.

Julia took his face in her hands, the warmth of his skin infusing into her chilled fingers. "I would've kissed you after our first date," she said.

Liam searched her face, those bright blue eyes filled with hope and sorrow at the same time. "I wanted to," he said, his voice scratching in his throat now. Probably because of the way he yelled everything else. "I was scared."

Julia pressed into him, and he finally put his hands on her waist, one of them moving up her back. "You?" she teased. "The tough, gruff police officer?" She studied his collar for a few moments before looking up into his face again. "I didn't think men like you got scared."

"Only of gorgeous women," he said. "After an amazing date which I never wanted to end."

"I have three sons," she said. "You could've told me."

He nodded as he held her close, close, close. Alice's neighbors sure were getting a show this morning. "I keep him close to the vest," he said. "He's an amazing kid, but I don't want him getting hurt again."

Julia noted the "again," and she'd like that story. Maybe not in the rain, with the whole neighborhood watching, but sometime. "Take me to dinner this weekend? Or are you working?"

"I'm off on Sunday until three," he said, his schedule right there in his mind. Julia had liked his intelligence when they'd first met, and again on their first date.

"So not dinner." She smoothed his collar down flat.

"Breakfast? Brunch? Lunch?" He listed them off, and Julia liked that it seemed like he wanted to see her. "All three?"

A smile touched her mouth, and Liam finally cracked too. He allowed a tame grin to spread his lips, and Julia fantasized about kissing him. Straightening that smile and really being able to taste the mint and raspberry jam on his lips.

"You can keep him to yourself for a while," Julia said. "Okay? I won't ask you to introduce me to him formally until you're ready." She regretted how quickly she'd reacted to the lies he'd told. She had a reason for that—a good reason—but he didn't know it. She hadn't told him about her cheating ex or the way she felt unworthy of the pure, undivided attention from others.

"Okay," he murmured. "Can I kiss you now?"

Julia put a couple of inches between them and looked him right in the eyes. "Out here? On the street in front of my friend's house?" She shook her head. "Mm, I don't think so, Liam."

He smiled again. "Not good enough for you?"

Julia had no doubt it would be the best kiss of her life. She didn't want to say that, though, so she shook her head. "I want to enjoy it," she whispered. "And I can't do that if I think everyone's watching us."

He looked over her shoulder to the house. "I think the curtains just fluttered, so you're probably right."

Julia backed up again, the idea of her friends watching her stand in this man's arms overwhelming for her. They separated, and she said, "I didn't block your number." Enough rain had accumulated in her hair that it ran down the side of her face. She brushed the droplet away, gave him a smile, and turned back to the house.

She ran on her tiptoes to the porch and out of the rain. Upon re-entering Alice's house, she caught Maddy herding several others back into the living room and dining room areas, and they'd definitely been spying on her.

A smile stuck in her chest, and she decided she didn't care. She still wasn't going to answer any questions about Liam Coldwater tonight.

She paused at the end of the hall, trying to decide if she should simply return to her seat at the table or try to get a little dryer in the bathroom. The living room had carpet, and Julia wiped another drop of water from her face as she took in the crowd there.

Alice wasn't in the living room anymore, and she came around the corner and into the kitchen. She held up a pale blue towel, effectively eliminating another decision Julia had to make. She went toward her, and Alice bustled her into the master bedroom.

"Thank you," Julia said. She took the towel and buried her face in it. Alice didn't ask any questions, but Maddy would. Tessa would. Eloise would.

She wiped her hair back and met Alice's eyes. "Did everyone run into your office?"

"Pretty much, yeah," she said with a smile. "Maddy yelled at all of them when you started backing up." She wore pure curiosity in her eyes, and Julia wanted to tell her. Maybe if she could get some other opinions, she'd know what to do about Liam.

At the same time, she knew what to do about Liam— keep seeing him. She didn't know if they'd work out, because her last relationship had ended when she'd left Nantucket. She wasn't like Tessa and Abe, who'd stayed together and then made plans to both settle in the cove. Maddy and Ben had done the same thing.

Julia hadn't been so lucky.

She actually did count herself as lucky, because she didn't want a man who wouldn't move heaven and earth to be with her. Liam had texted her seventeen times since their encounter in the food mart. He'd called three times, until she'd finally texted to tell him she didn't want to see him again.

Her phone buzzed now, and Julia finished drying her

hair before she checked it. *Breakfast on Sunday. Nine o'clock. Too early? I think we could try this place.* He'd included a link to the cutest little bistro she'd ever seen, and she smiled as she looked at the image that had populated with the text.

"Have you been here?" She showed Alice the phone, and she didn't mind that the woman took a few moments to obviously read the previous texts.

"Yeah." She grinned at Julia. "They have amazing breakfast. Fast too. Tell him to get a reservation if you're going on Sunday. They're busy on the weekends." She took Julia's towel and left her alone in the bedroom to confirm her date with Liam Coldwater.

Chapter Two

Madeline Lancaster noted the red SUV in her driveway the moment the RideShare car made the turn to join it. "Who's that?" she asked, swinging her attention to Ben.

"Don't know," he said. He usually wore a serious expression, and that didn't change. He smiled the most when with her, and sometimes she felt like she had to work hard to get that mouth to curl upward.

"Thanks." She tapped to pay the driver and got out of the car. Ben met her at the front of the car and took her hand. They went by the car, and she eyed it suspiciously. She wasn't expecting visitors, and her house on Rocky Ridge wasn't exactly on any tourist loops.

"It's a rental," Ben said. "Chelsea? Kyle?"

"They didn't say they'd be coming," Maddy said. Excitement leapt through her, because she'd love to see her kids today. She'd thought about ordering Thanksgiving dinner from a specialty market here on Rocky Ridge, and it would be perfect for a quiet meal at home for two. But she hadn't, because she could put together something easy for her and Ben.

Before the red SUV in the driveway, that was what her Thanksgiving was going to be. Just her and Ben, and maybe not even turkey.

She went into the garage as Ben held the door for her, the scent of sugar floating on the air. "Someone's definitely here," she said.

Ben darted in front of her and said, "Let me check it out." He went up the few steps to the landing outside the house and then opened the door. The sugar turned to frosting, and Maddy moved slowly as her boyfriend went inside the house fully.

The spring-loaded door slammed shut, sealing Maddy in the dark garage. She expected Ben to open it again immediately and tell her everything was okay, but he didn't. She couldn't hear any yelling or laughing beyond the door either, and she wasn't sure if she should go in or stay hidden in the garage.

She hadn't heard of much violent crime in Five Island Cove, especially out here on this furthest north island, but it was a holiday, and this less-populated part of the cove could be a good target for thieves for all she knew.

Maddy hadn't quite committed to entering the house

yet when the door opened again. Her daughter stuck her head out and said, "Mom, get in here and see what I made for you."

Joy exploded through Maddy, and she said, "Chelsea," before hurrying toward her. "What are you doing here?"

Her daughter laughed as Maddy flew into her arms, and they entered the house together. She hugged her tightly in the mudroom again, and then hung her purse over a hook while Chelsea went into the kitchen, chattering about how she was glad Maddy had a few staples here at the house.

Maddy followed her, coming to a complete stop when she saw Kyle and Bea there too. They stood in front of the countertop, both of them holding a sugar cookie the size of their hands. Chelsea skipped over to them and picked one up as well. She faced Maddy, whose heartbeat had started jumping like water droplets in a screaming hot pan.

The sugar cookies weren't shaped like turkeys or pumpkin pies, the way Maddy expected them to be. Fall leaves, maybe. Something with brown frosting, or oranges and yellows.

Kyle and Bea held pure white frosted cookies that Maddy suspected were wedding bells.

Chelsea lifted a treat that was frosted in fall colors— gold. It was a diamond ring, with blue lines for the facets of the gem on top of the gold ring, which had been cut out expertly.

"What is going on?" she asked. Ben entered the kitchen from around the corner that led into the living room, and he carried a black box.

Her breath caught in her throat.

"Madeline," he said, oh-so-serious as usual. "I'm in love with you. I'm crazy about you. I want to spend my life with you." He spoke in that sexy, *I'm-in-control-here* voice he often used, almost like he wasn't nervous at all. Maddy knew the man in ways others didn't, and she watched his pulse flutter in his throat.

He was nervous, and that only made Maddy's anxiety increase.

Ben arrived in front of her and got down on both knees. He slowly opened the black velvet box in his hand to show her the ring. He looked at it, and then up to her, and Maddy beamed down at him. "Will you marry me?"

Maddy looked over to her children and back at him. "Did you ask my kids to come here just for this?"

"Yes," he said. "I needed the help, and I figured you'd like to have them here for Thanksgiving. So I asked them to come."

Tears filled her eyes. "You're amazing." She loved him, and they'd been talking about marriage and weddings and an engagement for months now. She loved having him in her life, and in her children's lives.

"Is that Maddy-code for yes?" he asked. Those gorgeous blue eyes searched hers, and Maddy decided she didn't need to torture him.

"No," she said. "That's not Maddy-code for yes." She took his face in her hands and leaned down, almost touching her lips to his. "Yes, I'll marry you. No code necessary."

He kissed her, and Maddy kissed him back while her kids cheered. So many emotions ran through her, she couldn't categorize them all. She pulled away from Ben and held out her hand so he could slide the diamond onto her finger.

She'd never thought she'd wear another wedding band. She'd never thought she could love another man as much as she loved Ben. She'd never thought her journey in life would lead her here.

Ben stood and took her into his arms. "I love you, baby."

"I love you too," she whispered just before her squealing daughter arrived. Maddy hugged her again, laughing with her. Then she gripped Kyle in her arms, tears filling her eyes the way they had when he'd come to her for help when he and Bea's wedding venue had flaked on them.

She hugged Bea last, saying, "Thank you so much for coming."

"Of course," she said, grinning. "Kyle and I love the

cove."

"Where's my grandbaby?" Maddy asked, just now realizing that Knox wasn't anywhere to be seen.

"Asleep in his crib," Kyle said. "Come on, Mom. Try the cookies and tell us which ones you like best." He cast a look over to Chelsea, and Maddy sensed a competition between them. She took a bite of the wedding bell, and it was flaky and moist at the same time. There was a bit too much frosting for her liking, but she grinned at her son.

She took a bite of the diamond, and this frosting was too weak. She would never say so, and she said, "They're both amazing."

"Told you she wouldn't pick," Chelsea said. She rolled her eyes, and Maddy looked around for her fiancé.

"Where'd Ben go?" she asked.

He came into the kitchen then, another specialty market box marked with a Thanksgiving dinner, and she couldn't believe his level of detail. She wanted to kiss him again, this time without the audience, but she helped him get it unpacked and get the turkey breast into the oven to get heated.

"I'll do it," Bea said, coming to Maddy's side to take over. "Kyle, Knox is fussing. Will you go grab him for your mother?"

"Oh, this is Daddy," Chelsea said, lifting her phone as it rang. She bustled into the front of the house to take the call, and Maddy took the opportunity to grab Ben's hand and duck into her bedroom with him.

"You'll move in here permanently, right?" she asked as she closed the door behind him. He stayed with her sometimes now, but she wanted him to live here.

"Yes," he said. He took her into his arms again and lowered his head to kiss her. It started sweet and slow, but as things tended to do with Ben, it turned heated and passionate rather quickly. She tipped her head back, and he slid his mouth along the column of her throat.

"Thank you for getting my kids here," she said breathlessly.

"I'm regretting it a little," he admitted.

She grinned at him, feeling flirtatious and far younger than she actually was. "You want me to yourself."

He growled, his eyes meeting hers. "I want you to myself," he admitted before he claimed her mouth again.

When he pulled away, Maddy looked at him, not wanting to tease him anymore. She wanted him to *know*. "I want you to myself too," she said.

"When do you want to get married?" he asked, simply holding her now.

"Spring," she said. "Right here in the cove. I'll talk to Robin about the weather, but maybe April?" She looked at him. "Did you tell your parents?"

He nodded. "Showed them the ring last week."

Another rare smile came to his face. "She's going to drive you crazy at Christmastime."

Maddy groaned, but it was all in good fun. His parents were great, but his mother did like to shower Maddy in gifts, as if she needed another skin care kit. His brother worked for a huge skin care corporation, and his mother was simply regifting things.

"Mom," Kyle called, and Maddy pushed away from the door.

"Coming," she called. She looked at Ben again. "I'm so in love with you. You know that, right?" She needed him to *know*. She spoke her feelings quite often, actually. It was Ben who *showed* her how he felt.

"I know," he whispered. "I love you too."

She nodded and turned to go see her grandson. Then she'd call Robin and see about booking her to plan the spring wedding Maddy was going to have. She'd also need to talk to her boss, make sure she could have time off in the spring, and balance everything with The Glass Dolphin.

If Ben can get away from the Coast Guard, she told herself as she went out into the kitchen and saw her beautiful grandson. He kicked and squealed, and she laughed as she took him from her son.

Then you can make a spring wedding work with your job.

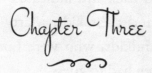

Chapter Three

When the doorbell rang, Kristen Shields dusted her hands against her apron and hurried out of her cramped kitchen. The only people who'd ring the doorbell were exactly the people she'd been baking for, and her pulse knocked against the back of her throat.

"Coming," she called. She very nearly tripped over the rug she'd put down between the kitchen and the doorway, but she managed to stay on her feet.

She opened the door to find Theo standing there with a man who looked very much like him.

His son.

Kristen hadn't met any of his children yet, and she wished she wasn't so nervous about doing so. Theo had made it clear his feelings for her wouldn't change based on his children's opinions, but Kristen still wanted to make a good impression.

"Terry, this is Kristen," Theo said. "Kristen, my oldest, Terry." He stepped back and indicated the woman there. "His wife, Cleo, and their kids, Marty and Violet." He beamed at his grandkids, who were both in their teens. Mid-teens, if Kristen had to guess.

"Hello," she said. "Come in, come in." She stepped back, pulling the door open further to make more room for them.

"It smells good," Terry said, and he smiled at Kristen as he entered first. "Dad said you were making cookies."

"So many cookies," Kristen said. "There's a whole bunch of them on the table. Help yourself."

The kids smiled at her politely as she entered, and once everyone was in, Theo put one hand on her hip and swept a kiss across her lips. "Did you make those snicker-doodles?"

"Yes, sir," she said, working hard not to giggle. The man loved cinnamon and sugar, and Kristen made snickerdoodles at least once a week, just for him.

Her cat, whom she'd named Sweetie, came down the hall to see what the fuss was about. Violet pulled in a breath and said, "Mom. Look at that cat."

Her mother turned and looked, and Kristen watched as she then exchanged a glance with her husband. "Is she allergic?" Kristen asked. "I can put her in her carrier in the bedroom." That wouldn't rid the apartment of cat hair, but Kristen had vacuumed meticulously last night and then again this morning.

She wanted everything to be perfect for today. She wasn't even sure why, only that she wanted Theo's kids to like her.

"It's fine," Cleo said. "Violet thinks she needs a cat."

The girl rushed toward Sweetie, who sat down as her eyes widened. She scooped the cat into her arms, and Kristen thought they'd be best friends before anyone else arrived. "She's so cute," Violet cooed.

"She might scratch your face off," Marty said.

"Martin," Terry said. "Don't antagonize your sister. Look." He pointed to one of the plates of cookies. "Kristen made thumbprints. Come get one, and then take these oatmeal raisin ones to your grandfather."

Marty, who was clearly older than Violet, did as his father said. Kristen's chest vibrated as he then bit into one of her thumbprint cookies. She'd made the raspberry jam and the apricot jam from scratch, and pure satisfaction poured through her when Marty leaned his head back and groaned. "This is so good," he said around a mouthful of cookie and crumbs and filling.

"They look so beautiful," Cleo said. "I love the thumbprint at Christmastime, but I'll take it any time of year." She picked up a cookie too, and she smiled as she took a bite of it. "Mm." Her eyes widened, and after she swallowed—she had more manners than her son, and Kristen liked them both immensely—she said, "Kristen, these are delicious."

"Thank you," she said. "I got the recipe from a fellow lighthouse wife." She rounded the counter as the timer on the oven went off. She bent and took out the last sheet of sugar cookies. By the time everyone arrived, they should be cool enough to decorate.

Theo had seven grandchildren, and Kristen had thought planning an activity for all of them to do made the most sense. Then she could finish dinner while they did that, and as snow had come to the cove for their not-on-Thanksgiving Thanksgiving dinner, herding them all outside wasn't an option.

To prove her point, Mother Nature drove a gust of wind into Kristen's windows, and they shook slightly.

"Rowena is here," Theo said. He started to get up, but his son told him to stay on the couch. He went to the door before anyone knocked or rang the bell and opened it. He went outside, and it didn't take long for the cold to leak in.

Terry started to laugh, his voice as big and as boisterous as his father's. He said some things Kristen couldn't decipher, and then he entered her condo again, this time with another woman.

They definitely belonged to each other, and to Theo, and Kristen put down her oven mitts and went to greet her. "Hello," she said, smiling with everything she had once more. "I'm—"

"Kristen Shields," Theo said, appearing at her side. His hand moved along her waist, and Kristen couldn't resist leaning into him. "This is my daughter Rowena. She's divorced, but she brought her daughter, Hailey. Where is she?"

"Sulking for a moment," Rowena said with a heavy dose of eye rolling. "I swear, I don't know how anyone survives seventeen-year-olds." She gave Kristen a smile that didn't seem as warm as Terry's or Cleo's, but Kristen could've imagined it. Or, Rowena could've been dealing with her own family situation and simply not felt like smiling at her father's new girlfriend.

Kristen told herself she and Theo weren't that new. They'd been dating for six months, and honestly, she couldn't believe it herself.

"What goes around, comes around," Theo said.

"Dad." Rowena scoffed and rolled her eyes again. "I don't need a lecture." She started to shed her coat, the awkwardness and tension in the room suddenly expanding to the rafters. Kristen looked over to Theo, and he didn't seem ruffled at all.

"She'll know where to come to?" Kristen asked.

"I'll go get her," Marty said. "I'll take these mint chip cookies, and she won't be able to resist them." He smiled at Kristen, the whole plate of double-chocolate chip cookies—yes, some of them were mint—in his hand. He ducked out of the condo, and Kristen sincerely hoped he'd come back with some cookies...and his cousin.

Rowena joined Cleo on the cusp of the kitchen and surveyed that spread. "Wow," she said, genuinely sounding surprised. "You said there would be cookies, but this is a *lot* of cookies." She didn't look at Kristen at all, but her brother and sister-in-law.

Kristen had made little labels for each kind by folding a small card in half and writing the variety of cookie on it. Some of them had themed plates that went with them, and she admired her cookie bar. Robin would be thrilled, and Kristen had snapped a few pictures before anyone had arrived.

"They're amazing," Cleo said. She pushed the last bite of a cowboy cookie—coconut, oatmeal, pecans, and chocolate chips—into her mouth. She didn't try to speak around it, but when she finished, she said, "I've eaten four already." She giggled, but Rowena didn't join in.

"Dad has the oatmeal raisin," Terry said.

Kristen hadn't joined them, and looking at them from across the room, she knew she didn't fit with them yet. They'd had their whole lives to mesh, to learn about one another, to become a family. She was the outsider here, though Theo still stood at her side.

Rowena lived in Connecticut, and her divorce had been finalized in the fall. Kristen knew women like her;

some of them were her own Seafaring Girls, and she knew Rowena likely needed time to heal. Having Kristen and Theo's relationship shoved in her face wasn't something she wanted.

Kristen stepped away from Theo and went around the people standing at the end of her peninsula. She started getting out the frostings she'd made and colored that morning and putting them on the dining room table. She'd already fitted in the leaf, and it still wouldn't hold them all for their dinner tonight.

Theo would probably have his sons set up the folding table that currently waited in Kristen's hallway, and they'd butt it up against the table to make one big long one.

"So," Rowena said as Kristen returned to the kitchen. "Are you and Daddy going to get married?" She took a bite of her shortbread cookie, which Kristen had decorated like a wreath, and looked at Kristen fully for the first time.

Panic shot through her chest, sending barbs into her ribs and fleshy organs.

"Row," Terry admonished. "Don't."

"What?" Rowena asked. "It's a valid question."

"One Dad said not to bring up." Terry gave his sister a pointed look and then Kristen a warm smile. "Don't mind her. She's—" The rest of his words got drowned out by a hearty shout from the direction of the doorway.

Kristen looked over to it and found Theo's final child

entering. Nelson carried more weight than his older brother, and he had far less hair. He'd shaved his head completely, but he wore a full beard. He laughed and practically yelled, "We're here!" as he held the door open for his four children to parade through.

Two boys and two girls entered, each of them wearing a bright red or green sweater. They were a festive bunch, and they were followed by their mother, who wore a red, white, and green plaid dress with a pair of four-inch, bright red heels.

Kristen had never met anyone like her before. Her blonde hair had been swept up into a ponytail high on her head, and she surveyed the condo like she could single-handedly transform it into a penthouse suite if given a few hours and a roll of duct tape.

"Nelson!" Terry boomed, and he went to hug his brother. Lots of greetings got exchanged, one where Nelson picked up Rowena and hugged her in a bouncing way while she loudly protested.

Kristen stood out of the way and watched Theo interact with his kids and grandkids. He glowed, as he obviously loved them all. He'd told her they hadn't gotten together like this in a few years, and he'd really been looking forward to having the holidays with his family back together again.

She swallowed as he finally looked at her. He held out his hand, and Kristen forced herself to move to stand

26

beside him. The door opened again, and Marty and another teenage girl entered.

"Ah, Hailey," he said. "Rowena's daughter. My son, Nelson, and his wife Victoria. Their kids, Raven, Fiona, Denver, and Dallas. The last two are twins." He beamed at the boys in matching red sweaters like they were the cutest things on the planet. They had good genes, and they were good-looking boys.

Kristen smiled at all of them, and said, "Welcome. Thanks for coming." She gestured to the cookie bar behind her. "It's great to meet you all, and I have dessert first today. We can decorate the sugar cookies when everyone's ready too."

All four of Victoria's children looked at her for permission to eat a cookie, and she gave it with a quick nod of her head. They then converged on the counter, nearly knocking Kristen out of the way.

She laughed as she moved into the safer recesses of the living room, Theo at her side. The noise from the kitchen only reached its current level when she held the luncheon for her girls here at the condo. She'd only done so once, because it was easier to meet at a restaurant. Then someone else cooked and cleaned up.

"They're great," she said.

Theo took her hand in his. "I think so too. Even Rowena. She'll come around."

Words gathered in Kristen's mouth, and she tried to

order the properly before they came out. She finally landed on, "You told them not to ask about our relationship?" She looked at him, searching those brilliant gray-blue eyes.

He suddenly looked nervous, and Theo never looked like that. "I didn't want it to be awkward for you."

"Why would it be awkward for me?"

"Because we haven't talked about it." He waved to one of the twins, who lifted a sandwich cookie Kristen had made from a boxed cake mix.

"Maybe we should," Kristen said, her voice dry and brittle.

Theo looked at her. "You want to get married?" He seemed genuinely surprised, and that sent a barb of uncertainty into Kristen's heart.

"Maybe," she hedged. "Do you?"

"To be honest," he said. "I—"

"Grandpa," Hailey yelled to him. "Get over here and look at this stained-glass cookie. It's amazing!"

Kristen edged away from him, the echo of his words in her ears. *To be honest. I—*

"Just a minute," he said to his granddaughter. But that only spurred her to groan and insist he come now, before Marty ate the artwork.

What came after that *I*? He what? He never wanted to get married again? He never thought he would? He liked things how they were?

Theo sighed amidst more insistence that he come join them at the cookie bar, and he said, "Be right back," and walked away.

Kristen stayed over by her electric fireplace, watching. Part of her mind whispered at her to *go join them. You can't be part of them if you stand over here.*

The other part really wanted to know what Theo was going to say. *Needed* to know.

Cleo met her eyes and gave her the tiniest gesture to get over there. Kristen would have to shelve her disappointment and rein in her imagination for now. Once Theo's children left, she'd ask him again. Oh, yes, she would, because she needed to know what the past six months had been, if anything, if it hadn't been building to a permanent, long-lasting relationship.

Chapter Four

Robin Grover needed more time to get used to, well, having her own free time. She'd dedicated so much of the last twenty years of her life to raising her children, and in more recent years, running her wedding planning business, that she wasn't used to unrushed lunches with her friends.

But the Saturday following Thanksgiving had provided her with that opportunity. Her eldest daughter, Mandie, had come home from college for the turkey festivities, but she was returning today.

Duke, Robin's husband, would be taking her and their younger daughter back to the city that evening. They'd stay over there—just the two of them—and return tomorrow afternoon. Robin would have the house to

31

herself—another luxury she'd given up years and years ago.

She sometimes didn't thrive in the quietness of a house without anyone else in it. Sometimes, she adored being able to make what she wanted to eat without consulting with anyone or worrying that they might not like it. Sometimes, she needed the silence to order her own thoughts and put her own life in order. But sometimes, it only reminded her of being alone—and Robin didn't like being alone.

"There you are," Alice said, and Robin blinked her way back to reality. Back to the present, where she sat on a plush bench in the lobby at The Glass Dolphin. She'd been the first to arrive for lunch today, but now she rose to her feet to hug one of her best friends.

Alice, in her fashionable slim-cut black slacks and a sweater with swirling black and white roses on it, embraced her back. "El says she's running late."

"When isn't she running late?" Robin asked, though she didn't mean it unkindly. "That inn is going to eat her alive." She pulled away from Alice and re-shouldered her purse so it wasn't slipping down her arm.

Alice wore concern in her expression, a similar vein of which ran through Robin. "She seems to love it, though," she said. "And she did just hire more help."

"Three managers," Robin acknowledged. "Plus her."

She looked out the wall of windows at the front of the restaurant. "I hope it gives her more time at home."

"I think it will." Alice turned to face the weather outside too. It hadn't snowed yet, but it would soon enough. Usually not until January, and it didn't stick for long, a fact Robin appreciated. Duke had to go out fishing every day, rain, snow, or shine, and she worried about him during the winter squalls.

He had a new boat now, however, and he'd been doing better than ever. Robin allowed a small smile to move through herself, erasing the tension in her muscles. This was an easy-going, Saturday afternoon lunch with her two best friends. She didn't need to be stretched so tight.

"Hey," Eloise said a couple of minutes later, breathless as she bustled into the restaurant. "I'm so sorry. I barely made the ferry off Sanctuary." She hugged Alice, who reassured her she wasn't late, and then she moved into Robin's arms.

"Mm, it's so good to see you," Robin said, squeezing Eloise. Both of her friends had dark hair and eyes, and Robin, as the only blonde there today, stood out among them. "How's Aaron? The girls?"

"Good," she said. "He's home this weekend, which almost never happens." Eloise stepped back, her smile glorious and her cheeks a bit pink, probably from the chill on the ferry ride from Sanctuary Island, which sat just north of Diamond, where her inn overlooked the world.

Alice stepped over to the hostess station while Robin stayed closer to Eloise. "How was dinner at his parents'?"

"Good," Eloise said with a note of falsehood in her voice. "I like his mom and dad."

Robin nodded. Her mother had spent the Thanksgiving holidays on the mainland, and Duke's parents lived in the Midwest. Robin hardly ever saw them, and her core family unit felt smaller than ever.

Her heart pinched once, and then she brightened as Alice turned toward them. "They're ready for us." She led the way, and all Robin had to do was follow. With every step, she reminded herself that she had more friends— good friends—than some people had family members.

They could've invited a dozen women to this luncheon—and they had. But everyone else had had plans, and Robin knew better than most that not everyone could attend everything. She took a seat on the bench next to Alice, and Eloise sat across from them in a chair.

The waitress introduced herself and handed each of them a menu she opened for them. The Glass Dolphin was fairly new to the cove, and they definitely catered to a high-end clientele.

That didn't normally include Robin, but she could come here with her friends for lunch and only order for herself. "Did the twins get back to the city?" she asked as she perused the salads. They had one here with roasted beets, goat cheese, and candied walnuts that made Robin's mouth water just thinking about it.

"They're not going back until tomorrow," Alice said. "They met up with some friends from high school and went to the beach today."

"It's cold for a beach day," Eloise said.

"Not when you're eighteen," Alice said wryly. She glanced at Robin. "Remember when we used to escape to the beach whenever we could? It didn't matter if the wind whipped our clothes off our bodies, we still went."

Robin smiled at the memories. So many of them marched through her mind, many of them with both Alice and Eloise in them. "I remember," she said. "I definitely feel the cold differently now."

"No kidding." Alice looked back at her menu. "Do you remember if we met up after going off to college?"

Robin startled at the question, because Alice didn't usually spend too much time in the past. She'd itched to leave Five Island Cove and go to her fancy law school in the city. She'd done just that too. She'd married a lawyer, and they'd had a big, beautiful home in the Hamptons. Right up until a handful of years ago, when she'd left the mainland, left her husband, and returned to her roots.

Robin cleared her throat. "I remember you didn't come home for the holidays," she said as casually as possible. She let her eyes roam the menu, but she wasn't reading any of the items. "At all. And then summer came, and you still didn't come back."

Alice met her eye, and Robin simply gazed back. "I remember missing you," Robin said next, her voice soft. "And then I met Duke, and I got sort of wrapped up in him." She offered Alice a small smile, and her friend reached over and gave Robin a side-squeeze.

That was all she needed to do, because Robin knew why Alice hadn't wanted to return to the cove. Even after she'd gotten married and had her twins, she'd rarely returned to Rocky Ridge, the northernmost island in the cove, where she'd grown up.

"I think I came back," Eloise said, drawing both Alice's and Robin's attention. "But I don't remember much."

Before Robin could answer, her phone zinged out the text notification that meant her mother had messaged. "That's my mom," she said with a sigh. They hadn't been on the best of terms for a while now, but Robin was tired of dealing with the tumultuous emotions that came with her mother. "Let's see what Jennifer has to say."

"Probably something about how *perfect* Stu's turkey was and how *beautiful* Anna-Maria is." Alice gave Robin an encouraging smile, which caused a flash of love and friendship to bolt through Robin.

"Probably," she murmured as she fished through her

oversized purse to find her device. "I don't know, actually. There's been some tension between them."

"Fascinating," Eloise said.

Robin found her phone and swiped to see her mother's message. Her heartbeat throbbed up into her throat for a moment, and then the organ deflated and sank to her toes.

Thanksgiving was wonderful here. I hope yours was too. I think I'm going to go on another cruise for Christmas, so we'll have to find a time to celebrate together.

A soft "pfft" came out of Robin's mouth, a noise she hadn't even realized she'd made until it had escaped.

"What?" Alice asked.

Robin simply handed her the phone and smoothed back her hair. In the drier winter, it didn't frizz much, and she'd just gotten it cut and the color fixed up last week. "How are Clara and Julia doing at the inn?" she asked Eloise.

But Alice handed the phone to Eloise, and she read the message. She looked up, worry in her pretty brown eyes. "You'll be happier without having to entertain her for the holidays," she said. She turned over the phone and set it in front of Robin.

"Yeah." Robin looked at her device, wishing working out her relationship with her mother came with a manual. She'd read it cover to cover and do exactly as it said if she could. She drew in a deep breath and shook herself out of what-ifs and worries. "It's fine. I like having my small family celebrations."

"We'll have our Friendship Feast at the inn," Eloise offered. "I've already told AJ and Jean about it, and Kristen said she tried a few new cookie recipes on Theo's family yesterday, and some of them were a big hit." She gave them a big smile, and it reached right into Robin and plucked out her unhappiness.

"We can never go wrong with Kristen's cookies." She glanced over to Alice's menu. "What are you getting?" That was her way of saying she was done talking about this, and Alice and Eloise graciously allowed her exit from the conversation.

"I think I'm going to go for the pumpkin gnocchi." Alice tipped her menu toward Robin. "You?"

"I can't pass up the roasted beet salad," she said.

"I'm going to get the lobster mac and cheese," Eloise said, folding her menu and setting it on the edge of the table. She put her arms on the table and leaned into them, her smile faltering. "Aaron and I..." She cleared her throat, and Robin set aside her menu too, sensing something worth hearing was coming.

Eloise waited for a waitress to walk by behind them. Then their waitress appeared, wanting to know drink orders. Both Alice and Eloise lifted their eyes at Robin's order of red wine, but she shook her hair over her shoulders and said, "I'm home alone tonight and into tomorrow. I got a ride here, so I'm not driving. I can have wine for lunch."

Alice laughed lightly, but she had not ordered anything alcoholic. She'd had a bit of an issue with drinking right after her divorce, and Robin hadn't seen her drink much since. Likewise, Eloise bypassed the margaritas and mojitos in favor of a soft drink. She'd never been much of a drinker anyway.

The waitress said she'd back with their drinks to take their orders, and Robin leaned into the table too. She wanted to prompt Eloise, but she'd learned a lot over the past few years of raising teenagers and mending bridges with her friends.

They'd been through so much together, Robin couldn't imagine something could come between them at this point.

Relief painted through her when Alice said, "You had something to tell us, El?"

Eloise suddenly looked unsure. "It's not really something I want everyone to know."

"You don't have to tell us," Robin said, but that was totally code for, *Tell us and we won't breathe a word to anyone.*

She wouldn't either. She valued her friendship with Eloise, respected her, and wouldn't betray her confidence. "But you also know if you swear us to secrecy, we won't say a word." She cut a look over to Alice. "Right, Alice?"

"I won't even tell Arthur," she said.

"It's a little crazy," Eloise admitted. "Just...seeing AJ and Asher, and now Kelli's pregnant..." She shook her head, her brown bob bouncing along her chin. "Aaron and I are trying for a baby."

Robin leaned back in the booth, surprise streaming through her veins where her blood should be. The only noise she could make right now would reveal her complete shock, so she kept her mouth closed.

"That's great," Alice said, and she sounded genuine and normal. "I mean, I wouldn't want to do it." She gave another of her light, elegant laughs. "But I see why you do." She reached across the table and took Eloise's nervous hands in hers. "You are an excellent mother."

"Those girls aren't mine," Eloise whispered.

"They are too," Robin said, glad she'd finally found her voice. "Billie and Grace adore you, and they know what a mother is—and it has nothing to do with blood."

Eloise nodded, untucked her hands from beneath Alice's, and swiped at her eyes. "It might not happen."

"But Kelli and AJ," Robin said, leaving the thought there. She also did not want a baby at her age, not when her youngest had just turned fifteen and her oldest was away at college. The very idea made her ill. She loved babies—holding them while they slept, feeding them, and rocking them while they babbled—but she wanted to give them back to their momma's when they got fussy.

"I think it's great," Robin said. "I hope it goes well for you." She realized what she'd said a bit too late, and she looked up as their drinks thankfully arrived.

That didn't stop Alice from saying, "I'm sure with the police chief for a husband, it'll go fine."

"Alice," Eloise said in a scandalized tone, but she laughed afterward. Robin reached for her wine glass the moment the liquid had been poured, and she swirled it around as her minor embarrassment faded.

They put in their food orders, and then Alice sighed. "We better talk about Charlie and Mandie."

"We better?" Robin asked. "Why?"

Alice pierced her with a dark, sharp look. "We know what dating leads to."

Robin's eyebrows lifted. "You think they're going to get married?"

"I don't know," Alice said. "Charlie won't say how serious they are." She took a long drink of her seltzer water with lime. "But I know if they get married, he won't finish school." Alice's eyebrows went up. "Will Mandie?"

Robin waved away Alice's concern. "They're not going to get married." But somewhere in her stomach, a tiny needle pricked at her. Mandie hadn't said anything about her relationship with Charlie, other than, "Yeah, we're dating. We go out, and see each other."

Robin hadn't felt the need to question her further, because Mandie was an adult. Barely, but still an adult.

She didn't want today's lunch to be filled with worry. "Only good news," she said next, giving Alice a slight glare. "What else is going on? Kristen said her dinner last night went well, right?"

AJ stayed home with her fifteen-month-old, writing freelance articles on the side. Laurel had quit the police force to do the same, but her baby was only two months old.

Before anyone could say anything, a beautiful blonde appeared at the end of the table.

"Maddy," Alice said, jumping to her feet. "Can you sit with us?"

"No." But she glowed with light, her blue eyes as radiant as the summer sky. "But look." She thrust out her left hand, where a diamond the size of her knuckle sat.

"Oh, my goodness," Robin said as the air left her lungs. Alice shrieked, and even Eloise got caught up in the engagement joy. That was just the kind of good news Robin wanted, and by the time they all settled back into their seats and Maddy had to get back to work, she'd forgotten about her barely-adult daughter dating Alice's barely-adult son.

Almost.

It's fine, she told herself. She couldn't control Mandie, and she and Duke had gotten married young too. They'd made things work, bonded together to fight against the world, and learned to love each other more deeply through their challenges.

She was *not* going to be the kind of mother hers was, and that meant she needed to trust her daughter. She should. She could. She absolutely would.

Chapter Five

Julia ran her hands down the front of her skirt, wondering for the tenth time if she should even be wearing a skirt. "It's Sunday brunch," she said. "On an island." People would be wearing skirts.

Maybe in the Hamptons. "Or Nantucket," she said out loud, as she'd just relocated from the upscale island off the coast of Cape Cod.

Five Island Cove was quaint and beautiful, much like the Cape or Nantucket. It had a small-town feel neither of those other places had, and Julia had enjoyed the past few months here. She'd found a small place to rent on Diamond Island—the biggest island right in the middle of the chain of five—and the ferry ride to Sanctuary for her afternoon management job at the Cliffside Inn only took about a half hour.

The RideShare system on the island was impeccable, and she'd sold her vehicle in Nantucket and moved forward on her life adventure without a car.

This morning, she expected Liam to pick her up, but she spun away from the front door and hurried back into the bedroom. "Can't wear a skirt," she muttered as she ripped it off. She wished, at times like these, that she still lived with Maddy and could ask her opinion. But Maddy had rented a big house on an island two away from Diamond, and she'd very soon be living with her fiancé, Ben. Then they'd get married, and Julia would be left to her own devices again.

A surge of bitterness came with her thoughts, but she fought against it. She was happy for Maddy, because she knew what paths she'd trod in the past. No one had a perfect life, even if it looked like it from the outside.

She and Maddy had become close over the year they'd managed The Lighthouse Inn together in Nantucket, and she wanted to be happy for her friend. She *was* happy for her and Ben. She absolutely was.

Julia was the first person Maddy had called to tell her about the engagement, and if the tables were turned, Julia would dial Maddy first too.

She'd just pulled on a pair of black jeans when her doorbell rang. It really started out strong, but quickly faded and warbled as the seconds passed. "That thing is dead," she muttered as she buttoned and zipped. "Coming!" she called as she dashed out of the single bedroom at the back of the house and hurried toward the front.

Her ankle boots sat waiting for her, but she didn't want Liam to stand outside for one moment longer than necessary. Then he'd be out there without her instead of in here with her. She opened the door, feeling flushed and rushed, and looked up at him. "Hey."

His smile already sat on his face, the lines of his jaw rugged and handsome. "Hey," he said in return. He wore a pair of blue jeans, thick-soled work boots—but not the police kind—and a black leather jacket.

Black leather.

It felt so much like Maddy's motorcycle-riding boyfriend to Julia. That kind of dark, dangerous man had never really been her style, which made the fact that Julia had once been married to Maddy's former boyfriend all the more confusing.

"Wow," she said before she could stop herself. "You look—" Her brain caught up to her mouth, and she cleared her throat before she could say something totally inappropriate. Or something someone thirty years younger than her would say. "Amazing." She reached out and brushed her fingertips along the zipper of his jacket, just because she could. "Very handsome."

"Passable?" he asked. He scanned her to her shoeless feet, his gaze rebounding to hers. "You look fantastic."

Liam crowded into the doorway now, fully entering her house. "Beautiful."

"I just need shoes." She realized her house had been filling with cold air, and she backed up. "Come in for a second."

He dutifully did what she said, and Julia's hair seemed to stand at alert as she walked the few steps to her shoes and retrieved them. She pulled out the small ball of her no-show socks, sat in a dining room chair only a few paces from the front door, and started to put on her shoes.

Liam stood there and watched, and while their first date had been full of fun, flirty conversation, this one felt charged in an entirely different way. Last time, she'd felt awkward, as a forty-something would on a first date with an incredibly good-looking cop.

This time, she felt like she might burst apart at the seams if she didn't kiss him before they went to brunch. Or was nine o'clock still considered breakfast?

Good thing you changed into jeans, she told herself as she stood. With the added heel on the ankle boots, she stood a little closer to Liam's height, but she still had to look up at him.

He took the few steps to her fluidly, the way she imagined he did everything, and took her into his arms as if he'd done it a thousand times before. "What I really wanted to say when I got here was how gorgeous you are." His voice rumbled in his throat, not quite escaping but not quite staying silent either. "And how much I've missed you, and how not a minute has gone by since Appetizer Hour where I haven't thought of you."

Julia smiled, because oh, the man knew how to charm a woman. He'd been personable and easy to talk to on their first date too, and Julia wanted to be as nonplussed as Liam. She slid her hands up his chest and allowed herself to lace her fingers behind his neck. "Thank you, Liam."

She hadn't felt gorgeous very often in the past few years. She hadn't realized how much she wanted to feel that way until she heard the sentiment come out of his mouth. In the calm, quietness of her tiny beach house tucked between several others, Julia dared to look up at him.

They moved simultaneously then, him pitching down slightly and her rising up to meet him. He kissed her hesitantly for the first stroke, almost like she was a fragile bird and would take flight with the merest of touches.

When she didn't, he growled somewhere deep inside himself, pulled her closer, and kissed her like he meant to do it. Julia lost herself in the swirling embrace of his touch, the scent of his skin—like a cool ocean breeze and a hint of clean sweat—his cologne—like spices cooked over an open fire in the woods—and his jacket—like cotton and sunshine, like he'd hung his clothes out to dry in an island summer.

Julia got pulled back to reality when she remembered

it was decidedly *not* summer. She breathed in through her nose, and Liam ducked his head enough to break their connection. Her heart hammered, and all she could think was she never wanted to leave this safe circle he'd enveloped her in.

Her phone trilled at her, a text from someone. It could've been one of her sons, or a friend here in the cove, or her new boss. It could've been her ex, or someone she'd left behind in Nantucket.

Right now, she didn't care. Right now, she stood with Liam Coldwater. Right now, she looked up at him as he said, "Are you going to check that?"

She shook her head and somehow applied just the right amount of pressure to convey what she wanted without having to say anything. As she kissed him for a second time in as many minutes, Julia decided dating in her forties far surpassed the fun she'd had in her twenties.

She knew more now—more of what she liked and what she didn't—and Liam ticked every box with every stroke of his mouth against hers.

Finally, he said, "We better go, Jules. We don't want to miss our reservation."

She did, and she didn't. "Okay," she said, her mind as soft as her muscles. She let Liam lead her out of her own house, and the shock of cold wind woke her right back up. She hurried toward his car—until she realized it was a police cruiser.

Then her feet planted themselves on the sidewalk, wintery conditions or not. "That's what you drove?"

He looked over to her, then back to the car. "I don't have anything else," he said. "I cleaned it up. There's not an ounce of dog hair inside."

Liam ran the only canine unit in the cove, and she'd first met him at a demonstration on Pearl Island this past fall.

She met his eye, trying to determine why riding around in a cop car unnerved her.

"I'm off-duty, sweetheart," he said with that sloppy, lopsided smile that should be trademarked. "I'm not going to suddenly flip on the lights and go into a high-speed chase."

She eyed him. "Knowing you, Liam? You might." She bumped him with her hip as she passed, which made him laugh. She kept her smile to herself and waited for him to catch up to her so he could open her door.

He swept one hand along her waist while the other pulled on the door handle. "The only thing I'm chasing today, Jules, is you." With that, he opened the door, and she slid into the seat.

The car was clean, and it smelled like he'd sprayed lemon air freshener throughout the whole thing. She smiled as he jogged around the front of the car, then panicked when she wondered what he'd seen in her—*her*—that he liked.

"Something," she muttered to herself as he opened his door. "So act like it."

"Ready?" he asked as he buckled his seatbelt.

She hastened to do the same. "Yes," she said. "I'm absolutely ready." Julia really had no idea what this relationship would bring. She knew she liked how he called her "Jules" and "sweetheart." She knew she enjoyed kissing him. She'd wasted a bit of time thinking about him too.

So she'd do what her mother had taught her to do long ago: Strap in for the ride. Hold on tight. And have fun.

Chapter Six

Eloise Sherman entered the office at the inn she'd owned for a few years now, her arms full of ingredients for dips and spreads. She'd been the one to send the text to everyone that they couldn't bring the same dishes they'd brought last year or the year before.

She and her mother had always made a buffet of dips for Christmas, and while the holiday still sat a couple of weeks away, for their Friendship Feast, she planned to do something similar.

"I got it," Clara said as she got to her feet. She rescued the sagging bag of cream cheese before Eloise could drop it. Not that it would've mattered. It was boxed cream cheese. "What are you making?"

"Artichoke dip," Eloise said, depositing the cans of artichokes on her desk. They rattled and clanked, but she smiled at her two managers. She actually had a third, but Rhonda didn't come in until eight o'clock at night, and she made sure the inn stayed secure and running overnight.

"I'm also doing a new corn and bacon dip this year," she said. "So Robin won't be mad."

"I'm glad I haven't been to this before," Clara said. "Then I can bring whatever I want."

Eloise pushed her hair out of her eyes, trying to tuck it behind her ear. She'd cut it too short this last time, however, and it just sprang right back out. "What are you making?"

"My mother said she usually brings rolls—that's what she makes every Christmas—but this year, she's bringing some thumbprint cookies. So I made potato rolls...with her help." Clara smiled, and she really had come to life in the past couple of months. Since she'd quit trying to take Friendship Inn from dilapidated to something someone could live in. Since she'd allowed herself to join their group of friends fully.

Clara texted back and forth with everyone now, and she'd shared her daughter's latest achievement with everyone, complete with a picture of Lena smiling with her boss at the supermarket as she held the Employee of the Month plaque.

Eloise had really enjoyed getting to know Clara, as well as Julia, Maddy, and Tessa. Tessa was off the island right now, as her boyfriend was retiring from his family deli on Nantucket and expected to move to the cove in the New Year.

Julia sat in the other corner of the office, and Eloise sank into her chair and started pulling out groceries. "Good. I love those rolls." She smiled at Clara and then switched her attention to Julia.

"What did you make? I'm sure it'll be something delicious." In her previous job managing an inn, Julia had had to cook for guests. It had been a smaller inn than what Eloise ran here, and she didn't promise breakfast, lunch, or dinner.

She did offer cookies during afternoon check-in, but they usually ran out in the first couple of hours. Clara had asked about bringing in bagels and muffins for a casual continental breakfast in the mornings, sort of a grab-and-go option for people checking out.

Eloise had sat down to go over the budget, had found a little bit of money to do it, and they'd implemented it in the past couple of months. Because of it, Eloise had updated her website and nudged up her prices. No one had complained. The inn was still booked six months out.

"For Christmas morning, I used to make bacon-wrapped cocktail sausages for my boys," Julia said. "I made those, and they're in the oven caramelizing right now."

"With sugar?" Clara asked. "Or maple syrup? In Vermont, they put maple syrup on them."

"Brown sugar," Julia said. "That's how we made them in New York."

Eloise's stomach rumbled, because she hadn't eaten breakfast in her mad dash to get out of the house that morning. The bus had been late, and Eloise refused to leave before the girls were off to school. A late bus led to a late Eloise at the grocery store, and then her being late for the ferry.

Ferries didn't care about buses or long check-out lines at the supermarket. She'd missed the ferry, and even now, her fingers had just started to warm.

"Did we get the heaters on outside?" She glanced toward the windows beyond Clara, who nodded.

"They're running," she said. "Check-out went well. We've got the majority of the inn staying over another night, so the two rooms checking in tonight should be easy."

"Easy," Eloise echoed. So much of what she'd done here at Cliffside had been easy, but so much had not. She'd worked and worked and *worked* for what she had now, and she'd almost lost it more than once.

She'd almost lost herself for a while there. She wasn't going to go there again. She didn't want the inn if she couldn't have Aaron, Billie, and Grace.

And maybe a baby.

Her hand wandered to her belly, but even if she was pregnant, she'd be three weeks along at most. As she'd aged through her twenties and into her thirties and never married, Eloise had slowly let the hope of motherhood leak out of her. It had gone slowly, like the last rays of sunset surrendering to the inevitability of night.

She hadn't realized it at the time, but she'd clung to that hope for as long as she could, but no matter what, darkness always overtakes the daytime.

But the sun rises again each morning, and Eloise glanced up and pulled in a breath when she realized she'd fallen into her own thoughts. "Okay," she said as she exhaled. "Everyone will be here soon. If the inn is humming along, I'm going to go get my dip made. Can you guys get the tables set up?"

"Absolutely," Julia said. "I'll get the tables out." She didn't normally come in until lunchtime, but she'd been invited to the Friendship Feast—as Eloise had started mentally calling this new tradition she and her friends had started a couple of years ago when a tsunami had brought dozens of people to the inn for shelter.

Eloise had lost track of who was coming. She knew her core group—Robin, Alice, AJ, and Kelli—would be there, as well as her husband. Clara and Julia, obviously, but she wasn't sure if Madeline Lancaster would make it, and she didn't remember seeing a text from Laurel either.

Her memory sparked, and she realized Jean and

Kristen would be coming together, with Jean's new baby girl. She and her husband had been able to adopt a little girl a few months ago, and Eloise's mind ran away from her as she melted together cream cheese, mayo, sour cream, and a couple of cheeses.

Perhaps she and Aaron should consider adopting if they wanted a baby. Eloise wasn't sure how she felt about that, and she didn't have the energy today to sort through complicated feelings. Then, she'd have to bring Aaron's feelings into the conversation, and as she squeezed the water out of the frozen spinach and chopped it up, that was a conversation Eloise didn't really want to have.

She folded the spinach into the cheesy mixture, then added the drained artichoke hearts. Now, all she needed to do was heat this through and get out the water crackers and chips for it.

"Hey, my love."

She abandoned her cooking in favor of smiling to Aaron, her gorgeous husband. They hadn't been married for two years yet, but Eloise fell further in love with him with every single day that passed. Today, he held up a white pastry bag and said, "Guess what Gina had?"

"If that's an apricot tart, you'll be my hero." He already was, and Eloise couldn't believe she'd somehow caught the eye of this single dad. The Police Chief here in Five Island Cove. A boy she'd had a crush on as a high schooler, and who'd been available thirty years later when she'd returned to her hometown.

Aaron grinned from ear to ear, but he shook his head. "Guess I fail today, then." He set the bag on the stainless steel table while Eloise's curiosity spiked. "She was out of apricot. You have to get there before seven to get those."

"So I've heard."

With his hands free, he easily wrapped Eloise in a hug and bent down to kiss her hello. "I left too early this morning." He was warm and wonderful and safe, and Eloise loved everything about him. Maybe not the snoring that happened when he finally got a day off and took sleeping pills to catch up on his rest. Maybe not some of the brusquer language he used with the girls when he felt like Billie was getting fresh or going out with the wrong boys.

She put an inch between them and said, "What did Billie say about the Christmas Ball?"

"She's going with a group of friends," he said, his eyes darkening. "Stag." He didn't believe in going to dances stag, especially when she'd been asked by a reasonable, respectable young man. His words.

He didn't understand Girl Code, but Eloise did, and she'd supported Billie in her decision not to go with Ian Coldwater to the ball. Her best friend liked him, and Eloise wondered if Billie had said anything to Ian about asking Addie to the dance instead. Sometimes, once a girl went out with a boy, the magic of it seeped away, and perhaps then Billie and Ian could go to something in the future. Billie didn't really care, because she wasn't the one with the crush on Ian.

Eloise pushed her step-daughter and her dating and friendship issues out of her mind as Aaron's hand slid up her back, bringing her closer to his chest. "Are you ready for the feast?"

"I need to get the dip in the oven," she said.

"Don't mind me," Julia said loudly, and Eloise and Aaron broke apart. "I just need to get the cocktail sausages out of the oven."

"I could've done it," Eloise said.

"I didn't know Aaron was here." Julia kept her head ducked as if Aaron and Eloise were still making out. They hadn't even been doing that.

"He comes to the feast." Eloise stepped out of the way and let Julia remove her sizzling, bubbling, ooey-gooey, sugary cocktail sausages from the oven. With the door still open, she slid her crock of artichoke dip into the oven.

"Tables are up," Julia said. "Kristen and Jean just arrived."

Of course they'd be early. But an early Jean meant a baby girl, and Eloise shot a glance over to Aaron. "I'll go see if they need help," he said, and he slipped away out the same door he'd entered.

Eloise sighed and reached for the pastry bag he'd

brought while Julia removed her sugary sausages from the pan before they could stick. "Oh, that man," she murmured when she saw the double chocolate mint brownie inside the bag.

"Something good?" Julia asked.

She pulled out the brownie. "He knows me too well."

Julia grinned as Eloise took a big bite of the brownie, not even caring if frosting gathered in the corners of her mouth. "You two are sweet."

Eloise chewed and swallowed while Julia laughed, and then she asked, "How are things going with you and Liam?"

Julia didn't flinch. She didn't stop working for even a moment. "Well enough," she said. "To keep going out with him." She lifted her head long enough to give Eloise a smile that said so much more. Julia wouldn't, Eloise knew that. She'd never met someone as vaulted as Julia, and that only made Eloise like and trust her more.

"Can I use the stove in here?" Robin asked, drawing Eloise's attention to the swinging plastic door as she pushed through it. She carried two casserole dishes in her arms, and Eloise went to help her.

"What's this?" It better not be ham and potatoes, or Robin would be disobeying her own rules. Eloise felt the need to step in front of the oven to hide the fact that her spinach and artichoke dip was the same thing she brought every year.

She didn't really care; she could handle Robin's wrath. Everyone would do what they wanted anyway, Robin included.

"Roast beef," she said as she slid the casserole dishes onto the table. "Cheesy mashed potatoes." She wiped her hair off her face, a smile finally appearing. "Phew. How are you?" She stepped into Eloise. "I feel like I haven't seen you in a while."

They didn't see each other as often in the winter months, to be sure. Eloise's job kept her plenty busy, and she was absolutely determined to put her family high on her list of priorities.

"Deviled eggs," Alice said, which elicited a sigh from Robin. She put her tray of beautifully filled egg halves on the table and met Robin's eyes. "Sorry," she said. "This is what my tradition is, and it's the *Friendship Feast*." She beamed at Robin, and Eloise quickly faced her too.

"I made the artichoke dip," she said.

Robin cocked her head to the side. "So I'm going to be the only one who brought something different."

"No," Eloise said quickly. "I know Kristen brought cookies."

"Yeah, but Clara brought the potato rolls." Robin rolled her eyes. "I know Kristen made those for her."

"They worked on them together," Eloise said. "This isn't a big deal. Your food will be the best anyway."

"I'm pretty sure AJ isn't bringing pumpkin pie," Alice

said. "And Jean brought an amazing ice cream cake I can't wait to dig into. So that's totally new and different."

Eloise wanted to tell Robin that not everything had to be new and different to be wonderful. They had new people at their Friendship Feast today, and that alone made it different.

"I had a feeling the kitchen would be hopping this morning."

Eloise turned to find her evening manager, Rhonda, entering the kitchen. "I brought clam chowder." She wore a big, bright smile, as she usually did. Eloise loved her, and she moved to give her a hug.

"Let's get the food outside that can be taken there," Robin said, and she started directing traffic in the very Robin-like way she had. Even that didn't bother Eloise, because she'd rather have someone else take charge than be the one to do it.

Her artichoke dip came out of the oven, and she took it outside, where a spot had been kept for it. The patio buzzed with friends and cheer, and Eloise didn't care that she'd eaten Alice's fancy deviled eggs before. They were good, and she'd eat them any day of the week.

She glanced around at all of these people she loved. Laurel had brought her husband, Paul, and their baby, James. AJ and Matt and Asher stood in a trio. Alice and Robin were there alone, but Jean and Reuben had brought their baby girl, Heidi, whom Kristen held.

She'd come alone today, which gave Eloise a moment of pause as she'd been dating Theo Sands pretty seriously lately. At least seriously enough to have met his children when they'd come for Thanksgiving.

Kelli stood with Rhonda and Julia, and all three of them had brought their favorite dish and themselves, no plus-ones. Aaron stood near Eloise's mother and Clara, who'd brought her daughter, Lena. Scott must still be driving the ferry, because he hadn't arrived yet.

And Eloise didn't see Maddy either. "Are we ready?" she asked, and several people nodded. "All right." She held up one hand and the chatter started to dissipate. She faced west, the whole of Sanctuary Island spreading before her. The water swelled at the horizon, and Eloise loved this view more than anything else.

It felt like she stood on top of the world, and she always gained a bit more clarity when she took a moment to *feel* how far she could see.

"Welcome to the Friendship Feast," she finally said. "I'm so glad to be hosting everyone at the Cliffside Inn again this year, and I'm thrilled to have new friends here with us." She indicated the impressive spread of food. "Everyone brings something to share—something meaningful to them. Something that says Christmas or holiday or tradition. For me, it's family." She exchanged a look with her mother, then quickly refocused on Aaron so the tears wouldn't crowd into her eyes and pinch her vocal cords.

"Let's eat," she said.

"Let's eat!" AJ and Alice chorused, and that got the group laughing. Eloise fell out of the spotlight, because it wasn't her favorite place to be.

She navigated to Aaron's side and stood in his circle of strength. She wasn't sure if they'd be blessed with a baby. She didn't know what this next year would hold for her, for them, for their children.

She didn't need to know, though Eloise liked plans and routines. As she let the vibrancy of life and friendship move around her, she let go of trying to plan everything.

And that was the most freeing thing she'd ever done, so no matter what curveball life threw at her next, she was ready to swing.

Chapter Seven

A blaring alarm made Madeline sit straight up, her heart pounding as she pushed herself back against the head-board. Panicked, she tried to see in the darkness still surrounding her.

She lived alone. Ben hadn't stayed over last night. Her kids had left weeks ago, and she was going back to Nantucket to see her father for an evening, and then she and Ben were continuing to Montreal to visit his parents.

Her adrenaline calmed enough for her to realize no one had entered her home. It wasn't the security system blaring at her, but her phone. She scrambled to reach it on her nightstand as the alarm started anew.

She managed to silence it, and in the next moment, her phone trilled out the loudest, screechiest ringtone she'd ever heard. She'd never heard her device make a noise like that, and she stabbed at the button to answer the call. "Yes, hello," she said breathlessly.

"This is Malcolm at Island Forces Security. Your restaurant, The Glass Dolphin, has had three—oh, four—windows broken."

Maddy flung the comforter off her legs and stood. "I'm on Rocky Ridge," she said. She'd been managing inns and restaurants for over a year now, but she had no idea what to do in a situation like this. Yes, she'd been listed as the emergency contact for The Glass Dolphin here in Five Island Cove, as the owners still lived in Nantucket and ran the original restaurant.

"Do you want me to call the authorities?" Malcolm asked.

Maddy appreciated his calm demeanor, and she quickly snapped on the lamp, her eyes squinting at the sudden light. "Yes," she barked out. "Do I need to get over to the restaurant?"

"The cops will likely want to speak to someone in authority," Malcolm said.

Maddy didn't even know if the ferries ran all night. She didn't think they did, and she certainly couldn't jump in a motorboat and get herself there in the pitch darkness that existed beyond her window. "Okay," she nodded. "Yes, please call the authorities. I can still login and see all the cameras, I'm assuming?"

"Yes," Malcolm said. "There's only one that's broken,

but we have all the others running. We're getting good images, and the assailant is still there."

Maddy's heart skipped over itself, flew up to her throat, and then settled back into place as she left her bedroom, switching on every light she came to. "Okay," she said. "I'm getting online now. I have to wait for the ferries to open."

A quick glance at the clock told her it was three-twenty-eight in the morning, and the first ferry left Rocky Ridge for the direct-to-Diamond route at five-thirty.

Two hours.

She had to wait here and watch her restaurant from afar for two hours.

"Do you need me to stay on the line?" she asked as she flipped open her laptop, which rested on her kitchen table.

"No," Malcolm said. "The police have reported they've sent two teams of officers. They're en route and should be there in six minutes."

"Thank you." Maddy sat heavily at the table, trying to get herself back to a place of calm. She stared at the picture of her, Ben, Chelsea, Kyle, and Bea—a selfie the five of them had taken at their Thanksgiving feast. Ben had proposed a mere hour earlier, and he'd then brought out a fully cooked and ready-to-eat meal.

Maddy blinked, trying to focus.

Her phone rang again, and one glance had her picking

it up quickly. "Hey, Teresa. I just got off the phone with the security team. They've sent the cops."

"There's a man throwing buckets through the windows."

Maddy's fingers began to fly over the keyboard and track pad, so she could see what was happening too. "The alarm woke me."

"He's not even trying to conceal his face," Teresa said. "Surely he's going to run away..." She trailed off, and Maddy clicked and typed in her username. Her password generated, and Maddy tapped to login. The cameras came up, and she scanned back and forth, trying to find the culprit. The cause of her three-thirty wake-up call.

Her eyes shook, scrambled, the way leaves trembled in the gusts of an approaching storm.

She found the man as he entered the screen from the bottom, and she hurried to enlarge the video. Sure enough, he only wore jeans and a black sweatshirt. No mask. No gloves. Not even high-top sneakers, but flat shoes, like Vans maybe. Converse.

He launched the steely gray bucket toward the only remaining window that hadn't been smashed, and her mouth dropped open as the glass shattered right before her eyes. The cameras didn't have any sound, and that only made the images playing out before her eve more eerie.

Surreal. Unreal.

"I can't—" she started, but she didn't know how to finish. Teresa likewise sat silently on the line. "I'm going to be on the five-thirty express ferry to Diamond Island," Maddy said. "I'll get this sorted out."

She wasn't even supposed to go into the restaurant today, as she'd arranged with her assistant manager to be gone for the holidays. She'd just gotten engaged, and she had several days of travel ahead of her.

Maybe she didn't. Not now.

Helplessness filled her at the same time flashing lights she imagined in red and blue illuminated the screen. She watched as a pair of police officers entered a different camera zone, then another pair from the opposite direction. They walked close to one another, only one of them with a weapon drawn.

Their bright, bright lights flooded the front of the restaurant with light, and Maddy saw everything in black and white.

The man turned toward them, and she didn't recognize him. Not that she would. She was a transplant to the cove. She saw hundreds of faces per day; they blurred by the end of the first rush. Sure, she'd made some friends here, but she certainly didn't know every citizen of Five Island Cove.

He surrendered to the police without a fight, and Maddy's breath eased out of her body as the handcuffs went around the man's wrists. He was led off-camera by the cops, and Maddy sank fully in the back of the chair.

"It's done," Teresa said, but Maddy had the distinct feeling this incident had just begun.

* * *

She rose from the RideShare three hours later, freshly showered and dressed the same way she'd be if she was showing up to open The Glass Dolphin. Maddy pulled her dark jacket closed across her stomach and marched past the yellow police tape in her low heels.

At the line where the glass had flown back toward the sidewalk and parking lot, she stopped. The police officer she could see lifted his head, and she put up her hand. He frowned and came toward her, but Maddy didn't care what he said.

"Ma'am," he said. "You can't be here. We're still determining if the building is structurally sound. It's not safe."

"I'm Madeline Lancaster," she said. "I manage this restaurant. Chief Sherman told me you'd have a complete report for me?" She'd never been happier to know someone—the right person—in her community until today.

Her call to Eloise had been answered promptly, and she'd given the phone to her husband after only a few questions. The officer wore a badge with the last name of Harmon on it, and Maddy catalogued it.

"Let me call in," Officer Harmon said. "Please don't come closer, okay?"

Maddy nodded, then returned her gaze to the damage of the building. Surely the windows didn't hold up the roof, but she didn't know much about architecture and load-bearing walls. She wasn't sure how long she sat there, but she turned when someone stepped beside her.

"This is unbelievable."

Maddy turned toward Alice, not sure how to move her feet or vocalize her thoughts. She had no thoughts. Perhaps that was the problem. "What are you doing here?" she finally asked.

Alice glanced over to her too. "Eloise called me. She said you might need some help, but she has a family anniversary at the inn and can't be here." She turned her face back to the restaurant and hunkered down into her collar. "Robin's on her way."

"I didn't need you to come," Maddy said, but her voice sounded tinny and pinched as it left her mouth.

Alice didn't say anything as she put her arm around Maddy's shoulders and folded her into an embrace. Maddy wasn't sure why that simple gesture meant so much, or why it broke her down so easily.

Tears pricked her eyes and then streamed so fast she couldn't call them back. She'd hitched smiles into place in the past at important political events. Maddy had been a professional at tucking away all emotion until the doors had closed.

But today, the simple act of a woman she'd become friends with recently showing up undid her composure. Maybe it was the early-morning alarm that had woken her. Or the multiple phone calls. The videos she'd seen. The waiting for the ferry to open and get running.

No matter what, Maddy suddenly felt like she was carrying the weight of the entire island on her shoulders, and it threatened to break her back. Break her completely.

"I need to text everyone," she whispered.

"Who, everyone?" Alice asked.

"My employees," she said, sniffling and then pulling in a long breath as if she could reel in her insecurities, her exhaustion, and her anxiety with only oxygen. She stepped away from Alice and removed her phone from the front pocket of her slacks.

Alice gently took her phone from her and asked, "Do you have a group message?"

"It's an app," Maddy said, tucking her hands into her jacket pockets. She shivered in the early morning chill, Christmas only five days from now. The sun had crested the eastern horizon now, and the grayness surrounding them turned into copper and then gold and then white, seemingly before Maddy could exhale and draw another breath.

"It's called Bob," Maddy said. "He manages their shifts and hours and paychecks. They'll all get notified from him when I message."

"I've got it," Alice said, her eyes down and her fingers moving. Part of Maddy wanted to manage her own employees, but the other part could only stare.

"My boss is coming." Maddy sighed and turned away from the ruined storefront. "I need to get everyone here to help clean up."

"Not today," Alice said.

"I'm supposed to be in Nantucket tonight." Maddy took a few steps away, tilted her head back, and sighed up into the sky. Everything she'd had on her agenda had been wiped away by one person and a bucket. She wasn't sure how life could be flipped so dramatically, but she was living in the moment where it was happening.

"You have an assistant manager, right?" Alice asked. "And the owner. Let them handle it."

Maddy didn't know how to do that, so she didn't say anything.

Officer Harmon returned, and he gave Maddy a badge. "Clip that on your jacket there." He frowned at Alice's back. "Ma'am, I only have authorization for the manager here to come in with me."

"I'm her lawyer," Alice said smartly. "But I'll allow it."

"The owner will be here as soon as the Clipper arrives from Nantucket," Maddy said. "She'll need to be able to come in, and when can I get my employees in here to help clean up? We need to be open for the holidays."

Robin pulled up in her minivan as Officer Harmon looked at the ruined restaurant and back to Maddy. "I honestly don't know if that's possible, ma'am."

"Anything is possible," Robin said, and Maddy started to feel like herself again. She'd been strong through her divorce. She'd almost lost her kids completely. She'd moved to Nantucket and opened a dilapidated inn with an enemy. She and Julia were best friends once again, and that hadn't been easy.

She could do this.

"Show me everything," she said. "I need detailed lists of what needs to be fixed. Should I call my general contractor? He'll need to come through all of this too."

Another police vehicle showed up, and everyone waited while Chief Sherman and Paul Leyhe got out. They wore their official uniforms from head to toe, and Maddy really had no idea how they walked with all of that equipment attached to their belts.

"Robin," Aaron said, but it wasn't in the casual, caring way Maddy had heard during Appetizer Hour. "Alice. Madeline."

"Chief Sherman," Maddy said before Alice or Robin could pipe up. "I need to get back in there. I need to get this fixed. We have a *very* full holiday schedule."

Aaron exchanged a glance with Paul, who happened

to be Laurel's husband. "Come with me, Maddy," he said. "Lieutenant, stay with these ladies, would you?"

Maddy exchanged a glance with Robin and then Alice, and then she went with the Chief. Her heels crunched over glass, and she stepped *through* the door frame while it remained locked.

"Maddy," Aaron said, his voice much quieter than outside. No one would dare to contradict him, though, even in a soft voice. He carried power no matter what he said, which reminded her of Ben.

Ben.

Her mind seized. Her fiancé was coming to get her that morning so they could make the trip to Nantucket together. She couldn't believe she hadn't called him after the cameras had gone still, after she'd hung up with Teresa, after she'd showered and prepped herself for today.

"Chief, I need to make a quick call," she said.

Aaron quirked his eyebrows. "Maddy, this is a clear case of vandalism to make a statement."

Maddy blinked, because her brain could only hold so much, and it already operated at maximum capacity.

He nodded toward a bucket that lay on its side only a few paces away. "Careful as you come this way. Look." Aaron took the steps, and Maddy gingerly went with him.

The bucket lay there, but letters had been painted on the side of it. *No more tourism.*

She blinked again, and another moment of her life began. "What does that mean?"

"Clint—Officer Harmon—took photos of all of them." Aaron took out his phone and started swiping. Maddy's eyes once again shook with the want of trying to see so much, so fast.

Keep the cove small, one read.

Stop building, another said.

This land is sacred, read a third.

No more tourism flashed by.

The cove is big enough.

Keep our small town small.

Aaron lifted his eyes to Maddy's. "We have the man in custody, and he claims he's the front man for a large group of concerned individuals in the cove."

"Who...what?" Maddy asked. "Think The Glass Dolphin is the reason why their island community is... what? Growing?"

Aaron tucked his phone away. "I don't know," he said. "But it's almost Christmas, and we won't have the glass you need to get this fixed before then." He sighed, and Maddy felt it move through her whole soul.

She suddenly didn't want to be in this restaurant. She'd loved working here. She'd found the space open and airy and beautiful, the ocean just beyond the back wall of windows inviting and playful.

Now, everything felt tainted. Scary. Dangerous.

Maddy walked away from Aaron, her fingers already dialing Ben. "Hey, baby," he said, his voice a bit groggy. "You're up early."

He had no idea, and Maddy could explain everything to him later. "Ben," she said. "We're still leaving the cove today, but I might have to work a little while we're gone."

"What's happened?" he asked as a media van pulled into the parking lot. Maddy didn't want to be here. She didn't want to be interviewed, and she glanced over to Robin and Alice. They flanked her and all three of them got into Robin's van, and she clicked the locks closed.

"It'll be on the news soon," Maddy said. "But The Glass Dolphin was vandalized overnight, and it's going to have to close until after the New Year."

This wasn't her restaurant, and while she was invested in it, she had to be able to walk away. She had plans with her fiancé, her father, and her family. Teresa would have to talk to the police, the reporters, and the general contractors.

This wasn't Maddy's problem to fix. "I'll see you at my house soon?" she asked, her voice wavering again.

"Yeah, of course," he said. "I've got the news on. You're okay?"

"I'm okay," she whispered, but she met Robin's eyes in the rearview mirror, and they both knew it was a lie. "I'll see you soon." She ended the call before she could cry, and then she looked out the window, seeing a bucket

come flying through it, shattering it, breaking into someone's dreams and crashing them to splinters.

Maddy pressed her eyes closed. "We should go."

"Yes." Robin cleared her throat and got the van
backing up. "Where to?"

"The ferry," Maddy said. "I'm meeting Ben in a
couple of hours for our holiday trip." She spoke almost in
a robotic voice, and she didn't like that. She noted that
both Robin and Alice accompanied her on the ferry,
though they both lived on Diamond Island. They took
her all the way to the front door of her house, where they
each hugged her.

Maddy nodded to them and said, "Thank you," in a
quiet voice before she slipped inside and locked the door
behind her. She'd deal with work when she had to, and she
spent the next hour making sure everyone knew she'd be
off the cove, who to call, and what to do.

Then she packed her bag and waited for her gorgeous
fiancé to arrive, to whisk her away from all this madness.

Chapter Eight

"That's what they're reporting." Alice Rice set down the basket of bread that she'd just pulled out of the oven and buttered. She cut a look over to Arthur, silently begging him to stop talking about The Glass Dolphin.

"So it's not going to reopen?" Ginny asked.

Alice didn't want her Christmas holidays to be laced with tension and worry. But she couldn't really control that, since the vandalism at The Glass Dolphin had made the national news, and the twins had seen it in the city before they'd even returned to the cove. Suddenly, the sanctuary and peace of Five Island Cove had been disrupted, all in the name of preserving the sanctuary and peace of Five Island Cove.

Alice couldn't seem to wrap her head around it,

despite talking things to death with Arthur and then Robin. Their text messages on the group thread had not been about holly and ivy, mistletoe or gifts. They'd been solely talking about the messages from a group of people on the island who wanted to stop the growth. Or at least slow it.

She sat down and looked at her daughter. "I don't know," she said. "That seems to be the answer everyone has these days." Eloise didn't know what was going on with the investigation. Or she did and she wouldn't say.

Laurel didn't work for the police force anymore, so their insider was gone. Robin usually knew all the hot gossip around town, but she and Duke had taken Jamie and gone to New York for the holidays. Her mother would be returning from her cruise around New Year's, and they were planning to meet her there and all come home together.

Surprisingly, AJ had some tidbits, as her husband ran the golf course and seemed to catch snatches of conversation from those who came to the driving range. She'd learned that the man who'd thrown messaged buckets through the windows was someone named Weston Bent, and when Alice had done some of her lawyerly online digging, he did seem to be a lifelong resident of the cove.

He hailed from Pearl Island, the southern most body of land, but Kelli and Shad lived there, and they'd never seen him. Shad Webb worked in the government for Five Island Cove, but he'd been very tight-lipped about everything too.

In general, Alice felt like she was one breath away from inhaling toxin and one step away from having the ground vanish beneath her feet. It wasn't a very festive way to celebrate Christmas, but she jumped to her feet when the doorbell rang.

Thankfully, AJ and Matt simply entered without waiting to be invited in, and Alice met them as she bustled toward the front door. "Is it still raining?"

"It's turned to snow," AJ said as she slicked the slush from her coat sleeve. She carried her little boy, who pushed his arms up to rid himself of the blanket she'd thrown over him. He emerged with chubby cheeks that made Alice's grin flip onto her face instantly.

"Come here, baby." She took him from AJ and started removing his coat. "Did you get wet?"

"Da-da-da," Asher said. Everyone shed their wet clothes and left them on the hooks near the front door to maybe drip-dry, and Alice led them back into the kitchen.

Arthur greeted AJ at the end of the hall with a quick kiss on the cheek and the words, "We got your favorite drink. It's in the fridge."

"Ooh," AJ squealed as she went past him. He laughed and shook Matt's hand, and their Christmas Eve party was complete. Alice had seen AJ come to life when she'd returned to the cove, then disappear again, and then rejuvenate all over again when she and Matt had gotten back together.

But she was currently in a phase of pulling away again, and Alice had noticed that AJ and Matt didn't particularly like the big parties, where everyone showed up, and they were expected to stay for hours on end.

They'd disappeared from the Fourth of July party after coming, and they hadn't come to the last three big dinners or beach days—besides the Friendship Feast, and Matt hadn't attended that.

Alice slipped Asher into the highchair she'd bought just for him, clipped him in, and moved to hug Matt. "How are you?" She stepped back and looked into his eyes. Really looked. "How's the golf course?"

"It's wet," he said with a smile. "We've closed it for the season, so now we just have to maintain the driving range." He sighed as he sank into an empty chair across from Charlie. "It's a relief, actually. I'm tired." He fisted his fingers and reached toward Charlie. "How are you, man? How's college and New York City?"

Alice watched her son, because she'd gotten very little from him about his college courses or his life in New York. His dad lived there, and she knew both twins were in contact with their father. How much Frank helped them, she didn't know. Ginny usually volunteered more information than Charlie, and she watched a flicker of...something move through his expression.

"It's great," he said, his voice the upbeat kind he usually saved for talking about sports or skateboarding. "The city has a great vibe. I passed all my classes." He shot her a look, and Alice planted a smile on her face that bloomed to life in a mere moment.

"What are you majoring in?" Matt asked, and Alice vowed to have him over more often while the twins were home. She got to her feet, keeping both ears on the conversation as she went to grab the butter from the fridge.

"I'm not sure," Charlie said. "I think maybe I'd like to do something with chemistry, but..."

"But what?" Matt asked as the question screamed through Alice. She set the butter that had been carved into a Christmas tree onto the table. Her son looked at her, and Alice's eyebrows went up before she told them not to.

Charlie very nearly rolled his eyes. "It feels really geeky."

No one said anything, and Alice knew better than to chime in first. In fact, she took her sweet time sitting down again, and then she reached for a roll. "Look at the butter," she said. "I got it from the bakery, and it was one of the last ones."

"It's adorable," AJ said as she sank into the chair beside Matt, her cherry Pepsi popped and open, ready to drink.

"Are we ready?" Arthur said as he came in from outside, the turkey he'd been smoking looking golden and delicious on the platter.

"I think so," Alice said. She tore off a chunk of a roll and put it on Asher's tray. The little boy took a couple of tries to pick it up with his chubby fingers, and then he mashed it in his mouth. Alice couldn't help smiling at him, and she even caught Charlie doing the same.

Their eyes met, and everything inside her son softened. He'd definitely had a wall up between them recently, and Alice didn't know why.

"I think chemistry is a great field," Matt said. "People are always going to need medicines and pharmaceutical companies pay really well."

"Yeah, you don't have to teach," Ginny said, bored as she kept her eyes on her phone. She and Charlie had obviously had this conversation before.

"What's wrong with education?" Arthur asked from the opposite end of the table, where he sliced through the turkey breast like he carved a bird every single day. Alice gave him a grateful smile, because he'd been nothing but good to her teenagers. Nothing but amazing for her.

"Nothing," Charlie said. "I just never want to step foot inside a high school again."

"Chemistry is way more than teaching high school," Alice said.

"All right," Arthur boomed. "We're ready." He twisted and put the knife on the counter, then faced them all again. No one had moved. Ginny hadn't even put down her phone. Alice crossed her legs and smiled, because they'd been so low-key around the house since the twins had both moved out. Sometimes she simply baked a frozen pizza, cut it into wedges, and left it on the stove for Arthur to graze on when he got home from work.

Other times, he brought take-out home for the two of them, and they ate right out of the containers while they watched TV. Sometimes in bed. Alice had worried over being an empty-nester, but she was loving every minute of it.

"No one wants turkey?" he asked.

"I do," Alice said as she picked up her plate. "Pass that to Arthur, would you?" She handed it to Charlie, who did what she said.

"We usually have ham, don't we?" he asked as he piled his plate on top of hers.

"Arthur's family has turkey," Alice said. "And he got a smoker for his birthday, and we wanted to try it." She smiled at him again, glad when she found the gratitude in his eyes, even briefly.

Food got dished out, and Alice chopped up a corner of her turkey for Asher. She took mashed potatoes and gravy, the roasted Brussels sprouts, and plenty of cranberry sauce. Neither of her children would let protein touch fruit, but Alice rather liked it.

Just when the conversation had turned away from "how's this going?" and "what's new with you?" AJ sucked in a breath.

Every eye moved to her, and she quickly finished chewing her bite of food. "I can't believe I forgot to tell you this when we got here." She looked hopped up on sugar, her blue-gray eyes brimming with light and life.

"What?" Alice asked when she didn't immediately go on.

"I got asked to write an op-ed piece for the Cove Chronicles."

Alice exchanged a look with Ginny, but neither of them said anything.

"It's about the recent vandalism," AJ continued. "And we're going to poll the residents."

"Oh, boy," Alice muttered under her breath. She didn't want to talk about this, but Matt beamed like this poll would be life-changing for everyone who read the results.

He put his arm around AJ and said, "Yeah, because what's wrong with a little growth?" He looked around at the six of them at the table. "We need tourists to fund the cove. It's insane to think we can close borders and keep people out."

Silence fell over the kitchen, and then Arthur cleared his throat. "I don't think they want to close borders. I think they want to protect the feel of the town."

"I read that The Glass Dolphin was built on ancient tribal lands, and no one even checked to make sure it was okay," Ginny said.

"Ginny," Alice said, though she'd read the same article. For some reason, the vandalism at The Glass Dolphin had pushed a curiosity button inside her, and she'd been searching for headlines and news about it every day since it had happened.

That had only been four days, and it sure seemed like there was a new piece, a new opinion, or a new development out every single hour.

"I'm just saying," Ginny said. "I see both sides." She'd always been very aware of things around her, and Alice gave her a nod and a smile. She didn't want to squash her daughter's voice or opinion, but there was a time and place for everything.

"We do need tourists," Arthur said. "I agree with that. But I do think the City Council needs to be more...judicious in who they hand out permits to." He nodded, as he and Alice had come to this conclusion in their own private conversations.

"I suppose the islands are finite," AJ said, musing thoughtfully. "There's just going to be so much in the article, I can't wait to write it."

Alice congratulated her, because she did want AJ to have the journalistic opportunities she needed. But this topic was particularly charged right now, and she prayed there wouldn't be too much blowback.

"All right," she said as she scooped up another bite of mashed potatoes. "I need a relationship update—and it has to be more than two words."

"Mom," Charlie said, really rolling his eyes now.

"Come on," she said. "I know you're dating Mandie, and you've given me *nothing*."

Ginny too looked at Charlie, her eyebrows up. He glared at her. "Why don't you go first, Ginny? You've got news."

Alice's eyes nearly fell out of her head she looked at Ginny so fast. "News? Ginny?" She'd dated a nice boy here in the cove, but they'd broken up when she'd left for school.

Ginny rolled her eyes now. "It's not *news*. This boy at the coffee shop asked me out, and I said yes. We've been out a few times." She shrugged like this was un-newsworthy, but Alice disagreed.

"First," she said delicately. "He's probably not a boy. He's an adult, right?"

Ginny blinked, like this was the first time she'd considered that. "Yeah," she said.

"Then he's a man," Alice said.

"Gross," Ginny said, volleying her gaze from Alice to AJ to Arthur. "I'm not dating a...man."

"I thought you didn't call it dating," Alice said innocently. She put another bit of roll on Asher's tray, because he shredded everything before it went into his mouth. She grinned over to Ginny, who still seemed to be catching on that she was, indeed, dating a man.

"They've been out more than a few times," Charlie said. "Just sayin'."

"Charles," Ginny barked. "Why don't you tell Mom about how you and Mandie are talking about getting married?"

The air left Alice's lungs. She didn't even have enough to sputter a single word. Matt started to chuckle, which so didn't help the panic parading through her. He looked over to Alice, his laughter growing in volume and intensity.

"Ah, raising young adults," he said through the laughter. "It's so much fun."

That was the opposite of the truth, but Alice caught the sarcasm in his tone. She finally thawed enough to say, "Is that true, Charlie?"

"We've talked about it once," he said, shooting lasers at his twin. "One time, Mom, and it's not really going to happen."

"Ever?" Arthur asked quietly. "Or what timeframe are we talking about?"

Alice appreciated having a level-headed partner in situations like this. She had Mom Lecture 101 ready to go, which would include how Charlie could barely pay his rent and feed himself, and how did he think he and Mandie were going to do that—with no education, no skills, no training, no nothing?

She pressed her lips together and gave her son a chance to answer.

"I'm not sure," Charlie said slowly. "I'm not going to rule out ever, but I don't think it's going to be soon." He looked from Arthur to Alice. As he reached toward her, Alice tensed. "Okay, Mom? So don't worry."

"Charlie, I am your mother," she said. "I've been worrying about you since the moment you were born." She gave him a small smile and let herself get distracted by Asher's squawking demand for more bread. When she focused on her children again, an overwhelming sense of love filled her.

"I love you two," she said, her voice turning somewhat misty. "You're adults. I've done the best I can with you— and I will keep doing the best I can." Her lungs shook as she filled them with another round of air. "I trust you, and I know you'll do what's right for you."

Charlie's jaw jumped, but he nodded. That was a decently emotional reaction for him. Ginny smiled and nodded and even said, "Thanks, Mom." She took another bite of turkey, chewed, and swallowed, the smile dropping from her face.

"Oh, my goodness," she blurted out. "I'm *dating* a *man*."

Only a heartbeat of silence passed, and then everyone in the room—except Ginny—burst out laughing, Alice included.

Chapter Nine

Clara Tanner switched off the television, though everyone she'd invited for Day-After-Christmas dinner was watching it. "Come on," she said. "I've called everyone to dinner three times now, and I'm sick of being ignored."

Her husband got to his feet first, followed by her brother. Reuben joined her in the kitchen and said, "This whole thing with The Glass Dolphin is wild, isn't it?"

Clara shot a look at him, then over to her mother. "Don't say anything about it to Mom, okay?"

Reuben looked over to her too, and Clara watched as she put her hand in Theo's and then stood. She'd been dating him for six or seven months now, and they sure seemed to like each other. Clara wasn't sure how she felt about her mom dating again. It felt surreal almost, like discovering a forgotten door in a well-known house, one that led to a room she never knew existed.

She'd had to get to know her mother and her brother all over again after sequestering herself and her family in Vermont for the past two decades. It still boggled Clara's mind that when everything had fallen apart, neither of them had fired questions at her. Neither had turned her, Lena, or Scott away. Neither had whispered about her behind her back.

They'd both simply opened their arms, opened their homes, and welcomed her back to the cove. She'd had friends in Vermont, but none as close as the women she'd met and knew here. And she and Scott had only been here for the past several months.

Again, Clara felt like she should know her life. She should be able to sweep out every nook and cranny and recognize the crumbs. But she barely recognized herself— or Scott and Lena—now that they'd settled in the cove.

"Why not?" Reuben asked. "She's talked to me about it."

"She thinks half the people in the cove should be evicted," Clara muttered as Lena joined them at the island in the kitchen. She smiled at her daughter and smoothed down her hair. "Hey, Lena-Lou. Do you want to tell everyone what we made for supper?"

"Yes," she said bluntly, the way Lena said everything. "Grandma, come on. The corn is getting cold."

"I'm coming," Mom said, her smile made of gold for Lena as she approached the counter. "What did you guys make?"

Clara didn't love cooking for her mother, because she wasn't nearly as good at it. Jean had a way with baking, so Clara had asked her to do the dessert. She'd shown up with a Marlborough pie and a cheddar cheese apple pie. Clara had added a maple cream pie to the mix, because she had enjoyed her time in Vermont, and Christmas wasn't Christmas without something maple on the table.

"Candied ham," Lena said. "I did the glaze. Mom made the potatoes, and they have so much cheese on them."

Clara smiled at her adult daughter, feeling more grateful in this moment than she ever had. She and Lena had had their struggles. The woman would never be able to live on her own, as her mental disability wouldn't allow it. But she had a good job she liked, and she functioned well enough for Clara and Scott to lead a somewhat independent life.

She was loved, and Clara had sometimes let the negativity in her life overcome the many blessings she'd been given.

"Then Aunt Jean made the pies," Lena said, and Clara had missed the introduction of the garlic-rubbed corn, the rolls they'd bought at the bakery, and the honey butter Lena had whipped together herself.

"And you brought the cookies." Lena smiled at her grandmother, who positively beamed back at her. Clara's spirits lifted, because her mother loved so completely. She had for hundreds of girls growing up in the cove as she led the Seafaring Girls program. She'd been instrumental in reinstating it in the cove, and Jean now taught the young women who lived in Five Island Cove all the things they needed to know to be seaworthy.

Clara had always known her mother loved her, but she hadn't felt it as keenly as she did now. "All right," she said. "That's the spread. If something isn't good, don't eat it." She picked up a plate and handed it to Lena. "You go first, Bean."

Lena loved candied ham and rolls with honey butter, so it was no surprise that she loaded her plate with those three things. Oh, and the corn. She'd always loved corn, and Clara moved around her mom and Theo to take Jean's little girl from her. "I'll hold her while you get food."

"I got the highchair ready," Scott said, dropping his unused plate back into the stack. "I completely forgot." He bustled off to get it from the garage.

Jean watched him go, then turned to Clara with big eyes. "You bought a highchair for her?"

"Yes," Clara said simply. It was something Jean would've done for someone else. Clara knew she'd had a highchair in the tiny apartment on the bottom level of the lighthouse, simply because she babysat for AJ Hymas sometimes. She'd sewn the boy the most adorable clothes over the past year or so, and Clara had never seen Heidi—the little girl Jean and Reuben had adopted in September—wear anything store-bought.

No, Jean made all of the baby's clothes. She'd once taught sewing lessons out of a room on the second floor of the lighthouse, but she'd given that up when Heidi had come to her home. She did still run the Seafaring Girls classes three days a week, and Reuben came down from his work in the lighthouse to tend to their daughter.

From Clara's perspective, their life was simple, but good. They were kind, hardworking, and deserving people. Whenever she looked at someone's life from the outside, the way she was now, she wondered what people thought of her life.

What did they see when they looked at her, Scott, and Lena? Did they see a woman who worked hard for a friend at a busy inn on another island? Did they see someone who loved her family, tried to forgive herself and others, and just wanted to find a few moments to enjoy her life each day? Did they see a couple who loved one another?

"Here we go," Scott said as he came bustling back into the kitchen. "You can sit right here, baby girl." He took Heidi from Clara and got her buckled into the highchair. When he returned to her side, he looped one arm around her waist and pulled her close. "This all looks amazing, sweetheart. Thank you."

Clara warmed under his praise, as she always had. She'd loved Scott for as long as she could remember, but they'd nearly broken apart last year. She stood out of the way as Theo went down the counter, Mom right behind him. They laughed and chatted about something, but Clara made no move to follow them.

She looked at Scott. "We've come a long way this year."

His expression changed from jovial to burning in only a moment. "We sure have." He kissed her quickly, then pressed his cheek to hers. "I love you, Clara. I so appreciate you not giving up on me. On us. On our family."

Clara didn't need the acknowledgement, but at the same time, she sure did. It was nice to be recognized for the hard work she'd done, whether it was seen or unseen. So much of what she did seemed to go unseen by those around her, by the world in general, but Scott had always been good to see it, see her, and tell her.

He moved away from her then, and they filled their plates with holiday wares too. Once everyone sat at the table, Clara glanced around at her core family. She hadn't been blessed with a lot of siblings or children. Neither had Reuben. Without Theo, there would be seven of them total. The last of the Shields in Five Island Cove.

Growing up, she'd found her small family to be

boring. Lacking. Now, she simply wanted them to know how much she loved and appreciated them. She cleared her throat, and since no one had really started talking yet, the spotlight fell on her.

Heat filled her face, because Clara wasn't particularly good at expressing how she felt. "I just wanted to say how grateful I am to be here with all of you today." A wobbly smile landed on her face, and she glanced down at her food, hoping it would distract her. "I sure do love my family."

"Thanks for having us," Reuben said, ever the rock in their family. "Jean and I have loved falling in love with the cove since we moved here." He smiled over to her, and Clara only caught the end of it. "And with each other again. And we love Heidi, and of course, we're thrilled to be close to all of you too."

Jean nodded, her face bright and full of hope. Clara knew the misery, the nights spent crying and desperately hoping for a particular outcome, and the resiliency that Jean possessed. It was one of those unseen things that not many people got to know or understand.

She hoped those closest to her could see those same strong qualities in her.

"I love you, my chickens," Mom said, and that made everyone laugh. She hadn't called them that for such a long time, but the words brought back such a sense of nostalgia for Clara that emotion choked up her throat.

"I'm grateful to be here with you," Theo said diplomatically. "Thank you for inviting me."

Clara nodded, and the mood loosened now that the emotional, hard things to say were out. Hard for her, at least. She wasn't sure what other people had a hard time saying.

They tucked into dinner, and the silence that came from eating good food never bothered Clara. Then her mother said, "Oh, dear." She scrambled to her feet, her gaze flying from her phone. "We have to turn the news back on."

She hastened to do it, and Clara checked her phone. They were on the same group text, but she hadn't gotten anything that would alert her. Mom switched the TV back on while Clara's heartbeat dove through her body— and not gracefully.

The picture showed a young reporter standing in front of the still ruined windows of The Glass Dolphin. The police had roped it off, and they'd even put an officer there around the clock to prevent looting and more damage. There hadn't been any incidents since the vandalism that had happened almost six nights ago now.

Someone had boarded up the windows to prevent weather damage, and the speculation around the restaurant and its fate had grown to proportions that even Clara, as a self-proclaimed drama-lover, had to walk away from.

"We're on?" she said.

"Yes," a male voice said, and because Clara had been listening to the news before she'd turned it off to start dinner, she knew it was the in-studio anchor. "Go ahead, Ophelia."

"Welcome, everyone who's joining us for this breaking news," Ophelia said. "Everyone in Five Island Cove has likely heard about the vandalism that took place a handful of evenings ago, right here at the acclaimed, new restaurant, The Glass Dolphin. This popular place to grab lunch with friends or enjoy a fancier anniversary dinner has been the buzz around town since it opened last spring. But there's been a new discovery after the vandalism that brought a group of concerned Covers out of the shadows."

She'd been walking slowly along the sidewalk in front of the yellow tape, and the last shot of her included the on-duty police car. Now, the picture switched to something else—something a graphic designer had most likely made.

"The group, which refuses to take a name for themselves, is concerned about the implosion of tourism and recent additions to the islands that make up Five Island Cove," Ophelia said as a voice-over. "They claim that rental space is almost gone, prices have increased dramatically for locals, and that there's simply not enough room on the islands for everyone who wants to come here. Businesses and commercial zoning has been largely ignored, something Mayor Sherman has vowed to address in the New Year."

The picture switched again, this time to a map of Five Island Cove, the dots out in the sea of blue mere nubs in Clara's vision.

Her tongue felt stuck to the roof of her mouth. She could handle contention, but she didn't like willingly inviting it into her home. Scott loved the headlines, and he often told her what was going on in the world.

"Some have wondered if The Glass Dolphin sat on ancient, Native American lands. Rumors have flown from here to the mainland, where even national news stations have picked up the story. But we're here to show you first...what the police department found when they searched this site after last Monday night's attack."

The screen went black, and Clara wanted to cry out that they couldn't stop there. What had the police found? Had Eloise known and not been able to say anything? Laurel?

They were both married to cops—the two top-ranked cops on the island—and they'd been silent.

Suspiciously silent, Clara thought.

"This is not good," her mother said, her phone clutched in her fingers.

Maddy had also left town for her scheduled vacation with her new fiancé, but she had basically given no details and said nothing about the vandalism at the restaurant. Clara hadn't found it strange...until now.

The TV brightened again, this time with Ophelia back on the sidewalk in front of The Glass Dolphin. "Here at Channel Five News, the only news station direct from Five Island Cove, we've learned that the police have indeed found something on the site of this restaurant. Something historic, something that's long been forgotten. I have Chief Aaron Sherman here with me tonight, ready to tell all of you what's really going on here at The Glass Dolphin."

She spoke with such drama in her voice, Clara almost rolled her eyes. Surely they hadn't found a mass grave, and anything less than that certainly didn't warrant Ophelia's big, wide, serious eyes and her almost hushed tone.

"Good evening, fellow Five Island Cove residents," Chief Sherman said, his eyes serious and staring straight into the camera lens. On the table in front of her, Clara's phone started to buzz and vibrate as text after text came in.

She couldn't tear her eyes from the television, though, as Aaron said, "We did discover an old time capsule buried on the northeast corner of the building which houses The Glass Dolphin. It is not Native American land, and it was never registered as such." He spoke in a clear, concise, firm voice, leaving no room for debate.

"We've recovered the time capsule in its entirety, and

the year on the lid is listed as Nineteen Hundred-Fifty. We've asked our town historians to research if this is indeed a time capsule, sealed up for future generations of Five Island Covers, but they have been unable to find anything in the records."

Her mother's phone rang, and she said, "It's Eloise," as she swiped the call to voicemail. "Of course we're all watching this."

"Therefore, I took every precaution," Aaron said. "Just because a barrel has a lid on it marked with a year doesn't mean it's safe. We've opened the barrel and we have confirmed its contents are indicative of a time capsule from the year Nineteen Hundred-Fifty." He blinked slowly. "I've met with my father, the Mayor, and we've decided to display the contents of the time capsule at City Hall, beginning tomorrow at ten o'clock a.m."

He cleared his throat, which caused Clara to rise to her feet too. She'd spent casual time with Aaron Sherman. She'd seen him standing on stages to make public announcements and directing his cops through a crisis. The man did not clear his throat, ever.

"There are some interesting documents inside the time capsule, and we're still working to validate and verify their credibility. But in the interest of full transparency, we'll be displaying everything at City Hall. Nothing will be held back." He glanced over to Ophelia with one final nod.

"Now," she said. "I'm told the public will need tickets to attend the display, and Mayor Sherman has assured me they'll be available from the Five Island Cove city government website, starting right now. They're free, but the police don't want a mob. You'll need a ticket if you want to see what was preserved from over fifty years ago." She held very still for a long moment, and then said, "Back to you in the studio, Ralph."

The picture changed to the two of them side-by-side, and Clara finally released her breath. She picked up her phone, trying to decide if she should read the texts from her friends or hurry to the Five Island Cove government website and get tickets for herself and her family to see whatever had made Aaron Sherman clear his throat on live TV.

"The maximum is ten tickets," her mother said.

"Get all ten," Clara said, not sure where the words had come from. Something seethed in her gut, and she didn't know why. She wondered how documents were "verified" or "validated" and what that meant.

"I got ten for tomorrow at two-thirty," Mom said triumphantly. Her fingers never stopped moving, and she could text fast for someone her age.

Clara turned her attention to the group text, where messages had started flowing in to *Turn on your TVs! Aaron's got an announcement!* and *Are you guys seeing this?*

"Eloise got ten for three o'clock," Clara said, relief

filling her. They should all be able to go with twenty tickets split among them. Her mother's message came in about the ten she'd secured, and they started splitting themselves into two groups.

I can't believe I'm not there, Robin said. *Someone tell me everything once you see it.* Then she asked, *How long will the items be on display?*

Eloise must've been glued to her phone, because she said, *At least two weeks. You'll get to see it all, Robin. Don't worry.*

Clara wished she could take that advice. But she'd wait until she saw what was on display at City Hall tomorrow before she decided if she could stop worrying or not.

Chapter Ten

Kristen didn't want to separate couples, but she wanted to walk down the wide hallway at City Hall with her daughter and her Seafaring Girls. As it was only two days after Christmas, and as the holiday had fallen on a weekend, most people had today off as their vacation day.

She wasn't sure if Aaron and his police force had done that deliberately or not, but when she got within three blocks of City Hall, she couldn't go any further. "Just let us out here," she said to the RideShare driver, who'd probably heard the same thing all day today.

She and Clara exited the vehicle. Lena had gone to work at the supermarket as normal today. Scott had gone to drive the ferry. There were some occupations that always had to be done, and those were two of them.

Clara had worked her shift as the morning manager at

The Cliffside Inn, and she and Eloise had ridden the ferry back to Diamond Island together. El had gone home first, but she planned to meet them for their two-thirty entry appointment.

Alice and Ginny, Laurel and Jean, and AJ and Kelli, took their party to nine. The last ticket had gone to Theo, and Kristen quickly texted him that they'd abandoned their RideShare and would be walking in.

The ten of them would be going through City Hall together, and the other ten tickets that Eloise had procured would be going to anyone else who wanted them. Julia and Liam had taken a pair, though surely Liam, as a cop, had seen the time capsule contents already.

Robin and Duke and their girls were off the island until next week, and Kristen knew that was slowly killing her.

Maddy and Ben weren't back from Montreal yet, but they'd gotten tickets for later in the week. Kristen knew they wouldn't allow photographs, and she could only guess at the texts and gossip that would be flying.

She'd deliberately stayed offline that day, choosing instead to walk with AJ and Jean despite the cold, then visit the lighthouse and her granddaughter. She loved all things Five Island Cove, and she couldn't imagine learning something damaging about this place where she'd grown up, loved, and lived for her whole life.

Tessa and Abe were still in Nantucket, as he was planning to move to Sanctuary Island with Tessa in another week. So they had plenty of tickets for Arthur and Charlie, Matt, Shad, and Reuben.

Unsurprisingly, Aaron and Paul hadn't wanted tickets, probably because they'd been over the contents of the time capsule with a fine-toothed comb. Both Laurel and El had spent several texts last night assuring and reassuring everyone that their husbands had not told them a single thing. There had not been a single picture shared with them.

Finally, Kristen had detected some defensiveness in El's texts, and she'd told everyone to calm down. They either believed Eloise, or they didn't. And she had no reason not to believe her. Everyone had taken things down a notch at that point, but the situation only showed Kristen that even the closest of friends could have sharp talons when different opinions got raised.

When someone felt betrayed, they could transform into a portrait of desolation, with eyes like vacant windows and smiles as brittle as old parchment, their joy packed away as if fragile heirlooms, until trust could be stitched back together thread by fragile thread.

Kristen had seen it before, with her girls—the very women she was going to meet. She'd seen them disperse as young adults, then forget about one another as they each made their own separate way in the world. Their paths had really only intersected again with the death of Kristen's husband, and she pressed her lips together as she put one foot in front of the other, each step taking her closer to City Hall.

To the truth.

Hopefully not to witness something that would fracture the friendships she'd carefully nurtured and watched reseed, rebloom, and regrow over the past few years.

The women she loved so dearly definitely didn't always agree. They'd weathered familial storms, a literal tsunami that had nearly torn them apart, and old secrets buried inside even older walls.

They'd had a fairly quiet year, despite a semi-scandal between Clara and Robin's mother. Oh, and there'd been that squall that had nearly left Reuben a widower while Jean was out at sea with her Seafaring Girls...

And the drug case that had caused Laurel to leave the Narcotics division and return to the streets as a beat cop.

Fine, so they'd been through a lot together. That should've comforted Kristen, but somehow, it only made her dread what she might find inside City Hall.

"El says she's on the plaza," Clara said. "Alice and Ginny are walking, like us." She kept Kristen up to date, so all she had to focus on was walking. Her phone chimed, and it alerted her to the fact that Theo wasn't on her girls' text.

She checked her device and read his message out loud.

"I'm coming up on the south side of City Hall. I should be there in about five minutes."

"There's time," Clara said. "We're going to be early, even with the walk."

Kristen wanted to seek reassurance from her daughter, but she didn't. She didn't want to know what Clara thought they might find. She hoped it would be something simple and classically Five Island Cove, like a recipe booklet of the time, or black and white photographs, perhaps a diary, or artwork, or an article of clothing portraying the time period.

She didn't really know what people from over half a century ago would find valuable enough to bury in the earth for a future generation. She let her mind go down the road of what she might want her posterity to glimpse about her life. If Kristen Shields made a time capsule for her grandchildren and great-grandchildren to open in forty or fifty or sixty years, long after she'd gone, what would she want them to have? And why?

Cookie recipes, she thought with a smile. Perhaps her logs of the time she'd helped her husband in the lighthouse. Those were unique and certainly portrayed what she'd spent a lot of her life doing.

Her Seafaring Girls manuals. The old, yellowed and curled photographs she had from her time as their leader, from their activities. All of the things she'd kept when she'd cleaned out the tiny cottage she'd shared with Joel after his death.

There isn't much, she thought, and her curiosity piqued at how big this "barrel" of items had been. "Do you think we'll get to see the time capsule itself?" she asked Clara.

"I don't know, Mom." Clara had been saying that a lot since the broadcast last night. Kristen hadn't really expected another answer.

She'd already walked that morning, so her feet ached by the time they arrived on the plaza outside City Hall. The line of people had been marked off, and several cops were keeping un-ticketed people behind another roped-off barrier.

"Clara," El called. "Kristen." She waved her hand, and Kristen detoured over to her. Within a few minutes, the ten of them had congregated, and Kristen pulled up the tickets on her phone. At her age, not much really got her heartbeat revving, but joining the queue of people who would be admitted for the two-thirty time slot definitely did.

"You'll have thirty minutes to view the contents of the time capsule," Paul said into a megaphone. "There are some items preserved behind glass. Please do not touch them. Do not touch anything. Stay behind the barriers. Photographs are not allowed. If you take a photo, we'll have to confiscate your device."

He repeated the information as the line started to inch forward. Kristen estimated that they'd joined it about halfway through, and she reached for Laurel's hand and squeezed it as they walked past her husband. He met her eyes and nodded from where he stood above the crowd, no smile in sight, and then the entrance loomed only steps away.

Kristen's pulse raced now, and she wasn't even sure why. She walked at the front of their group, showed the tickets to another cop, and entered the building. The queue went right, and she followed it. Most people spoke in a whisper, though they hadn't instructed them to do so. A sense of reverence hung in the air, and Kristen hardly dared to breathe lest the sound be too loud.

She turned left, the items ahead of her now. The tall arms of an easel stretched above the crowd, but otherwise, she couldn't see much. Another ten feet, then five, and the first item on display was the "barrel" itself.

Kristen had expected it to be made of metal. Something hardy that would last the test of time, at the very least. What stared back at her really was a barrel, like the kind that Kristen had played with as a small child.

It was nothing more than wood, and while sturdy, it had definitely started to rot slightly. It looked like something she'd seen at the lighthouse as a little girl, and then thrown away after she and Joel had taken over the care and keeping of the lighthouse.

Her heartbeat throbbed against the back of her tongue, but she didn't dare speak. She didn't even know what she'd say. The couple in front of her whispered to each other, breaking Kristen's attention on the barrel. She didn't know why, but it felt like she'd seen it before.

Of course, there were a lot of barrels around Five Island Cove. Everything they used, everything they built, everything that came here had to be shipped in. A lot of those shipments came in crates, buckets, or barrels.

The next display was a felt board with several photographs dotting it. Kristen sucked in a breath and came to a complete stop. Most people were quietly shuffling, moving an inch or two at a time but never stopping.

Not her.

She froze, her eyes blitzing from one familiar face to another.

"These are my grandparents," she whispered. The words lashed through her head, increasing in volume until she turned toward Clara and said right out loud, "These are my grandparents."

Clara frowned at her and then looked at the photographs for several long moments. Long enough that the other women they'd come with had piled around Kristen, all of them examining the photos. "Mom, are you sure?"

She had photos of Grandmother Rose and Grandfather Clancy. Pre-WWII, when they'd first purchased the lighthouse. Then her grandfather had been called off to war, and he'd never returned.

Her favorite photograph, one she'd taken from the walls of the cottage at the lighthouse after her husband had died, and one she still owned, was her grandmother, standing on the rocks at the lighthouse which she had lovingly and painstakingly taken care of—alone—for many years.

She knew her face. She had parts of her grandmother's features. As she stood there, she reached up and touched her cheek, almost expecting something to happen. What, she didn't know.

"Keep moving, please," someone said in a quiet voice, and Kristen jolted into action.

The next display held two leather-bound books. To the casual observer, they might be perceived as diaries. Kristen knew instantly that they were logbooks from the lighthouse. She'd written in many of these over the years, creating a record of every day, every swell, every ship, and every supply it took to keep the sailors and others safe on an island community.

She knew this time capsule was not really a time capsule. This was a storage container for her grandmother. There was a reason the historians hadn't been able to find a record of the time capsule—it didn't exist.

The next display also held something a bit fun and whimsical. A shiny black record with gold lettering across the top. *CAPTIOL* it spelled, with Nat "King" Cole below the center hole, and the song *Mona Lisa*.

Her grandmother had loved Nat King Cole, and one of Kristen's earliest memories was listening to her grandmother sing while she worked in the kitchen.

She suddenly didn't want anyone else to see her family heirlooms. She hadn't even known they'd been misplaced, but everything she'd seen testified to her that this wasn't a time capsule for the entirety of Five Island Cove.

"Oh, wow," Alice whispered, and Kristen moved to the next display, which was a glass case that held newspapers. Some were just clippings, and they came from the Cove Chronicles. Little things like a new ferry line opening or the fifth annual Kaleidoscope of Colors Event.

Some were entire newspapers out of the mainland, with the most prominent one being the screaming headline of KOREAN WAR STARTS: NORTH KOREANS INVADE SOUTH KOREA.

She'd been born two years before the Korean War had begun. Her father had served overseas for a while, but unlike her grandfather, he'd returned. He'd helped his mother run the lighthouse until he'd passed it to Joel and Kristen to carry on the legacy.

Such fondness for her ancestors, for the roots from which she'd sprung, filled her. Tears heated her eyes, and she allowed herself to be moved in the crowd down the case.

Another Cove Chronicles headline sat there, this one still attached to the full newspaper as well. Kristen took in the headline all at once—ROSE WORTHINGTON SELLS LIGHTHOUSE—and the first of her tears fell.

"No," she whispered. She leaned forward, trying to read the article. The paper was almost seventy-five years old, and the letters faded at best.

"Come on, dear," Theo said, his hand slipping into hers. How he didn't know the level of her distress, Kristen couldn't comprehend. He tugged, but she pulled her hand away.

She needed to see that newspaper. The whole story. Right now.

Her adrenaline shot through her body, and she suddenly felt like someone had put a heated blanket over her head and around her shoulders.

"Kristen?" Theo asked.

"Mom," Clara hissed.

All of her girls stood near the exit, as there wasn't anything else to see in this "time capsule display." They watched her with expressions ranging from confusion to wariness to something else entirely.

Frantic now, she spun around, trying to find a police officer. The one who'd asked her to keep moving met her eyes, and he came her way. "I need to see Chief Sherman," Kristen said out loud, her voice strong though so much of her shook. "Right now."

"What's this about?" the officer asked. Kristen knew him, because she'd been very active in the Five Island Cove community for a long time.

"Brandon," she said calmly. "This is not a time capsule. This is a remnant of my family history, which is why Chief Sherman couldn't find any record of the capsule in Five Island Cove history." She drew in a breath. "Now, I want to see him immediately so I can reclaim my property."

"Let me get him," Brandon Watts said, and he turned away from her and spoke into the radio on his shoulder.

Kristen couldn't help turning back to that last newspaper in the case. How many people would realize the significance of it? Who had her grandmother sold the lighthouse to? Had she ever repurchased it?

If she hadn't...then Kristen didn't own what she'd always thought she had, and Reuben had no right to be living at the lighthouse, running it.

She had the strongest urge to storm over to the case and rip the paper from it. She could burn it, and no one would ever learn the truth. *She* didn't even know the truth.

"Ma'am," Officer Watts said. "He said you can come back." He took her elbow and led her away from everyone waiting for her at the exit.

"Kristen," Alice said helplessly.

"Mom, what's going on?" Clara called, her voice so loud in the quiet hall.

Kristen said nothing as she followed the officer through a doorway and into a much more private hallway. Chief Sherman appeared near the end of it as he came out of an open doorway. He didn't smile as she approached, and Kristen wanted to run at him and shout her questions in his face.

She maintained her composure, however, and Aaron gestured her into the room. "All right, Kristen," he said. "Tell me what's going on."

Chapter Eleven

Kelli Webb couldn't stand the silence in the lighthouse. She strongly disliked getting online and reading the speculation and rumors about the items on display at City Hall. She hated the fact that she'd come to Diamond Island today to meet her husband, and then they were on their way for the ultrasound that would tell Kelli what gender her baby was—and this joyous event that should be the big thing on the friends' text would be overshadowed.

She normally wasn't a very jealous person. She didn't need to be in the spotlight—and in fact, she'd spent a large portion of her life trying to keep people from looking at her.

She groaned and pressed one hand to the side of her belly. The baby had shifted and she'd forgotten how uncomfortable it was to grow another person inside her body. She'd do anything for the baby inside her, so she moved over onto her hip and sighed.

"You okay?" Jean asked, and Kelli looked over to her. She'd been feeding Heidi when Kelli and Parker had arrived, but she'd since laid the little girl down for her nap.

"Yes," Kelli said with a smile. She wasn't going to complain about her pregnancy. Not to Jean, who'd longed to carry life inside her and had never had the chance to do so. "Are you sure it's okay if I leave Parker here? He was completely disinterested in the ultrasound."

"Of course," Jean said. "Reuben is showing him the new weather system, and then I told him I'd take him down to Seal Beach."

"Is it safe down there?" Kelli worried about almost everything, though she'd found some relief from that after her divorce and through yoga and meditation. "This winter has been a bit strange."

It had been cold and windy for a couple of months now, with lashing rain one day and then a gloriously blue sky the next. Kelli wasn't cold at all these days, not with an extra bun in the oven to keep her warm.

Parker had brought a jacket, and Kelli reminded herself that her son wasn't a little boy anymore. He'd be thirteen—a teenager—in only a few months. Not only that, but she trusted Jean. If she said Seal Beach was safe, it was safe.

"I'll check the waves," Jean said, lifting her phone up.

"We've got a camera that points that way on the lighthouse." She flashed a smile that didn't stay long, and Kelli wondered how this mystery surrounding Kristen and the time capsule display had affected her.

She wasn't sure how to ask. The words didn't just order themselves in her head the way they might've for AJ or Eloise. Alice and Robin spoke their mind, even if the sentences were a bit harsh or jumbled.

Kelli generally waited and watched until she could lay out all the pieces and make sense of them. The problem was, no one was offering any pieces. Kristen had disappeared with an officer, and no one had seen her since. She'd texted exactly one time to say, *I'm okay. I have some things to figure out, and I'll let you all know everything as soon as I can.*

They'd gone through the display together. Kelli could still hear Kristen say, plain as day, "These are my grandparents."

She hadn't been able to figure out why Kristen's grandparents would have their picture in the time capsule. She'd spent so much time at the lighthouse with Kristen and Joel after her father had lost everything. Without Kristen, without the safety she'd felt at the lighthouse, Kelli would not be here.

She wouldn't be in Five Island Cove right now, expecting a baby with her second husband. She wouldn't be on the friends' text at all. She wouldn't even be on the earth. Kristen and the lighthouse had saved her during a crucial time of her life, and unrest filled Kelli as she thought about it all being a façade.

It wasn't fake, she told herself. Her past wouldn't change because of whatever she learned in the present or the future. She reminded herself of that, but the hope only went so far. When new light got shed on something —as had happened a few times over the past several years since she'd returned to the cove—feelings changed. Experiences didn't seem the same. They didn't *feel* the same. Kelli desperately didn't want her fond memories of Kristen and the lighthouse to diminish or dull, wane or warp.

But she'd seen the pictures in the display. She'd heard Kristen claim them as her ancestors. Kelli had heard the stories of how Kristen's grandparents had bought the lighthouse before World War Two, but then her granddad had gone to war.

She knew he hadn't come home. She knew her grandmother had then dug in and run the lighthouse by herself —seven days a week, twenty-four hours a day. She'd built the cottage up on the rocks to house and hire extra help, and she'd lived in this underground apartment alone.

Kristen's father had then taken over the lighthouse duties with his family, and eventually, the task had fallen to Kristen and Joel, and now Reuben and Jean. History couldn't be changed, but the truth of it emulated a kaleidoscope, ever-shifting with the tilt of perspective, casting the same events in a myriad of colors and patterns, each equally vivid and real.

She didn't want her past truths to tilt. To change. To be shown through a different lens.

"The waves look a bit big," Jean said. "But there's plenty of beach, and he'll just toss bread to the birds." She looked up from her phone, her smile a tad bigger and definitely brighter. "Okay?"

"Yes, of course." Kelli got to her feet, and because she only had ten more weeks of her pregnancy, she couldn't actually see her shoes. "Jean."

The other woman looked at her again, her expression open, unassuming.

"Have you heard anything more from Kristen? Do you and Reuben, perhaps, know something? It's eating me alive."

Jean's face clouded, and she started shaking her head before Kelli had finished speaking. "I wish we did," she said. "Reuben's so perplexed by it all. He's gone to the display three times now."

"Those are her grandparents in the picture," Kelli said. "She used to keep them on the wall in the cottage. We all came to help her clean out the house, and I know she took them."

Jean nodded, her eyes focused on something far away now. "They're her grandparents. Rose Worthington. That headline that says Rose sold the lighthouse..." She seemed defeated, and Kelli hadn't meant to dampen the mood.

"I just want to know what's going on," Kelli said. "Shad won't say much, because Aaron's really trying to control how much information gets out there."

"Eloise mentioned that," Jean said.

Kelli nodded, though she didn't like it. "We just live in this world where we expect answers in less than two seconds," she said. "And it's frustrating that there's literally been nothing for days."

"Well, that Ophelia Francis seems to have plenty to say." Jean rolled her eyes and stood up. "Take a cookie with you. I wish I could tell you more. Kristen left no photo albums here. The library is in lock-down mode— Clara tried to get over there to look at their microfiche, maybe to find more newspaper articles."

She went into the kitchen and opened her freezer. "Reuben's tried to read the article to see who Grace sold the lighthouse to, but it's so faded and hard to read. It wasn't properly preserved."

"Yeah," Kelli said. "I don't think it was a time capsule."

Jean turned toward her with a bag of chocolate chip cookies in her hand. Her eyes widened. "You don't?"

"No." Kelli shook her head thoughtfully. "It wasn't preserved properly, like you said. The city doesn't have any record of it. I think it was just...some stuff they found that belonged to Grace Worthington." She lifted her eyebrows, asking Jean if she agreed.

Jean didn't say anything, but that didn't mean she believed Kelli. Another sigh filled her. "Okay," she said. "I have to go meet Shad for our appointment."

Jean flew into motion then. She squeezed Kelli tightly and put one hand on her belly. "What are you hoping for?"

"If I'm being honest..." Kelli allowed herself to smile. This *should* be one of the best days of her life. She didn't *have* to let this cloud of uncertainly block out the good in her life. "A girl. Then I'd have one of each."

"Baby girls are the sweetest," Jean said with a blissful smile.

"I'll bring back dinner," Kelli said, and then she made her way up the two flights of stairs to the navy blue door on the lighthouse. She didn't bother calling up to Parker that she was leaving, because he wouldn't hear her anyway.

She tapped to get a RideShare to City Hall, where Shad worked. They'd walk over to the doctor's office from there, as it was just behind the Hall, across a large grass quad. She got one and tucked her phone away for the three-minute wait.

Her phone buzzed, and she plucked it out of her pocket again. Her ride had just been canceled. She frowned and tapped to get another one. Sometimes that happened if a driver had taken another job almost simultaneously with hers.

No one would pick up the ride, and Kelli actually did start to feel a little cold. She'd forgotten to grab a cookie, and the time of her appointment neared. She tapped to call Shad, and he answered with, "Are you here? I need another five minutes."

"I'm still at the lighthouse," Kelli said. "No one will pick up my RideShare."

A long sigh came from her husband's mouth. Kelli had no way to get there if she couldn't use RideShare. Very few people owned cars in Five Island Cove, and their infrastructure was awesome—if it worked.

"Are you trying to come here?" Shad asked.

"Yes," Kelli said.

"Put in the address for the doctor's office," he said. "I'll meet you over there. They're not driving to City Hall right now."

Kelli frowned, because she'd never heard of RideShare limiting where they'd take a person. "Okay," she said. "I hope I get there before I freeze to death."

"Hon, just go back inside the lighthouse to wait."

"Okay," Kelli said, but she wouldn't do that. She ended the call, amended the location she wanted to go to, and tapped to get another ride.

This one got accepted immediately, and she had a six-minute wait. She could handle that, because it wasn't terribly windy right now, though the gusts tended to kick up every now and then.

Shad didn't understand why Kelli wouldn't go back inside, and she could admit she barely understood. She simply didn't like imposing on people. She didn't like good-byes—and she'd already said good-bye to Jean.

"Oh, dinner," she muttered to herself. She texted Shad that they were going to grab dinner after their appointment and eat it with Reuben and Jean. She didn't expect him to answer, because he'd sounded rushed on the phone and she'd see him in person in only a few minutes.

Sure enough, her ride came, and the woman behind the wheel smiled her into the backseat. "To Doctor Willis?" she asked, glancing down at Kelli's stomach. "Seems like it. People have been putting in addresses on the other side of City Hall just to get there."

Kelli managed a tight smile. "I really do have an appointment with him today. Ultrasound."

"Oh, that's great," the woman said. She chattered the whole way downtown, but Kelli didn't mind. She didn't have to say much, and the noise actually distracted her from her own thoughts.

Inside the doctor's office, only a receptionist waited. She looked up as Kelli entered, and she bloomed to life. "Kelli," she said, rising to her feet. "We're ready for you."

"You—are?" Kelli looked around, but the lobby was empty.

"Yep," the receptionist said. "You're our last appointment of the day, and we've just been waiting." She smiled like this was no big deal, but Kelli had the impression the woman was ready to go home, and only Kelli stood in her way.

"My husband isn't here," she said.

"I'll just take you back and bring him when he comes," she said, gesturing for Kelli to get on over there to where she stood. Kelli did, and she followed the woman down the hall to a room with a long table in it and plenty of equipment.

She'd just pulled out her phone to text Shad when Dr. Willis entered. "All right," he said. "Let's check on your baby." He also beamed, but the sunlight felt false, like that of a tanning bed. Bright, but almost lethal.

"Shad isn't here," Kelli said. "He's coming from City Hall, and he was going to meet me."

"City Hall." Dr. Willis scoffed and shook his head. "It's incredible what's going on there, right?"

Kelli didn't know how to answer, so she simply blinked at him.

"Did you see that article that said the Planning and Zoning Commission approved over two hundred building permits this year?"

Kelli took a breath. "The Planning Commission doesn't actually approve permits," she said, her voice growing hoarse. "They *recommend* them to the City

Council, and they get reviewed there." She swallowed, because she wouldn't have known that without Shad's knowledge and expertise in city government. "Then they go to the Building Permits Division for final approval."

Dr. Willis took his turn to blink at her. "It's still a lot of building permits. Two hundred?"

Kelli wanted to tell him that number might not even be true, but she held her tongue. The tension between them broke, and Dr. Willis took a big breath. "Okay," he said, his voice moving back into the bright zone. "You did want to know the gender, right?"

"Yes," Kelli said. "But we're waiting for Shad."

"Oh, we can get started without him." Dr. Willis stood and picked up a tube of gel.

Kelli did not lay down and expose her belly. "I want to wait for him before we start."

"He's late," Dr. Willis said.

"And you don't have any other patients after us," Kelli said pointedly. "So can we please just—?" She cut off when the door opened and Shad hurried inside.

"Sorry," he said. "Sorry, doctor. Hey, honey." He smiled at her and pressed a kiss to her forehead, obviously oblivious to the mood of the room. He'd broken it, and the awkwardness had fled through the open door. He looked from Dr. Willis, who still held the tube of gel, to Kelli. "Did I miss something?"

"No," Kelli said quickly. "We were waiting for you to

start." She laid back and lifted her shirt, her heartbeat suddenly tumbling through her veins. "Let's see how this baby is doing."

Shad smiled at her, but Kelli had a hard time returning it. She'd always liked Dr. Willis. She'd known there would be differing opinions on the growth happening in Five Island Cove.

She and Shad lived on Pearl Island, the one furthest from the center of the cove. Life there was slower, quieter, easier, and she had no desire to be in the thick of anything political like how many building permits were issued this year.

All of that disappeared when the steady, drumming heartbeat of her baby filled the room. "Oh," she whispered, looking over to the screen. She let Dr. Willis talk about the size of the baby, and how things looked like they'd been developing properly.

He adjusted her due date from March tenth to the fifteenth, and a rush of adrenaline filled Kelli. Five more days? She didn't want to be pregnant for an extra five days —especially by the end of all of this. Not only that, but March fifteenth was the Ides of March—a day of misfortune.

She shook the superstition out of her head. March fifteenth was just a date, like the fourteenth before it and the sixteenth after it.

"All right," Dr. Willis said. "Right here, I'm seeing

that you two are going to be the proud parents of a little girl."

Kelli's smile burst onto her face then, and it was the first real one she'd experienced since the windows had been shattered at The Glass Dolphin.

"A girl," she repeated. Shad laughed and leaned over to kiss her. As he gazed at her, they smiled at one another and both said, "A little girl," at the same time.

Kelli would like to think she could retreat to her bubble on Pearl Island and let all the other things slide around her. She knew that wasn't possible, but for this one moment, with Shad, it totally was, and she seized onto it and committed it to memory.

She couldn't wait to tell her friends, and she hoped her news would be a ray of light in the darkening uncertainty hanging over all of them.

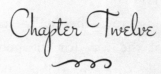

Chapter Twelve

Maddy twisted the key, and the new glass doors to The Glass Dolphin opened just like they had before the vandalism. She breathed a soft, nearly silent sigh of relief even as Ben pressed close behind her.

"Okay," he said, because that was what he said to steady her. He'd asked her if she was okay two weeks ago, before they'd left for Nantucket. She'd said she was.

She'd taken him to her father's house, and they'd enjoyed their stay there before continuing up to Canada.

Maddy leaned back into his body. "Okay," she repeated. On her next breath, everything solidified inside her again, and she drew strength from the fact that she'd been in much worse situations before.

For this, she'd been out of town for a large portion of the rebuild, and it hadn't taken that much. The assailant had thrown seven buckets through the windows, but those buckets had been empty. They hadn't contained water, coins, or anything toxic that would've ruined flooring, tables, or chairs.

A good cleaning crew—her staff—had moved everything back out of the way for the general contractor, who'd come to make sure everything was still structurally sound and ready for windows.

Then, the waiting started. Maddy hadn't needed to be here to wait for the glass to be shipped from New York. So she'd done her best to enjoy herself in Montreal. She'd laughed with Ben's parents. She'd met his sister and her husband. She'd let his mother exclaim over her every morning and tell her how pretty she was and how she'd been praying for Ben to meet someone like Maddy for so long.

Ruth did have a strong personality, but Maddy didn't mind. She'd been married before, and Ben's mother had taken the news that they would be getting married in the cove pretty well. She still wanted to be involved, and she claimed she could fly down "at any time" to go dress shopping with Maddy, or help her pick out flowers, or to do taste testings.

The thought of it all exhausted Maddy. That tiredness went with her as she entered the restaurant she'd returned to last week. She'd met with Teresa and the building inspector, and they'd laid out a timeline for tonight's grand re-opening.

"It's not a re-opening," she said out loud. "We just need to get everything where I want it, and then you can go."

"I can stay as long as you need me to," Ben said. "I'm not working today or tonight."

Maddy went past the new seats that had been put in the waiting area. The other ones had been ripped and nicked with glass shards. The hostess station remained, as did their bar area. None of that had been damaged beyond repair, and as Maddy inspected every inch, she couldn't tell what was new and what was old.

She marveled that broken things, shredded things, ruined things could be made whole again. If she hadn't stood on the sidewalk in pre-dawn light, she wouldn't believe that The Glass Dolphin had ever been anything but how it was now.

Her mind wandered as she made sure the menus were wiped down and set in the right spot. She hadn't gone to see the display of items from the time capsule. She'd read and re-read every message on the chat she'd been added to months ago, and she could picture every item in her mind's eye without having seen them.

She and Julia had gone through plenty of old pictures and heirlooms at The Lighthouse Inn, and frankly, Maddy didn't want to see the old LP or the weathered photos. She didn't need to read the headlines from 1950, or try to piece together who'd gathered the items and placed them in the ground.

If they even had. Maddy directed Ben to help her straighten chairs and curtains, and systematically, they moved through the restaurant. After several minutes of silently working together, Ben looked over to her, something dark and dangerous on his face.

Maddy paused, and Ben softened. "I'm worried about you," he murmured from the other side of the table.

She wanted to reassure him that he didn't need to worry about her, but it honestly felt nice to have someone care enough to fret over her. All she could offer him was a small smile, which she did. "I'm okay," she said. "Really."

"Work gives you a purpose."

"It helps," she admitted.

"Have I ever told you how sexy you are when you're thinking about something?" He quirked up one half of his mouth, and Maddy couldn't stop the smile that spread her lips fully.

"You're not scared here, are you?" he asked.

Maddy shook her head, though a tremble of anxiety moved through her. "I maybe invited you along to help so I didn't have to come alone," she said. "But I'm not really scared to be here alone, no. He didn't show up at peak dinner time and start throwing buckets."

He'd waited until the middle of the night, when absolutely no one would be on this street, let alone inside the restaurant. He hadn't run. He'd allowed himself to get caught. "This was about the message, not the mess."

Ben straightened another chair and fixed the vase of flowers in the middle of the table. "It still caused a mess. It can still unnerve you."

"It can," she said, glancing around. She wondered how she'd feel if she was there alone. The front and the back of The Glass Dolphin were made of glass. Pure glass, with slim metal pieces holding them together. Anyone could see in or out; anyone could see her, alone, inside the restaurant.

Ben drew around the table and paused in front of her. "Sweetheart." He didn't really say much, but that word said so much. She brought her attention to him, feeling like she'd been sandwiched between two pieces of glass and then put under a microscope.

The planes pressed against her, squeezing tighter and tighter and tighter.

"Mads."

The word snapped her back to the present. Ben still stood in front of her, one hand wrapped loosely around her wrist. She looked at their point of contact, then moved her gaze to meet his. "I'm okay," she said.

"I don't think you are."

She had no reason not to be, so she smiled at him. She'd learned through her divorce and everything that had happened since, that human emotions couldn't be explained. They simply swarmed onto a person at the most random of times, consuming them until there was nothing left.

Maddy had learned to tame hers during her time in the political spotlight. She hadn't liked how cold and detached she'd become, and she'd vowed never to return to that state. "Could you stay?" she asked. "Just through opening. I'm sure once there are other people here, I'll be fine."

"I'll stay all night," Ben said. "Whatever you need." He gave her one last look, then bent down and gently touched his lips to hers. For the thrill-seeking, fast-moving, motorcycle-riding Coast Guard Captain, that simple, elegant, gentle touch told her how much he loved her.

Maddy let herself bask in that instead of the negativity of uncertainty and fear. She invited those feelings in, hoping they'd attack the others and drive them out.

Ben pulled away and said, "Let's finish up the back wall, okay?"

In that moment, Maddy realized she hadn't allowed herself to work by the windows yet. She looked that way, saw all the bright afternoon sunlight pouring in through the glass, and bravely nodded. "Yeah," she said. "Let's finish up."

* * *

Hours, a hundred and fifty tickets, and two ferry rides later, Maddy sank into bed. She'd set the text messages from all the women here in the cove to silent, so she could focus on dinner service at The Glass Dolphin.

Ben breezed into the room wearing only his boxers. He brushed his teeth as he looked at her, and Maddy gave him a smile. He tried to return it with his foamy mouth and that made her giggle.

Simple things, she told herself. *Quiet moments.* She needed to find them and appreciate them more. Not everything had to be big and grandiose to be worth having. Ben went back into the bathroom, and Maddy faced her phone.

That text string had over a hundred messages on it, and she finally found the strength to tap it open.

Good luck tonight, Maddy! Alice had said. *I'm sure the re-opening will go well.*

Thinking of you, AJ had said, which meant a lot, as Maddy had spent minimal time with AJ.

Aaron's got officers nearby, Eloise had assured them all. She hadn't had anything to say on the items retrieved from the ground near The Glass Dolphin. Maddy had read a dozen articles, all of them speculating on what those items meant, who they belonged to, and how they'd gotten to be where they'd been discovered.

It seemed no one had any answers, even two weeks later. No answers they were sharing anyway.

Every message of well-wishes made her heart lift, and eventually the conversation turned to the young adults who'd gone back to college, Robin's mother who'd returned from her cruise, and then a luncheon that Kristen had invited everyone to this upcoming Wednesday.

Maddy knew some of the women got together in smaller groups. She lived out on Rocky Ridge, and she didn't feel the need to ferry in to go walking for an hour, and she usually worked the day shift, so lunches were out.

Ben returned to the bedroom, and he sank onto the mattress beside her. "You're not working, are you?"

"No," she said. "But I do need to do the schedule for the rest of the week and next week." She hadn't been sure how dinner would go tonight. Neither she nor Teresa had wanted to commit, but they both wanted the restaurant open again.

She looked over to Ben and then handed him her phone. "What do you think? Should I go to lunch with everyone?"

He took a few moments to read through the last several texts, and when he looked up, he wore a light in his eyes that Maddy loved. "Honey, I think you want friends here, don't you?"

"Yes," she whispered. "I have Julia."

"Yeah, and from the things you've said about her, she'll be married before us."

Maddy smiled and took her phone back. "She won't, because Julia is cautious, but yeah." She set her device on her nightstand and looked at the selfie she'd put in a picture frame in front of the lamp. "She sure does like Liam, and he's treating her right."

"Yeah?" Ben slid his hand down Maddy's leg. "Like, treating her right the way I treat you right? Or…"

Maddy ducked her head and wove her fingers through his. "Julia is tight-lipped about Liam." She turned into him and pressed her lips to his. "Just like I am about you. You don't want me talking about how you…treat me right, do you?"

"Absolutely not," he growled as he laid her back and kissed her. He didn't linger long before he broke the kiss and whispered, "You should go to that lunch, sweetheart. I think you want to, and I think you *need* to."

Maddy let his words sink in, and then she nodded. "I'm going to go."

"Good," he said. "Now, let me take care of you, okay?"

And all Maddy had to say was, "Okay."

Chapter Thirteen

Robin Grover hesitated in her office, the white binder with the sketched-out plans for Maddy and Ben's wedding accusing her from the corner of her desk. Maddy would be at lunch today, and Robin could just pass her the binder afterward.

"You could just text her and set up a time to meet," she told herself, and she pulled out her phone to do that. She adored the big group text, but even she could admit it was hard to keep up with from time to time.

She knew everyone on it and had for a while, and she couldn't imagine how someone like Maddy or Julia might feel. At the same time, Robin had hearted the picture of Clara, Eloise, and Julia in the kitchen at The Cliffside Inn, where they all worked. They obviously had a close friend-ship, and Robin didn't know Clara or Julia as well.

She went to lunch with Laurel and Alice the most, and she definitely talked to Alice the most off the group chat. AJ had posted a picture of her, Jean, and Laurel bundled up and walking with their tiny kids yesterday morning, so smaller off-shoots of the larger group definitely existed.

It wasn't worth being upset about, and Robin wasn't upset about it anyway. Her thoughts strayed to Kelli, though, because Kelli wasn't as loud as some of the others, and she lived on the farthest island.

"So does Maddy," Robin said, though Rocky Ridge sat in the opposite direction from Pearl.

She sent a quick text to Maddy about bringing the binder, and then she grabbed it and left. It could ride shotgun in the minivan to lunch and back, and no one would be any wiser.

Kristen had called this luncheon, and she'd said she'd gone back and forth about where to have it. A restaurant? There were plenty of places to eat on a Wednesday afternoon that could accommodate twelve people, but Kristen had chosen the cottage at the lighthouse.

Robin could drive to the iconic landmark on the east side of the island with her eyes closed. She'd gone there so often growing up, and she alone had continued to visit Kristen and Joel Shields after everyone else had moved on to college, careers, and life.

The small parking lot only held two cars when she

arrived—Eloise's and Alice's. She wasn't sure if that made her third to arrive or not, as everyone else could've easily used RideShare and been dropped off.

She paused again, the car stopped and off in the stall. Her phone chimed, and she picked it up from the cupholder. Maddy had texted to say she had all day today to meet, *if you want to stay after the luncheon?*

Sure, Robin said. *I have your binder, but we can go back to my house.* She sent the text and looked up and out the windshield. The sky hadn't been blue for a couple of days now, but an ominous shade of gray. Not dark enough to indicate a storm, but the lighter kind that simply told Robin she'd not be seeing the sun that day.

Since she'd returned from New York City, where she'd welcomed her mother back from her fifteen-day Christmas cruise, Robin had found herself staring a lot. She'd been beating through life to the rhythm of her mother's drum for her entire life. Almost fifty years now.

She'd hated the sound of it, and she'd tried to find her own beat to march to. In some ways, she had. She and Duke no longer lived in her mother's rental house. They no longer relied on her for anything.

"And because of her, you no longer have the boat payment."

Her mother had done exactly what she'd offered— she'd gone with Robin to the credit union, and she'd paid for Duke's fishing boat, right down to the last penny. She had millions of dollars, and she was trying to figure out how to be a person again.

Someone knocked on her window, and Robin yelped as she startled away from the sharp sound. Laurel opened the door, her smile big but falling fast. "I'm sorry," she said. "I called to you through the glass a couple of times. I even waved. You didn't move a muscle."

"Just thinking." Robin collected her purse, her news about to spew out of her. She hadn't wanted to tell it over the group text, and she wasn't sure why. Perhaps she needed more time for everything to make sense inside her head before she put it down in black and white.

She stood and immediately stepped into Laurel's arms. "It's so good to see you."

Laurel held her back perfectly, and Robin got reminded of how good it was to expand borders. How right it felt to include everyone. How empty her life would be without Laurel in it. She occupied a piece of Robin's heart that no one else could, and she beamed at the younger woman as she stepped back.

"Are you surviving James's first tooth? For real?"

"Only by the grace of God," Laurel said wryly. She didn't carry her son in her arms as she moved up onto the sidewalk.

"Where is he today?" Robin asked as she followed her. "I assumed you moms would have your kids."

Laurel gave her the side-eye and pushed her blonde

hair off her face as the wind tried to plaster it to her cheek. "You really were out of it. I walked right in front of you with James. He's in the lighthouse with Reuben and Heidi."

They didn't go down the sidewalk that would branch up toward the lighthouse. Robin looked that way, because she'd traversed that path so many times. Happy times. Sad times. Mad times. Kristen and the lighthouse had always been there for her, and she'd tried to repay the favor as much as she could over the years.

Laurel led the way down a different sidewalk, this one leading parallel to the lighthouse and toward a cottage that had been built back behind it. Robin had trod this path many times too, to visit Kristen and Joel, to bring them food when she'd learned of his illness, and to help Kristen finally clean everything out and move on after his death.

It was funny how the same path could exist over time, but every time a person walked over it, they were different.

Neither of them knocked as they reached the cottage; Laurel simply twisted the knob and went right in. The weather basically demanded that, and Robin scurried in after her and pushed the door closed behind her.

They definitely weren't the first and second to arrive. The cottage held physical warmth, and as Robin shrugged out of her coat, she found at least six women turning toward her and Laurel, smiles on all of their faces.

Jean came forward first as Clara said, "Robin's here."

"Finally," Alice said, a fruity drink—most likely non-alcoholic—in her hand and a knowing smile on her face.

Robin let herself get swept up in Jean's embrace, and then she joined the others in the kitchen, making a space for herself between Julia and Maddy. "So." She exhaled. "What's going on?"

"They're talking men," Alice said, leaning toward them, her smile more impish now. "Jean and Clara and I are talking about the inn; Kelli had to go to the bathroom—"

"Again," Jean said with a grin."

"Again," Alice echoed. "And believe it or not, AJ won't come out of the kitchen, where Kristen is currently hiding too."

The cottage wasn't big enough to hide, though Robin had seen Kristen try to do so before. AJ too.

"So only Eloise isn't here?" Robin asked, glancing around. "No, wait. And Tessa."

"Oh, she can't make it now," Julia said. "She came down with a nasty cold, poor thing."

"Eloise's car is outside," Robin said, hooking her thumb over her shoulder. She watched Kristen in the kitchen, but the older woman kept her back to everyone. She hadn't greeted Robin, which made her stomach thunder in the most uncomfortable way.

"We drove it," Clara said. "Julia and I, from the ferry station. She said she'd get a RideShare when she came."

The door opened again, and a wind-blown Eloise got swept in. Her hair had started to grow out again, but it still sprouted from her head in curls, and she huffed as she wiped them out of her eyes. "Sorry I'm late," she said, which had become a mantra for Eloise lately.

Robin had hoped that she'd find some relief by hiring more people, and perhaps she had. Maybe Robin hadn't asked her. There was so much she'd missed out on in the past couple of weeks, and as she met Alice's eye, they both raised their eyebrows.

Alice actually smiled, but Robin felt like bursting into tears. "Who's gonna call it?" she asked as Jean went to greet El too.

"You better," Robin said. "No one wants to hear me do it."

"Call what?" Maddy asked, looking from Robin to Alice and back.

"All right," Alice yelled into the small space. The smaller two-person conversations that had started dried right up. "I'm calling a Tell-All. I know people have things to say, and to quote Robin, these things keep us close. If there's something you don't want to tell us, you probably should."

"I have never said that last part," Robin said, shooting Alice a look she hoped was filled with pure venom. "I do think telling each other things keeps us close, and well, I feel far apart from some of you."

"Only because you've been out of town," El said, slipping her hand around Robin's waist. She grinned at her. "We're right here. You're right here."

A surge of love for Eloise moved through Robin. "Thanks, El," she whispered.

"Do you want to get food first?" Kristen asked. She now faced the group as she leaned into the small peninsula that separated the tiny kitchen area from the small dining area. A big round table had been set up in what had once been the living room, and Robin sure did like that. She'd be able to see and hear everyone.

"Always food first," El said, deciding for everyone.

"I would like to go last," Kristen said, nodding to Alice. She couldn't seem to look at Robin at all, and as Alice granted her permission to participate in the Tell-All last, Robin skirted around behind El, Maddy, and Clara to get to the kitchen.

She waited on the peripheral as Kristen and AJ laid out the food. Then chatter broke out as paper plates got picked up and people put food on them.

Robin edged into the kitchen and finally wrapped her arms around Kristen. She remained stiff for a long moment, and then she relaxed into Robin's embrace. "How are you, dear?" she asked in that voice that had comforted Robin for nearly five decades.

She pressed her eyes shut and just held on, no words

needed to convey how she was. She finally stepped back and met Kristen's eyes. "I have a lot to tell everyone."

Kristen smiled in that loving, matronly way she had. "Good thing Alice called the Tell-All then." They laughed together, and with a happier heart, Robin filled a plate with a brownie, a roll, and plenty of salad. Then, she selected the Dijon chicken stew for her main dish and went to sit at the table.

Alice had kept a spot next to her, and Robin took it, assuming it to be hers. Alice side-hugged her, pressing her cheek to Robin's. "I missed you so much. Never go to New York again."

Robin laughed, because they'd talked every day. Maybe not verbally, but definitely through texts. "What are we going to do about our kids?" she asked almost under her breath. She even tried to hide the fact that she'd spoken by lifting her spoon to her mouth, as if a plastic spoon with a bit of soup on it would conceal anything.

"You know what?" Alice looked right at her. "I've decided they're adults. Of course I'm going to worry about them. I'm going to counsel them the best I can. But *doing* something? There's nothing I can *do*."

"You've already done it," Julia said from a few seats down. "That's one thing I learned from my adult sons. I'm already the voice in their head." She smiled at Alice and Robin. "Right, Maddy?"

"Usually," Maddy said. "I was surprised at how much

my kids had actually listened to me. There are years where you feel like you're shouting at the walls."

"Don't I know it?" Alice joked.

Robin definitely felt like that. Jamie, her fifteen-year-old, had already brought the drama to the house, having had two boyfriends in the past year alone. Robin did not enjoy the teen girl stage of life, and she told herself she just needed to make it through to Jamie's senior year. That had been when Mandie had matured a lot.

"You're right," she said to Alice, who blinked at her. "Charlie and Mandie are adults. If they want to get married and face the world together, why would we say no?'

"Because they're nineteen?" Alice asked. "And not even that."

"I met Duke when I was nineteen," Robin said, and she actually put the bite of soup in her mouth.

"Yeah, but you didn't marry him for several more *years*," Alice said.

"All right," AJ said from across the table. "Are we doing this or not? Some of us would like to then enjoy the luncheon." She cut a look over to Kelli, whom Robin had not seen return from the bathroom.

"Sure," Alice said smoothly. "Why don't you go first?"

AJ rolled her eyes, but her fun smile negated the action. "I don't have a lot, but I will say this—if there's a vote or poll about the growth in Five Island Cove, Matt and I are going to vote in favor of it. Tourism and having a positive image of our islands fuels the golf course. It's literally our livelihood."

Kelli didn't miss a beat as she asked, "When's your op-ed piece coming out?"

AJ's expression turned a bit dark. "They keep giving it back to me to 'edit.'" She made air quotes around the last word. "Hopefully soon."

A beat of silence passed, and then Kelli said, "I'm having a girl." Her face pinked up, and Robin only delayed cheering so she could swallow her bite of salad. Then she lifted her voice toward the rafters along with everyone else congratulating Kelli.

Kristen sat next to Kelli, so Alice looked at Clara. "Clara?" she prompted. "Something for the Tell-All?"

"Uh." Clara quickly put down her spoon. She'd taken the winter minestrone soup, and that had tempted Robin. She glanced at her mother on one side and Jean on the other. "Nothing much, I guess? I really love working at the inn." She smiled at Eloise, who sat next to Robin. "Lena's loving her job. Scott and I are getting along. It's a pretty boring life."

"Boring does not mean bad," Alice said, and Robin wondered what she'd say for her Tell-All. She usually knew all of Alice's news before the others, but she didn't have anything for her.

"Jean?"

"I miss my sewing students," Jean admitted. "And, this is probably crazy, but Reuben and I are going to put our application out there for another baby. We love Heidi so much, and we both think it would be fun if she had a sibling."

Robin nodded, though shock coursed through her. Their baby girl wasn't even four months old yet, and birth mothers didn't usually pick a couple until they were almost due. Jean and Reuben could have two tiny babies very close together.

She'd always thought it took a special person to do that; that was why her children were four years apart.

"El, you're up," Alice said, glancing past Robin. Her heart started to pound, because after Eloise, she'd have to talk. Her mind blitzed, because she didn't even know where to start. She hadn't been on the island when Aaron had announced the time capsule. She hadn't been able to walk through the display with everyone else. She'd told no one about her mother's offer to pay for Duke's boat, and then the fact that she'd done it.

"I'm going to brag," El said. "In the past week, I've only worked fifty-two hours." She smiled out at everyone, and she was the prettiest one there in Robin's opinion. "I'm home more with the kids and Aaron, and I'm still able to be at the inn."

"Amazing," Robin said, and that started another chorus of congratulations, this time for El.

Robin wiped her mouth, her throat already narrow. Most of the women here knew of her rocky relationship with her mother. Those who didn't, Robin trusted. She glanced over to Clara, then Maddy and Julia. She *did* trust them, and this was exactly why she loved the Tell-All.

Alice looked at her, and Robin cleared her throat. "Some of you know my mother is a bit difficult." Her voice came out stronger than she'd thought it would. "But I...she's trying. She's recently told my brother and I more about her financial situation, and she's paid for Duke's boat."

Her eyes met AJ's for some reason. Perhaps because Duke had lost his boat in the Christmas tsunami two years ago, and it had been AJ's absent mother who'd swept into the cove with financial offers to fix everyone's problems.

Robin had almost taken her up on it too.

AJ had stopped eating completely, her eyes wide as she stared at Robin.

"Like, paid for his boat," Robin said. "We asked her to do that two years ago, and she wouldn't. She has the money. She has some attachments to it, because it came from my dad." Robin's throat closed again, and wow, she had not been expecting that. Tears burned her eyes, and she shook her head in tiny, micro movements, trying to rationalize her way past the emotions.

"Anyway," she said, her voice like that of a cartoon character. "It's done, and she wants to start meeting with me to go over her will and trust, so Stu and I know what to do when she passes."

Alice linked her arm through Robin's and leaned her head on her shoulder. "That's great, Robin," she said.

"Yeah," El said. "Really great." She squeezed Robin's other hand.

Robin didn't dare look at anyone else. Instead, her eyes dropped to her bowl of chicken stew, and she scooped up another bite. She knew better than to put anything in her mouth before Alice said something, though, so she waited with it poised in the air.

"I'm a little bored now that my kids are gone," Alice said, her smile absolutely huge. "So Arthur and I have decided to learn a new hobby together." She paused, ever the dramatic one in the group. She'd performed in plays in high school and everything. "We're going to audition for *Kiss Me, Kate* at the Cove Community Theater next month."

Stunned silence filled the cottage, and it filtered through Robin too.

"Good for you," Julia said first, and that got everyone else's vocal cords unfrozen.

"Yeah," Robin echoed with a few others. "Wow, theater."

"Arthur has a good singing voice," Alice said, her smile going nowhere. In fact, the wattage of it only increased.

"So we'll see." She looked at Laurel, who hastened to wipe her mouth.

"I thought you'd say more," she said. "I'm a lot like AJ. Not much going on. I have to admit, being a full-time mom is more...daunting than I imagined. Most days, Paul gets home before I've had time to shower, but what I've been doing is lying on the floor, reading books to a baby." She didn't smile, and Robin wondered if there was more to what she'd said.

Laurel reached up and wiped her eyes. "I don't know why that makes me emotional. I feel like I used to be so put together, and now I can't even shower before evening."

"Oh, honey." Alice put her arm around Laurel. "It's a big adjustment."

Laurel nodded, but she shot a look across the table to Jean. What that meant, Robin couldn't decipher quickly enough.

"I think it took me a year to figure out how to be a mom," Julia said. "And that was just getting up and getting us both dressed and fed." She grinned around to the group. "After that, the job description changed every day, and I felt like I was putting together a jet plane while flying it into battle. Every single day."

"That's about how it is," Robin said with a smile.

"And I had twins," Alice said. "And no co-pilot." The conversation stalled for a moment, and Alice shook her head. "I'm sorry. I didn't mean to make it sound like anyone here has it easier than me. Or anyone else."

Laurel nodded and hugged Alice. "Thanks, Alice," she whispered.

"Bring sweet baby James over anytime," Alice said. "I'm just reading boring stuff most of the time, and I can at least hold a baby while I do it." Her face brightened. "I know. I can read him my family law briefs. It's reading, right?"

That got a few laughs, and Robin reached past Alice to squeeze Laurel's shoulder. She gave Robin a grateful look, and then the baton got passed to Julia.

"Okay." She took in a deep breath through her nose. "Liam and I have been seeing each other since Thanksgiving," she said, glancing around at everyone. She spoke slowly, evenly. "And he's already started talking about 'when I'll live with him' and what our life will be like together."

"That's great," Maddy said.

Julia gave her a look like, *no, it isn't*, and Maddy clamped her lips closed. "I'm meeting his son, Ian, on Friday night."

"Do you want to meet Ian?" Kelli asked.

Julia looked like she'd swallowed poison that had no known antidote, but she nodded. "I do, because it's the next step for us, and I don't know. It feels huge."

"You like Liam, right?" AJ asked.

"Yes," Julia said.

"She more than *likes* Liam," Clara teased, and that caused Julia to flush and shoot Clara a death glare all at the same time.

"What's scary about this?" Robin asked.

"Robin," Alice admonished.

"What?" she asked. "Until you identify what you're afraid of, you have to keep being afraid."

"Thanks, O Wise One," Alice said.

"No, I think she's right," Julia said, and Robin shot Alice a look she didn't see. "I guess I'm afraid it's moving too fast."

"Julia doesn't move fast," Maddy said. "For anyone who doesn't know. She likes to examine things for a while. Lay out all the pieces and make wholistic decisions." She smiled at her friend, and Julia returned the gesture.

"It might slow down once you meet his son," Alice said. "That's a big step for Liam, too, and I doubt you'll be like me and Kelli and get married on a whim." She glanced across the table to Kelli, who nodded soberly.

"Maybe," Julia said. "I guess we'll see." She looked over to Maddy. "You're last."

"Kristen is last," Alice said loudly, and all eyes went back to her. Her lunch was completely gone, as she hadn't said more than a couple of congratulations at this meal.

Her dark eyes burned in a way Robin hadn't seen in a

while, and she looked to Alice to judge her reaction. Alice simply gazed steadily back at Kristen.

"All right." Maddy cleared her throat. "The Glass Dolphin reopened on Monday, and I had to have Ben stay for the service, but I worked all day yesterday without him, so I'm going to count that as a win." She smiled around the table. "My trip to Montreal was a big success. He was right, and his family really seemed to like me." She leaned forward and looked at Robin. "And Robin and I are meeting today to go over some wedding things."

She nodded, her smile finally feeling natural as it settled on her face.

"You were scared to go back to The Glass Dolphin?" Kelli asked.

"I...I watched him throw those buckets through the glass." Maddy swallowed. "We have online security cameras I can see from anywhere. He seemed so... unhinged."

"He wasn't unhinged," AJ argued. "He had a point to make."

"The point you don't like, you mean?" Alice asked. "The point that he doesn't want tourism to expand here in the cove?" She folded her arms, but AJ didn't back down from Alice. She never had.

"I didn't say I agreed with his point."

"Vandalism is not a good way to make a point," El said quietly. "It's illegal."

"But it's got people talking now," AJ said.

Robin wasn't sure where to weigh in, so she said nothing. That wasn't usually like her—she had opinions and she vocalized them. But this idea that Five Island Cove was growing too big, too fast... She hadn't had much time to really think about it. She and Duke hadn't talked about it.

He was a fisherman. If there weren't people to eat fish, he didn't have a sustainable business.

There's always Alaska, she thought, and that only soured her stomach. She couldn't imagine moving from the only home she'd ever known, from these women here at this luncheon.

"All right," Kristen said loudly. "All right, enough. We're not going to bicker over the expansion of Five Island Cove." Her voice got them all to quiet, the way it had when they were teens and arguing over something.

She twisted and retrieved a manila folder from the bookcase behind her. It didn't hold anything else, and Robin hadn't seen that folder there either. Kristen's hands shook as she flipped open the folder.

"My news is simple, yet complex. I think—I know—it'll impact some of you here. Maybe some of you in ways you don't even know or I couldn't anticipate."

She took a single sheet of paper out of the folder. It was white, not aged, but Robin couldn't see it from her position at the table. "My grandmother sold the lighthouse in Nineteen-Fifty," she said smoothly, though her voice was half the volume as previously. "She simply couldn't afford to keep it. I didn't know this. My parents didn't know it. I grew up here at the lighthouse, and I thought it belonged to my family."

She glanced at Jean, who wore a nervous, wide-eyed look. "This is the full article of that paper we saw on display in City Hall. It says Rose sold the lighthouse to the Cove Fisherman's Coalition."

Robin's heartbeat thumped against her neck. Duke was the current Vice President of the CFC. This couldn't be true.

"They had an agreement with Rose to continue to run the lighthouse," she said. "They paid her, not the city." She took out a couple more pieces of paper. "There was a fire at the downtown city office buildings in Nineteen-Sixty-Two. All of the records burned, and from that date forward, the city of Five Island Cove started paying my grandmother, then my father, then us, and now Reuben, to run the lighthouse."

"What does this mean?" AJ asked as she peered at one of the papers.

"I've asked Alice to sort through all of the documents I could find," Kristen said. "I found some pay stubs from the CFC. Then some from the city. I couldn't find the title to the lighthouse, and I couldn't find any bill of sale for it..." Her gaze switched to Maddy. "Or for the land where The Glass Dolphin sits. You see, that was a plot of land that my grandparents owned. They had a small house there before they bought the lighthouse. They kept it, because my grandfather got called to war before they could do anything with it, and...well, I have no idea when or if my grandmother ever sold it."

"A fire?" El asked, looking at her phone. "Oh, the big one in 1962. Yes." She looked up. "What does this mean?"

Kristen had been passing out the papers, and one reached Robin. She looked at it, and it was the same newspaper as the one she'd seen on display in City Hall. She'd gone with Duke, and it honestly hadn't meant much to her.

The only reason she'd known there was anything afoot was because of Alice's and El's texts to her privately about what had happened with Kristen.

"Alice?" Kristen prompted.

Robin looked up and to Alice, who wore a grim line of determination across her lips. She said nothing, and the tension in the cottage rose and rose and rose, until Robin thought she might burst.

"Alice," she barked.

Alice didn't move a muscle. She stared straight across the table to Kristen as she said, "In a nutshell, the fact is, Kristen—and thereby Reuben and Jean—does not own the lighthouse. According to the Chronicles, the Coalition does. But there is no paperwork. There is no one claiming they own the lighthouse."

Alice finally blinked, and she looked at every woman at the table, all the way around it. No one looked at their phones. No one studied the photocopies Kristen had passed out. No one spoke.

Robin trembled when Alice let her gaze land on her. "So the real question is—what does she do about it?"

Chapter Fourteen

Alice watched as Kristen poured coffee into mugs. She'd needed the escape from the tension at the table, and Alice understood that too. Currently, Robin stood huddled with Jean and Clara, and all of them seemed to be whispering furiously at the same time.

Kelli had immediately hunched toward AJ; no surprise there. They always liked to bounce things off each other to make sense of them.

Julia and Maddy looked like they'd been hit with water balloons, only to find out the water had been frozen inside first.

Laurel and El stood with Alice, and she nodded over to AJ. "What do you think they're talking about?"

"Could be baby clothes," Laurel mused.

"Or what Kelli should name her baby," El said. She

lifted her mug to her lips and took a sip. Alice didn't want coffee. She already felt too keyed up—she'd been buzzed this morning when she'd rolled out of bed.

She'd known about Kristen's dilemma for a week now, and she still wasn't sure what the solution was.

"So," Laurel said, and Alice appreciated her level head so much. "Under the Destroyed Public Records Act, what, exactly, does she need?"

"Private records," Alice said. "We're trying to find a bank ledger, a title company that kept private books, anything like that, where we can find the record of sale. If we can, then we can recreate the title."

"But it won't be Kristen's," El said quietly.

Alice didn't have to shake her head to affirm. "According to the newspaper and Rose's private logbooks here at the lighthouse, it did transfer ownership to the Coalition. The problem is, neither of those are complete enough to recreate the official, public record."

Robin joined them, her face somewhat flushed. Alice needed to stay cool around her, because this news could potentially impact her. Alice had known Duke was the Vice President of the Coalition when Kristen had dropped this bomb in her lap. In fact, Robin had been her first thought.

Kristen worried endlessly for Jean and Clara, though Clara and Scott didn't have any role at the lighthouse. Alice had been over every shred of paperwork, any photograph she could find, and through every inch of microfiche in the library in the past week. She'd put together everything she could, and it still wasn't enough.

Newspapers didn't always report things correctly, and when she'd inquired at the Chronicles to find out if anyone was still alive who could help her, she'd come up negative. The Coalition changed leadership every two years, and the President and Vice President for the time period in question were either deceased or unable to remember. There was no paperwork at the Coalition, as they only took notes of their meetings.

Alice had requested the notes for the entirety of 1950 and 1962, when they'd allegedly bought the lighthouse, and then when they'd stopped paying Rose Worthington. Surely those things would've been discussed at their monthly meetings.

She'd come up empty. Yes, the Coalition had turned over the notes. No, there was no mention of the lighthouse anywhere.

Bank records from almost seventy-five years ago were impossible to get. Rose hadn't saved paystubs or taxes from that long ago, and even if she had, Kristen—her granddaughter—certainly didn't have them.

"There's literally no proof to show that the Coalition purchased the lighthouse," she said. "The problem is, there's no proof that says they didn't."

"No one has questioned this in decades," Laurel said. "Why does it matter now?"

Alice had laid awake at night, wondering the same thing. "It does," she said with a sigh. "Because you need legal documents to hold up in a court of law. For example, let's say I file a lawsuit against Reuben and Jean for ownership of the lighthouse. Me, Alice Rice. I walk into court and I contest their ownership." She pressed her palm to her chest. "I tell the judge *I* own the lighthouse, and the city of Five Island Cove should be paying *me.*"

"They have to have some way of proving you wrong," Robin said, a hint of resignation in her voice.

"Right." Alice needed something to do with her hands, so she moved over to the plate of crispy rice treats Kristen had made and picked one up. The sugary marshmallow made her taste buds rejoice, and she forced her shoulders to go down a little.

"So we need to recreate that title somehow," she said. "But who it belongs to...I don't know. We need documents to prove it, and I'm not sure where else to look."

"Aaron didn't have any ideas?" El cocked her head, her eyes thoughtful. Out of all of them, she'd freaked out the least. Honestly, none of them had gone into hysterics or anything, but the news had definitely hit some women harder than others. Jean would not leave Clara's side, and they both kept looking at Alice like she'd set the records building on fire herself, back in 1962.

"He led me to several people I interviewed," Alice said. "It was a *long* time ago, and most of those people aren't with us anymore."

"Things get lost," Laurel murmured.

"Or stored in attics," Robin said. "Forgotten."

Lost and forgotten. Alice honestly felt like that herself sometimes. She watched everyone for a few more moments, and then she stepped over to Kristen. "Listen," she said as she hugged her. "I know it's not the answer you want, but I'm going to keep working on it, okay?"

"I know you will, dear." Kristen hadn't shed a tear today. When she'd first met with Alice last week, she had. She simply didn't understand how things could've gotten so mixed up. Alice didn't either, but as a lawyer, she loved a good mystery.

She'd find the evidence…somehow. Now, what it showed still might not be what Kristen or Jean or Clara wanted. But Alice would find it.

"I have to take off," she said to the group at-large, and that caused Julia and Maddy to turn toward her.

"Already?" Julia asked.

"We finished eating an hour ago." Alice smiled at her as she left the kitchen and entered the living space. "How long were you planning on staying?"

"I don't know," Julia said. "All day?" She trilled out a light laugh and then smiled at El. "I have to get back to the inn anyway."

"I'll head out with you," El said, and that made three of them.

"We should go over your wedding binder," Robin said to Maddy, and the blonde woman nodded. Two more.

Alice turned back to Kristen. "Do you need a ride? I can take you home."

"I'm going to get a RideShare with Laurel," Kristen said. "But thank you."

Laurel looked up from her phone, her eyes catching on Alice's. She nodded to Laurel, who nodded back, Alice's silent way of saying, *Please make sure she's okay and inside her condo before you leave.*

"All right, you two," Alice said as she faced AJ and Kelli. "Let me see if the baby will kick for me." She grinned widely as she put her hand on Kelli's bulging belly. She would rather do anything than be pregnant right now, but she knew the joy it had brought to Kelli's life. Shad had never been a father, and he glowed every time Alice saw him.

"She's not moving," Kelli said as she placed her hand over Alice's. Their eyes met, and Alice wanted to reassure her that everything was fine. Nothing had changed. Adjusting wasn't Kelli's strong suit, that was for sure.

Kelli pressed Alice's palm into her belly further. "Sometimes, if you annoy her, she'll kick back."

"So she's like you already." Alice grinned, laughed, and took Kelli into a hug when her baby steadfastly refused to be budged. "I'm so happy for you, my friend. Being a girl-mom is the best."

"Thank you, Alice," Kelli whispered. "For helping Kristen, too."

Alice moved back, her smile waning. "I hope I can," she said. "It's hard to recreate records from a time when there were no computers."

"I thought they went back and scanned in hand-written records," AJ said. "That's what they did in the collegiate sports programs." She cut a look to Kelli. "When I was covering those stories, I learned that."

"Sure," Alice said easily. "Because then, if the hand-written paperwork gets ruined with say, water or fire or other damage, it's in the computer somewhere, right?"

"Right."

"But, AJ, there was no record to scan. Computers didn't exist until the mid-seventies. This record burned fifteen years before that."

AJ pressed her lips together. "Yeah, I get it. It just feels..."

Alice knew exactly how it felt. "Unjust," she supplied, and AJ's eyes filled with tears. Alice grabbed onto her too, and she hugged her fiercely. "I'm going to keep working on it."

As a lawyer, Alice was always very careful not to promise something she couldn't deliver. So she couldn't tell AJ and Kelli not to worry, that she'd handle this, that she'd find what they needed. It was very possible what they needed did not exist. That she may never find it.

She simply needed to do her best work and try until all the options had been exhausted. She loved Kristen so much, and she would do that for her.

Smiling her way past them, she swung her attention to Clara and Jean. It was obvious who the protector was and who was submissive. Jean's chin shook, but she raised it to Alice. "Thank you for helping us with this."

"Of course," Alice said easily. "I hope we can reach the outcome everyone wants."

Clara cut a look over to Kristen. "She hasn't even told Reuben."

"But she will," Alice assured her. "I actually advised her to tell you and Scott, as well as Jean and Reuben first, before this luncheon." She glanced over to the older woman too. She'd put cream in her coffee and now stood with Robin, who hadn't said she was leaving yet. "But she does what she wants."

She smiled at Clara and Jean, hugged them in a three-way embrace and let Maddy and Julia precede her out of the cottage.

Outside, the sky had turned darker, like it might actually thunder and lightning and rain. Alice didn't mind the chilled wind as she paused and tilted her head back, her eyes squinting though the light was only gray and not that bright.

She breathed, and for the first time since she'd arrived here at the lighthouse, it felt like oxygen entered her lungs. She wasn't sure how a body could live without oxygen, she only knew she'd grown more and more tired the longer she stayed inside the cottage.

The sound of a car door slamming met her ears, and that was when Alice realized she hadn't moved. She made to follow Julia and Maddy and found the second door closing behind Julia in the RideShare vehicle that had pulled up.

Alice managed to put another smile on her face and lift her hand in a universal sign of good-bye before the other two women left. Then she got behind the wheel of her car, got it started, and rolled down the windows. It wasn't too hot inside, but she simply wanted the extra air. She craved the cool breeze as it kissed across her cheeks and entered her nostrils.

She had work to do at home—Kristen's wasn't her only case—but Alice sighed and leaned the seat back so she could just lay down and relax for a moment before making the drive across the island.

The winter wind had such interesting things to say, and Alice thought of how the trees had become barren as they shed the heavy load of last season's leaves. Yet they stood tall and stalwart against the wind, the winter, the world.

As she lay there, she definitely felt like winter was a

pause. A fresh of breath air between two vibrant seasons. A time to rest before the awakening of spring.

"...I'm just saying," AJ said. "You should find out what you can and tell Alice."

Alice's eyes opened, but she didn't move.

"The Coalition surely wouldn't stand to profit from owning the lighthouse," Robin said. "What would we gain? What would Duke gain?"

"I don't know," AJ said. "But that's why you should find out. The lighthouse is a symbol of community and power. That alone might be worth something."

"I can't imagine what," Robin said. "But I'll talk to Duke."

"You guys, what about Jean and Reuben?" Kelli's voice sounded unsure, hesitant.

No one said anything, and Alice had had more time with all of these questions, all of this uncertainty, than the others. She'd wondered if Robin would benefit if the Fisherman's Coalition owned the lighthouse. She'd wondered how it had become a private enterprise in the first place. Usually, the keepers at a lighthouse worked for a federal agency—the US Lighthouse Services. In some areas, lighthouses had been privately funded, or they were run by state organizations.

With Five Island Cove being the easternmost land mass in the United States—technically part of the state of Massachusetts—Alice had assumed that the lighthouse here had fallen under county jurisdiction. Namely, the Cove County which only comprised of the five islands in Five Island Cove. They were a city *and* a county, all governed by the state, and then the federal government.

Something new to look into, she told herself, and she listened as Robin, AJ, and Kelli all got in Robin's car and left the parking lot. If they'd found it odd that Alice's car was still there when she'd left before them, none of them had commented on it.

She raised her seat and took her phone out of her pocket. Arthur worked as a counselor at the high school, and Alice allowed a small dose of nostalgia to flow through her as she remembered meeting him in his office for the first time.

"Hey, sweetheart," he said brightly after he'd answered. "What are you thinking for dinner?"

Alice had just eaten lunch, but she honestly couldn't remember what she'd eaten. "Can we get those really cheap chicken sandwiches from Gardenia's and then go sit on the rocks at Rocky Ridge?"

Arthur heard so much more than that, and he paused to absorb it all. "Rough lunch?" he asked.

"I just don't want to think about anything for a while," she said.

"I can finish up here and be home in twenty minutes," he said almost under his breath.

Alice smiled, so grateful and glad to have a safe place

to retreat to when one part of her life turned tricky. "Thanks, babe," she said. "I'll see you there."

She hung up and left the lighthouse as well, watching it in her rearview mirror. She'd done so in the past, usually with a sense of angry-longing to stay. But now, the symbol that had once been so comforting for Alice only held uncertainty.

"I'll find what I need," she vowed once more. "One way or the other."

Chapter Fifteen

Julia came out of her bathroom and back into the bedroom. "This is the second option," she said to her phone, which she'd leaned up against the mirror on her dresser. She'd called Helen Ivy, a little old lady who still lived in Nantucket. She owned a bakery there, and Julia had hated leaving her behind the most.

"What do you think?" She spread her arms out to her side so the bell sleeves could register their full effect, and she turned in a slow circle. When she faced the phone again, she wore a bright smile to match the loud floral print of the dress. "It's got keyhole sleeves up here, but I made sure you can't see my bra."

She was meeting her boyfriend's fifteen-year-old son for the first time as his father's girlfriend. She didn't need to be showing too much skin. Or the wrong kind of skin.

"The flowers are magnificent," Helen said with pure kindness in her voice. "You look ravishing in either one."

"Yeah." Julia looked over to the more subdued, a bit sexier, dress. "It's Friday night, but I'm not going to be alone with Liam." She fingered the fabric, which did stretch a lot and had some sequins across the bust of the eggplant fabric. "I think I'm going to go with this one."

Number one, it had a wide, brown leather belt that sat around her waist, giving her body great shape without being form-fitting. Two, the skirt flowed like warm water around her legs, and Julia felt like a million bucks wearing it. Three, it was different than a "little purple dress" she might wear to make Liam think about kissing her.

She wanted him to think she'd be a good maternal figure for his teen son. Over the past eight or nine weeks since Thanksgiving, Julia had learned that Liam's first wife had left the cove five years ago this coming summer.

She hailed from New York City, and she simply didn't like small island life. Liam had grown up here in the cove, and he loved everything about it. They'd started their life in the city, and he had wanted to quit the police force almost as soon as he'd started it.

Too much violence in the city, he'd told her. He hadn't wanted to raise a child there, and he'd gotten a position at the Police Department here in the cove—which didn't happen as often as Julia thought it might—and they'd moved here.

His ex had lasted a couple of years, and then she'd confessed how unhappy she was. He couldn't take his ten-year-old back to New York, so they'd split up. She'd forfeited her right to custody, but Ian still went and saw his mother from time to time.

Julia knew there were a multitude of sides to every story, as lives were like gemstones. Each facet held a different story, and that facet could shine light out in an infinite number of directions. Every story could be seen through those rays of light, and that meant they could mean an infinite number of things to different people.

She'd accepted what Liam had told her as his truths, because they were. It was possible Ian saw things differently, and she knew for a fact that Liam's ex-wife did. And those were just three sides to the story

Julia fidgeted with the necklace she'd put on to complete the outfit. "What do you think? Is this too much?" The chunky beads almost felt like rocks against her collarbone. "I think I'm going to lose it."

"I think you're worried about too much," Helen said with a laugh. "Just go have fun. Where's he taking you?"

Julia picked up her phone and sank onto her bed. Her small bedroom didn't have room for a chair, a fact she lamented often. "It's winter and nighttime, so we're staying in."

"His house?"

"I don't think so," she said. "I actually think he

decided on the bowling alley. We can bowl and get dinner all in one spot, and apparently Ian is a master bowler." She smiled at Helen's white hair as she'd set her phone down and had busied herself with something else too. "What are you doing tonight?"

Helen looked up, then held up her crochet. "I'm finishing up the coasters for tomorrow's winter market."

Julia smiled at her. "That sounds fun. I wish I could come."

"Then come," Helen said. "It's a thirty-minute ferry ride, and they'll have peppermint hot chocolate and that candy cane popcorn you love." She smiled, the lines around her eyes so wise and so deep.

"They know it's January on Nantucket, right?"

"We milk Christmas for everything we've got," Helen said with a smile.

Julia sobered. "I wish you'd come here," she said wistfully. "You could open a bakery here. A second branch like The Glass Dolphin."

Helen snorted and dropped her eyes to her crocheting again. "Yeah, I heard what happened to The Glass Dolphin. No, thanks."

"It was an isolated incident," Julia said. Nothing had happened to any other new business that had come to the cove in the past year. The man who'd vandalized the restaurant had been released on bail, but the city was pressing charges. He would likely have to pay a hefty fee, and he could get jail time. The damages to the windows at The Glass Dolphin were estimated to be over five thousand dollars, and that carried a strict penalty.

Julia could worry about whether the sky was blue or not, and she didn't need the extra stress in her life right now. She sighed, trying to push the tension out of her shoulders, but it only partially left. "No one was hurt, so who knows what will happen?"

Helen nodded, at least Julia thought so. "Maybe you can just come for the summer," she said. "You can help me start a book club." Helen snorted, but Julia only smiled. "I need you here to do it, Helen. It's like no one reads here."

"People read there," she said without missing a beat. "People read everywhere." She did pull herself away from her stitches for a moment. "Don't you have like, ten new best friends? Start a book club with them."

"Yeah." Julia looked past her phone to the open doorway of her bedroom. "I'll think about it. It would just be so much more fun with you here."

"Everything is." Helen grinned, and Julia returned it.

"I have to go," she said. "They'll be here soon."

"I want an update tomorrow," Helen said. "I can't believe you're just now getting ready to leave the house. It's dark already."

It wasn't even six o'clock yet, but Julia's smile only deepened. "Don't go to bed too early," she said.

"I'll go to bed when I want," Helen griped back. "I get up at three to make doughnuts, you know."

Julia laughed, but she didn't argue that Helen had passed the early morning baking shifts to her younger assistants. "Love you, Helen. I'll talk to you tomorrow."

"I love you too, dear." The video call ended, and Julia sighed as she dropped her phone to her lap. She couldn't quite figure out where to look, and she ended up meeting her own eyes in the mirror.

She could only see herself from the neck up, and instant alarm wailed through her when she realized she hadn't finished her makeup. Jumping to her feet, she yelped and then hurried back into the bathroom. Helen had wanted a fashion show, and what Helen wanted, Helen got.

A few minutes later, Julia left her bedroom and bathroom behind and entered the main living area of her house. The clock ticked to six, and Liam didn't immediately ring the doorbell. He hadn't texted, but Julia didn't need to worry. He wasn't always precisely on time, because clocks varied, and he'd never been more than a minute or two behind hers.

Her phone vibrated, and she checked it, only to see the women in her new friend group had started texting while she'd been on the video chat with Helen. Over a dozen messages had come in, and they were all something similar to the one Robin had started with.

Have an AMAZING time on your date tonight, Julia! I'm sure it'll be incredible, and I can't wait to hear how it goes.

Her heart warmed that she had friends—actual friends—concerned about her. After her divorce, she wasn't sure anyone even knew she existed anymore. Time had a way of healing and erasing, and she spoke more often to her sons now. Her parents...Julia still had a hard time with them—mostly her father. Or maybe her mother. She wasn't sure which. They'd both made mistakes, and on the outside of their relationship, Julia could see clearly what they each should do.

But she'd been on the inside of relationships before, and nothing was as ever clear as it seemed.

Her sister also knew about tonight's date, but she hadn't texted. Alice, El, Laurel, AJ, and Kelli had though. Jean had just added her voice to the mix with, *Remember, he's only fifteen right now. He won't be that age forever*, and that somehow reassured Julia that while she viewed tonight as important, it wasn't pivotal.

It wasn't now or never. Ian might not like her, but as Jean had said, he wouldn't be fifteen forever.

The doorbell rang, and Julia almost dropped her phone as her head jerked toward the front door. Her pulse clamored through her body, ringing like a big church bell meant to signal to everyone within ten miles that the service was starting.

Surely Liam would be able to hear it, see it throbbing against the skin in her neck. Julia pressed her hand there, felt her pulse against her fingertips, and took the first step toward the door.

It's fine ran on a loop in her head, and she felt like she was swimming through quicksand as her arm—reached—out—to—open—the—door.

Then a tidal wave rushed inside, and she blinked at the tall, curly-haired man standing on her front porch. Liam's hair was the stuff of legends, and he claimed not to put any hair products in it. It had full body and wave, and while it didn't hang lower than his ears, it curled back in glorious waves Julia had had the extreme pleasure of burying her fingers in.

They tingled now just thinking about kissing him while she tangled her fingers in that hair.

His bright blue eyes beamed a hello at her, though he hadn't said anything. His son, who had slightly less curly hair and slightly less electric eyes, looked at her from his side. Liam put his arm around his boy and said, "Ian, this is Julia Harper. Julia, my son, Ian."

A smile crept across her face as she took in the teen's reaction to her. He clearly recognized her, but he might not have known from where. She stood up a few inches, but she still only reached his height.

"Hello," she said pleasantly. "It's so great to meet

you." She stuck out her hand, and Ian didn't look at his father first.

He took her hand and said, "You too," as he pumped it a couple of times. "My dad can't stop talking about you." He did shoot his father a wry look then.

Julia laughed a little. "Well, he talks about you all the time too."

"Like you stop talking about Billie," Liam said to his son right before he rolled his eyes. They both looked at her again, and Liam added, "Are you ready? Do you need us to come in?"

"I'm ready," Julia said. "Let me just grab my purse." She backtracked a few steps and picked up her purse from where she'd slung it over the back of the couch. She shouldered it and faced the porch again.

Liam now stood there alone. He stepped into her house, glanced over his shoulder, and pushed the door almost all the way closed with his foot. "You look incredible tonight," he said. "That dress is…" His eyes dropped to the belt, then her feet, and came back to her face. "Stunning. I am so lucky to go out with you."

He knew all the right things to say, and Julia stepped easily into his arms. His hands on her waist fit just right, and she took a deep breath of the crispness of his shirt, the woodsyness of his cologne, and the maleness of his skin. Warmth crept through her as she tipped her head back to look at him.

"He's a nice kid," she said.

"He said two sentences," Liam said. "It'll take time for you two to get to know one another." He leaned down to kiss her, but Julia pulled back an inch, stalling his progress. "What?"

"And that's what you want? More time with me? With all of us?"

"Yes," he whispered.

Julia's vein pulsed in her neck again. "I wasn't sure, because we've been..." She swallowed. "Moving so fast."

Liam kept his hands on her body but put more space between them. "Have we?"

She gave him a soft smile, because Maddy had been right. She'd said that for Liam, he was probably moving at normal Liam-speed. To her, it felt fast. "I think so," she whispered. "I'm not upset by it, but I think it's been pretty fast, yeah."

He looked thoughtful for a moment, and then he leaned in again. He pressed his cheek to hers, and she let her eyes close in bliss. "It's because I wanted to stay here over Christmas, isn't it?"

"Yes," she said. She'd turned him down, but they'd parted with a semi-understanding that she wasn't ready yet. It hadn't had anything to do with the speed of their relationship—until now.

"Noted," he said. "You're just so..." He didn't finish

the sentence, and as he lifted his head, Julia didn't need him to. He wore the desire right there in his eyes, and Julia realized the speed at which their relationship had been or was moving was her issue to resolve.

He wanted her. She could see it plainly in his expression. She could hardly believe it, but she couldn't deny her own eyes. She could close them and bridge the gap between them, so she did that, landing the kiss squarely against his lips.

Liam pulled in a fast breath through his nose, this kiss electrifying and bone-meltingly hot at the first touch. He kissed her roughly for a stroke, then two, before he settled himself and turned the action into something that resembled a cherishing touch.

"I just...want you," he said, breaking their kiss and then diving into a second one. "You're so...good." He kissed her again. "And kind." He moved his mouth to her neck. "And smart."

Julia clung to his shoulders, taking every compliment and touch from him freely. "Your son knows what we're doing in here."

"I doubt that very much," Liam whispered, his mouth lingering along the neckline of her dress. He lifted his head. "But he does have a vivid imagination." His eyes sparkled with mischief mingled with desire, and he backed up, taking his delicious hands with him. "Let's go."

He took her hand and turned to leave the house. Julia went with him, her legs feeling very much like stiff logs. He wasn't driving the police cruiser tonight, and Julia squeezed his hand. "Where did you get this car?"

"It's Ian's," he said, looking over to her. "Don't worry." He chuckled and brought her hand to his lips. "I had him clean it out, and it passed my, and I quote, military inspection."

Ian sat behind the wheel, and surprise once again poured into Julia. "He's driving."

"He's going to chauffeur us," he said, like this was totally normal.

"He's coming on the date with us, right?" Julia asked.

"Yes." Liam glanced over to her and then opened the back door on the driver's side for her. "We're going bowling. That's still okay, isn't it?"

"Absolutely," she said as she sank into the narrow back seat. "I love bowling."

Liam waited while she tucked her skirt under her leg and out of the doorway, and then he closed the door and started around the car. Julia looked up to Ian, though he sat directly in front of her. "You're driving."

"Yes," he said. "I'm not bad."

"You're not sixteen."

He met her eyes in the rearview mirror, and his contained that same glint his father's had. Oh, this boy would break a lot of hearts, Julia knew. "If I'm with a licensed adult, I can drive."

Liam opened the door on his side, and Ian twisted around to face them as he settled into the seat. "All right," he said. "Ready."

"Okay," Ian said, his voice tight. "Now, look here. I can't have any kissing or canoodling in the back seat. It'll be too distracting, all right? So hands to yourself and behave." He glanced over to Julia and back to Liam. "I'm mostly talking to you, son. You hear me? You keep your hormones in check while I'm in the car."

A moment of silence beat through the car, timed perfectly with Julia's jumping pulse, and then Liam burst out laughing. Julia's nerves scattered as Ian's laughter joined his father's, and she joined her fingers to Liam's as his son turned around to face the front.

"You've given him that lecture before, haven't you?"

"I think word-for-word," Liam said, still chuckling. "I had to drive for the Christmas Ball, and he was with a *very* pretty girl. He needed the lecture."

"Who did you go with?" Julia asked.

"This girl named Addie," Ian said. "And I told you, Dad. I don't like her."

"I know," Liam said dryly. "You went with her to get on Billie's good side."

Ian said nothing, and though Julia's view of him was

limited, she still caught the tightening of his jaw in the mirror.

"Ah-ha," Liam said. "He doesn't deny it."

"It's not a secret," Ian said. "I know she likes me, too. I don't get why she can't go out with me now that I've gone out with Addie."

"Girl code," Julia said at the same time Liam said, "I don't get it either."

She looked at him, blinking. "You don't get it? Of course you get it. It's Girl Code. Addie is Billie's best friend, and Addie *does* like Ian. *Of course* Billie can't go out with him." She glanced back to the mirror and then Liam. "Even if she wanted to."

"Girl Code?" Liam asked.

"Why not?" Ian asked.

Julia couldn't believe they didn't know this. "The only way Billie will be able to go out with you, Ian, is if Addie says it's okay. So you have to wait for Addie to stop liking you, and then Billie might—*might*—be able to go out with you."

"That's insane." He shook his head and made a very careful turn to get onto the main highway that led around the island.

Liam blinked at her like she'd just revealed something no man had ever heard before. "There you go, son. Who knew?"

Ian muttered something, but Julia didn't understand

it. She did want to slide over a little and sink into her boyfriend's side, but she settled for focusing out the window and letting him play with her fingers in the darkness down on the bench seat where they sat.

Only a few minutes later, Ian pulled into the parking lot at the bowling alley. "All right," he said as he killed the engine and started to get out of the car. Julia had barely unbuckled her seat belt before her door opened.

Ian stood there, and he offered her his hand. She beamed up at him and put her hand in his. "Thank you, good sir." She laughed as she stood, and Ian didn't hold onto her hand the way his father would've.

Liam came around the back of the car in his rugged jeans and black leather boots. He wore a dark jacket over a dark blue T-shirt, and every cell in Julia's body felt pulled toward him. He did take her hand, and then he said, "Okay, our goal tonight is to see if our combined scores can beat Ian's."

"That's not fair," his son protested, but Liam only laughed.

"I can't remember the last time I went bowling," Julia said, happiness flowing through her.

"See?" Liam said. "Trust me, son, you're still going to win."

In the bright lights of the bowling alley, with her hot boyfriend and his son, it was easy to forget about the politics swirling through Five Island Cove. It didn't matter that Kristen and Jean didn't have the title to the lighthouse.

There was just too much fried food, bright lights, loud music, and the way Liam interacted with his son when he got a strike, and then as he swung Julia around in his arms when she knocked down four pins that told her life could still be good, right alongside the bad.

Chapter Sixteen

Eloise looked up as Aaron set a plate of eggs and toast down in front of her. "Thank you, baby." She kept her face tilted back so he could kiss her. She held a pencil in one hand, her paper calendar open on the table beside her.

"Almost done?" he asked. He turned to go back into the kitchen, and El watched him for a few moments while his back was turned.

"Yeah," she said as he twisted toward her, his eyebrows up. He wasn't wearing his usual cop-black today. No uniform at all. Just jeans and a tee, and El still found him to be the sexiest man alive. "Your hair is getting long." She set aside her pencil, the schedule for the next couple of weeks almost done. Having three full-time managers had helped so much, and El couldn't believe she could still pay her bills and have profit, but she did. Month over month, she did.

Aaron sat at the table beside her. The girls were already off to school today, and he wasn't going into the station, to that office that consumed him whole while he was there. El had learned so much from him about leaving work at work, and she glanced to the calendar.

She did bring home more menial, secretarial tasks like this, and she always did them outside of family time. She gave him a kind smile, the roots of it sown in love, and reached out to run her fingers along the tips of his hair, which was long. For a cop, at least.

"Do you want me to cut it this afternoon?" she asked. "After lunch and the movie?"

"Sure," he said easily, like they weren't going to an appointment that morning that could change both of their lives. They were, and they both knew it. Aaron just handled things like this better than Eloise.

"Are you nervous?" she asked.

He finished his bite of toast and nodded to her breakfast. "You haven't eaten."

"I don't feel well," she murmured. Just the sight of the scrambled eggs turned her stomach, and she switched her gaze to her hand as Aaron's covered it.

"That might be good," he said. "Right?"

She loved it when he spoke in his tender voice, the one that didn't have any hint of Police Chief in it at all. She nodded. "Yeah, could be." She looked up at him again. "Or this just could be a January flu bug."

"You've missed your period," he said.

El pressed her lips together and nodded, as if she didn't know. She'd told him the very next day when she should've started and she hadn't. Then they'd waited another week. Then she'd called a doctor, and they'd waited four more days to be able to go together.

She could just run by the grocery store and pick up some at-home pregnancy tests, but she really didn't want to. Despite the protests and recent act of vandalism, Five Island Cove was still a small town. Everyone—literally everyone—knew who she was. She'd married the single Police Chief whose father was the Mayor, for crying out loud.

The last thing she needed was a rumor flying around about her pregnancy—or the lack of it. She wasn't sure what she'd do if the test came back negative today. She hadn't had to take one in November or December—her body had told her she wasn't carrying a baby.

"At least have a couple of bites of toast," Aaron said as he pulled her plate closer to him. "I'll eat these or give them to Prince." He fed his dog a chunk of egg from her plate, his smile popping onto his face because of it.

El picked up a piece of the toast he'd made for her and took a bite off the corner. She'd had a few sips of coffee too, and she could admit that by the time she finished her toast, she felt marginally better.

She scratched on the last few shifts for her schedule, and then she tucked the pencil into the pages and closed the calendar. A sigh slipped from her lips as she stood, and she leaned down to kiss Aaron again. "We want this, don't we?"

He paused, his head moving slightly closer to hers. He'd been looking at his phone, but he'd come to full attention at her question. "I'm afraid it's too late if we don't," he said. He scooted back and looked fully at her. "Why are you scared?"

"Because." El settled onto his lap, glad when he drew her even closer, his strong arms around her tightly. "I'm... not twenty-five," she said. "Neither are you. We have two girls we adore. Maybe I let my heart run away from me." She played with the ends of his hair, hating this second-guessing inside of her.

Eloise was a scientist—or at least she had been before moving back to the cove to open her father's dilapidated inn. She knew how to think logically and rationally. She understood data and facts, and she based a hypothesis off of those things. Not her silly heart.

"Sweetheart." Aaron ran one hand through her hair. He looked at her with those dark, dreamy eyes, and El closed hers.

"I'm being silly."

"*I* want this," he said with plenty of punch. "I want you, whether we have a baby together or not, but I'm going to be *thrilled* if you're pregnant. I don't care how old we are. We're together, and that means we can do this."

El nodded, absorbing his words in a world where she couldn't see him. "Thank you, Aaron."

"I know you want this too," he murmured, his lips landing lightly against her collarbone. "So doubt yourself for a minute, but don't let it ruin today."

"But what if—?"

"If you're not, then we just get to keep trying," he said, his lips sliding along her skin until the crested her jawline. "I'm having a lot of fun doing that. Aren't you?" He didn't let her answer, because he claimed her mouth before she could.

She didn't need to anyway. Aaron was an attentive, excellent lover, and yes, El enjoyed their time in the bedroom. Whether she got a baby out of it or not, she certainly couldn't complain.

"All right, then," he said, though she hadn't said anything. He pushed her curls off her face. "I love you. Let's go see if we're going to have a baby." He smiled at her, so much love swimming in his eyes. "No matter what, we're getting a fun date out of today, right?"

"Lunch and a movie," she confirmed. "Before the girls come home."

"Right." He shifted, and that was El's cue to get up. She stood, and he did too. She let him lead her into the garage, and they drove her SUV to the health clinic with only silence between them. It wasn't strained, or awkward, or even upsetting. She simply liked to exist inside her mind sometimes, and Aaron let her.

She got herself checked-in, and they sat side-by-side in the waiting room. Only a handful of other women sat there, no husbands with them. Her appointment time came and went, and a couple of other women got called back.

Aaron leafed through a pregnancy magazine, which Eloise found funny, and she smiled to herself.

"Eloise?" a woman finally called, and she got to her feet as he tossed down the magazine. He followed her now as she went past the nurse and into the back of the office. "We'll be in room three."

She detoured into the appointed room, the younger woman right behind her. With the door closed, she said, "So you think you might be pregnant?"

"Yes." Eloise hated sitting up on the tables in the smaller doctor's rooms, so she settled into one of the two chairs, Aaron right at her side. She liked how sometimes he led, and sometimes she did, but that she could always find Aaron beside her.

"Have you taken a test at home?" The young woman

wrote something on her chart, but El couldn't imagine what.

"No." She glanced over to Aaron. "Everyone...I thought I'd like to do it privately."

The young woman looked over to Aaron and visibly flinched. "Oh, of course." She recovered quickly, a little laugh coming out of her mouth. "I have to admit, I didn't even see you. You go a little face-blind when you work in a place like this."

"I'll bet," Aaron said kindly.

She drew in a breath as she looked up. "Well, if we're just testing, I can get you going on that. It only takes a few minutes, and if you want to see the doctor after that for vitamins or due dates or..." She trailed off, her eyes growing wider. "Let's take the test first."

"Yes," El said. "We should probably do that first." She left Aaron sitting in the room while she went with the nurse alone this time. She provided a sample, and she couldn't believe that something she normally never thought about could hold the answer to something she desperately wanted.

"Ah," she said to herself as she dried her hands. "So you do desperately want this." Of course she did.

A child bonded a mother and a father into a family, and she'd be forever woven into the intricate tapestry of their shared existence, each thread imbued with laughter, tears, whispers of love, and moments of wonder.

She'd seen AJ and Matt and Asher. They *belonged* together.

Eloise wanted to become part of something greater than herself; she wanted to belong to a story being written with each beat of her heart, Aaron's heart, and their baby's tiny heart.

Exhaling, like she'd done all she could do for now, she left the bathroom and returned to Aaron. The nurse wasn't there, and she found him frowning at his phone. "Work?" she asked.

"Yes," he clipped out. "Councilman Hodges just reported a threatening letter." He looked up and tucked his phone away, his face clearing quickly. "Done?"

"They're testing," she said as she sat. She'd dealt with a lot of up and down emotions since dating and then marrying Aaron. She knew how to worry about him and when to start letting go and trusting in his other officers, in his expertise, and in God. "A threatening letter?"

"Paul's handling it," Aaron said easily. "I'll look at it tomorrow—or when he texts it to me."

"Something about the building permits?" The same group that Weston Bent claimed he belonged to had been posting semi-threatening messages on social media, citing that "more will be coming" unless certain changes were made around the cove.

"Yes," Aaron said, practically exhaling out the word. "We're not even doing building permit approvals right now. They should be happy about that. They've basically gotten what they want."

El nodded, though she didn't quite agree. "The Council did approve over two hundred last year."

"Those still have to go through the Building Permits office," Aaron said. "And a building permit isn't just issued willy nilly. It has to have an address assigned to it, and more than half of those were for residential houses, not retailer space."

Eloise looked up. "They were? You didn't say that."

"Well, they were." Aaron pressed his lips into a fine line. He'd been spread thin for the past several months, first with his father's Cleaner, Safer Beach Initiative, and now with this. He'd been in a constant hiring loop, and El wanted to provide a slow, steady, safe place for him to come home to.

They rarely talked about his job at home, though he did bring up topics from time to time. When she'd learned of the vandalism, she'd asked him questions, because it was Maddy's restaurant. He'd informed her five minutes before he'd gone on-air that he'd be doing so, and Eloise hadn't appreciated that.

He didn't like keeping secrets from her either, but he hadn't wanted to put her in an awkward position with her friends.

"Like, hey, we're adding a deck and need a building

permit?" she asked. "Or permits for big subdivisions of condos and townhomes?"

"Both," he said. "Everything is on the website. There are only three building sites in the cove right now, and they were approved prior to last year. They still need permits for various things from time to time. There's not *that* many new houses going in."

El watched his face flush slightly. "You think their argument isn't valid."

"I think the cove has to grow in order to survive," he said, meeting her eye. "How can people not see that? We get swamped with tens of thousands of tourists every year. Who serves them in restaurants? Where do they buy groceries? How can we get them from island to island, and then around on each island? People who live here. We can't force our full-time citizens out of the cove and expect to support our tourism in the summer." He shook his head and looked down at his phone again. "Yeah, I think Weston Bent has his knickers *bent* the wrong way."

El smiled, because she actually liked it when her husband finally started talking. She could've guessed how Aaron felt about this topic, but now she didn't need to. She owned an inn on Sanctuary Island, so of course she wanted all of the things he'd just said. She wanted the cove to run like a well-oiled machine, from the airlines who flew here, to the drivers working for RideShare, to the ferry operators who brought her travelers up to Cliffside.

She needed truck drivers to deliver food, and laundry services to keep her sheets and towels sparkling white. She wanted more tourism, not less, and she threaded her fingers through Aaron's. "What is the outcome of this going to be?" Her stomach, which already clenched angrily at her, seemed to double down in its protest to her introducing a stressful topic.

"I honestly don't know," he said. "We can't silence them. If they operate outside the law, then we use the law to punish. That's all we can do."

"So they can show up at tomorrow night's meeting and picket."

"Of course they can."

El nodded, but she didn't like it. "I don't want you getting hurt."

"It's not me I'm worried about." He sighed and looked down at their joined hands. "I don't think they'll be violent, to be honest. There's a reason Weston threw those buckets into The Glass Dolphin at three-thirty in the morning."

"Why send a letter then? That reeks of terrorism, almost."

"It could be nothing," Aaron said. "Paul texted, wanting to know if I wanted to be there to meet with the Councilman. I said no. He can handle it. He said he would." He ducked his chin toward her without truly looking at her. "Okay? There's always something like this out there, El. We handle it when they break the law. That's my job."

"I know what your job is," she whispered. "And it's to keep me, Billie, and Grace safe. It's to keep everyone in the cove safe."

"Right." He swept a kiss along her hairline. "And Paul's doing it. We'll go from there." He looked up as the door opened, and El's emotions got yet another surprise as the doctor entered first, the nurse right behind her.

"Good morning," she said pleasantly. "Chief Sherman. How are you?" She extended her hand to shake, and Aaron half-rose to do it.

"Great, Shandy. How are you?" He'd switched to passionate about the law and keeping Five Island Cove from regressing into the past to smiling, bright Police Chief in less time than it took to shake hands.

"Just fine." Dr. Shandy Grishal looked over to El. "How are you feeling, Eloise?"

"Uh, okay," she said, somewhat surprised the doctor had switched her attention away from Aaron so fast. El was used to being overlooked at his side, as everyone did it —including his own father. "I missed my period last week, and I've felt shaky and weak in the morning."

Dr. Grishal looked down at the manila folder that El assumed held her chart. "That's because you're showing high levels of hCG, and that increased hormone in your body throws everything off." She set the folder on the counter and grinned at El and Aaron. "Congrats, Eloise. You're going to have a baby."

El could only stare at her. For some reason, despite the signs her body had given her, and despite her instincts, she'd been expecting the test to be negative.

"That's great," Aaron said, laughing as he wrapped one arm around El.

"Yeah," she said, coming to her senses. "That's really great."

"Oh, good," Dr. Grishal said. "I'm never sure if I'm walking into a room where the couple wants to be pregnant or not." She laughed too. "Okay, so I'm going to get some vitamins prescribed for you, and we can come up with a due date..." She fiddled with something on her computer. "Do you know the starting date of your last menstrual cycle?" She looked up at El, once again not paying much attention to Aaron.

Eloise liked that for some reason. "Uh, the exact date?" She looked over to Aaron, and he stared blankly back at her. Her mind raced. She'd been pretty regular her whole life, and her most fertile periods were near the end of the month. "I was supposed to start in January on the fifteenth, and I didn't. So probably December fifteenth. Or close to that."

"We can work with that," Dr. Grishal said in a somewhat distracted voice as she typed on the computer. "This is telling me you're due on September twenty-first."

"September," El repeated. "That feels so soon."

Dr. Grishal grinned. "It is still January, so...you've got time." She handed something to her nurse, and then returned her attention to El and Aaron. "I want to see you every month for the next little while. Sooner if you're really ill or you start bleeding. In extreme cases, you should go to the ER, of course."

She flipped something on the chart. "This is your first pregnancy?" She looked up, wide-eyed, at Eloise.

"Yes," she said.

"And you're forty-seven."

"Yes."

Dr. Grishal leaned against the counter, her expression sobering. "I'm sure you know this, but I have to say it. Getting pregnant at this age is pretty rare. It's only a three or four percent chance, and the odds of having something wrong with the baby are far higher for you than for younger women."

El nodded, because she did know this.

"You're automatically considered a high-risk pregnancy," she said. "You have to do more than moms in their twenties."

"Do more?"

"Avoid stress, eat right, get enough rest," Dr. Grishal said, listing them off on her fingers. "It's *really* important, Eloise, if you want this baby to be healthy." She switched her gaze to Aaron. "And you work the most high stress job there is. That has to bleed over into your household."

Aaron swallowed and squeezed Eloise. "I will take care of her," he said, and Eloise fell in love with him all over again. He smiled at her, and then the doctor. "We'll do everything we can on our end, Doctor. I can promise you that."

"I'm sure you will, Chief." She didn't smile, but she turned to her nurse and said, "Let's change those vitamins to be for our older moms, and let's put Eloise on an anti-nausea pill too." She smiled back over to El. "No reason you should be more uncomfortable than necessary." She straightened and sighed. "Protein drinks are great in the morning. So are vitamin waters and those sports drinks. You need to stay hydrated, and you need to give this baby every chance you can."

El nodded, her world shrinking down to only this office for a moment. When it expanded again, her mind burst with all the other things she had going on in her life —the girls, her friends, the inn, her employees.

"I can do it," she told the doctor, but mostly, she needed to remind herself. "I've already been taking steps to slow down at work, and this'll just be extra motivation."

"All right," Dr. Grishal grinned at them both again, then turned to leave. "The girls will check you out up front." They left El and Aaron alone in the room, and neither of them moved.

"I can do this," Eloise repeated, this time in a fierce whisper only for her husband. She looked up and met his steady, strong, cop gaze.

"Yeah," he said. "You can, and I *will* take care of you."

"Starting with lunch?" she teased.

He stood and offered her his hand. "Yeah, starting with lunch for my sexy wife." He grinned at her, and El took it from him and hid it away in her heart. Sure, the odds might be against her, but she'd already watched two of her friends—three, if she counted Jean—get their babily-ever-after, and she would work hard for hers too.

Chapter Seventeen

Kristen secured her hair at the nape of her neck, then bent to pull on her shoes. The winter weather had taken a turn in the past couple of days, but she still went out walking with Theo most mornings. Sometimes, she went with Laurel, AJ, and Jean, the three of them pushing their children in strollers.

The wind rattled her window, and Kristen glanced over to Sweetie, who liked to perch on the edge of the dining room table and watch the passersby as they moved past the sliding glass door. She had a tiny patio where she kept a big potted plant and not much else. There wasn't room for much else, though Sweetie did have a cat toy there she liked to scratch on in the spring, summer, and fall.

She shrugged into her coat and opened the door to her

condo, thinking she'd meet Theo down the sidewalk toward his place. She'd only been there a few times, as they spent the majority of their time together at her house, with her friends, at a restaurant, or walking around their senior community.

"Oh." She nearly plowed into the man, who was in the motion of reaching to ring her doorbell. That alone struck her as odd, because Theo just came in, calling, "I'm here, Kris," when he arrived to go walking in the morning.

A gust of wind shot down the stairwell between the buildings, but Theo smiled anyway. "Good morning," he said.

"Morning," fell from Kristen's lips, because Theo wasn't alone. Another woman in her sixties or seventies stood a half-step behind him, her pasted-on smile as bright as the noon-day sun at mid-summer.

"Ready?" Theo offered no explanation. He didn't introduce the woman. Kristen looked for similarities between them, thinking her a cousin or sister, but Theo hadn't said any of his relations would be in town. Kristen couldn't see anything the same about them either—other than their snowy white hair.

"Yes," she said, continuing the movement she'd started to leave her condo. She smiled at the other woman. "I'm Kristen Shields."

"Gladys Carrole," the woman said. She extended her hand for Kristen to shake, which she did.

She also cut a glance over to Theo, who seemed to wake up in that moment. He started to walk out of the stairwell, and Gladys followed him, with Kristen bring up the rear. "Gladys is the historian for the Cove Fisherman's Coalition."

Kristen's feet came to a complete standstill, then grew roots. "She is?"

"Was," Gladys said with a playful laugh. "My husband was a fisherman here in the cove for, oh, at least sixty years. Just retired a few years ago."

Kristen's heartbeat bounced through her body, and if she'd been hooked up to a monitor, she was sure the blips would be rapid and close together. A whoosh moved through her, leaving her lightheaded and pressing one palm to her chest.

"Are you okay?" Theo asked from several paces down the sidewalk. He'd left the shadows of the building, and the weak February sunlight lit him up.

"I..." Kristen didn't know how to answer. Why would he bring Gladys on their walk? He hadn't mentioned doing anything of the sort. She didn't even know he'd contacted someone from the Coalition.

She hadn't asked him to do that, and in fact, Kristen didn't want to alert anyone there of the fact that their organization might own the lighthouse. She had Alice—a trained, professional lawyer—working on the case.

Theo's face stayed blank, and Kristen wished she had

such leisure. "Do you and your husband live here?" she asked as Gladys turned around.

"Oh, Rodney died last year," she said, her smile sticking in its spot. "Theo and I have become good friends since I moved in next door to him." She glanced over to him, and he smiled fondly at her too. She definitely had eyes for him, and she laughed as she patted his arm.

Funny how Kristen had never heard of Gladys until today. She wasn't sure what emotions stormed through her, but she knew she didn't want to go on this walk. "I don't feel well now that I'm up and about," she said. "You two enjoy your walk."

She opened her door and went back inside the condo, a bit surprised when the door didn't close behind her. Theo had caught it with his hand, and he entered after her. The door did spring closed then, sealing them inside together.

"Are you sure you're okay?" he asked. "Do I need to call Clara or Jean? One of the girls?"

Kristen paced away from him, going past her small galley kitchen to the mouth of the hallway. Her thoughts tumbled, and she'd endured enough surprises in her lifetime to never experience another one. Memories of her life with Joel, at the lighthouse, on this island, streamed through her mind. She'd thought she'd known him. Loved him. They'd spent decades together and raised two children, then had many years together again, just the two of them.

After he'd died, Kristen had learned so much about him. So many things she'd thought were true that weren't. That would not happen to her again.

She turned to face Theo, heat flowing through her so fast, she probably could've shot it out of her fingertips. "Gladys Carole has lived next door to you for over a year?"

"Longer than that," he said easily. "Rodney lived there with her too, before he passed. It's probably been three or four years." He didn't seem to think this was a big deal at all. Kristen could admit she didn't spend a lot of time at community events and activities, because she had family and her Seafaring Girls in the cove that took up a great deal of her time.

"What did you tell her?" she asked.

"I said you might have some questions for her about the Coalition," he said.

"Did you tell her about the lighthouse?" Kristen had trusted him with that information; she hadn't thought for one moment he'd tell anyone else.

"No," Theo said, his eyebrows pulling down. "I thought you might want to tell her yourself."

Kristen took a series of quick steps toward him. "I don't want to tell them at all," she hissed. Perfect clarity rang in her ears. "You should just go on your walk with her."

"Kristen," he said.

"I don't feel well," she said again, though the lie rang in the air between them. She maintained her eye contact with Theo, who continued to watch her back. "I'm sure she's wondering where her 'good friend' is."

"Kristen," he said. "It's not like that."

"Maybe for you," she said.

He blinked, then nodded. "All right." He fell back a step and then turned around. "I suppose I can call on you later?"

Kristen's memory brought forward another memory. This one from Thanksgiving, when his daughter had asked if Kristen was going to marry her father. "Actually, Theo," she said. "I need you to answer something for me."

He faced her again and waited.

"At Thanksgiving, I said maybe we should talk about our relationship, and you asked if I wanted to get married. You seemed very surprised. You were about to say something when your grandchildren interrupted." It had been a couple of months since then, and neither of them had brought it up again.

He still hadn't talked to her about any sort of future together. Kristen's mind had lingered on it, but she'd then had quite a few other things happen that had stolen her attention and mental energy.

"I'd like to know what you were going to say then."

"I can't remember," he said with a chuckle.

"Then tell me if you think you'll ever get married again."

The grin vanished from his face, and while he didn't say anything, Kristen had her answer. She wasn't sure she necessarily wanted to tie the knot for a second time, especially at seventy-nine years old, but then, what was the point?

"Are we just friends then?" she asked. "Because bringing Gladys over feels like something a friend would do. Like, we're *all* walking together in the morning, not just the two of us."

"I'd rather have a companion," Theo said. "But no, Kris. I don't want to get married again."

She wasn't sure why the words hurt—she probably felt the same way. "I wish you'd have told me from the beginning." There it was—the source of the betrayal. He probably hadn't meant to hurt her, or hide things from her, or lie to her.

She wasn't even sure he'd done any of those things, but the hot river of foolishness carving through her sure testified that he had. She couldn't smile. She couldn't stand to look at him for much longer, not with that sad look on his face. "I'll see you later.

Kristen turned and went down the hall, entering her bedroom and closing the door. Theo did not come after her this time, and since these condos weren't the best build on the island, she felt the slight rattle in her walls when her front door slammed closed.

Sweetie had come into the bedroom at some point, and Kristen lay down on her bed, still fully dressed and ready to go walking, and stroked her cat. "Why does this hurt?" she wondered, because she and Theo had only been together for about nine months. She hadn't fully engrained her life into his, and she had so much separate from him.

But it still hurt, and she didn't need an explanation as to why. Some things were simply allowed to hurt, and she'd have to carry this pain with quiet dignity, like a bruise-colored bloom, until it faded and healed.

She'd been through battles like this before, and she'd won. She'd find resilience in the aftermath—if she could survive the turmoil in the present.

* * *

A couple of weeks later, Kristen set out paper plates while Jean and Clara continued to work in the kitchen. Well, Jean had parked herself in the kitchen, while Clara worked on the opposite of the bar.

"Let's put six on this plate for Robin," Kristen said as she stuck a sticky note to the plate. "That's two each."

"So six for AJ too," Jean said.

Kristen wrote the number and AJ's name on the

notepad and stuck it to another plate. "Four for Alice and Arthur," she mused. "Six for Kelli." She and her daughter and daughter-in-law were making Valentine's Day cookies, and the simple act of putting together a dough, baking it and watching it do what it should, cooling the cookies, and then decorating them into something that would make someone else smile had brought more light to Kristen than she'd had all month.

She'd told no one of Theo's departure from her life, and in all honestly, the only difference now was that she sometimes walked alone in the mornings. Her girls likely assumed she was still seeing him, and Kristen hadn't corrected them. She already saw the way they looked at her over the issue with the lighthouse, and she didn't need more pity.

"I'm just going to ask her," Clara muttered as Kristen went around the end of the table closest to her and Jean.

"I think you should let her bring it up," Jean hissed back.

Kristen pretended like she didn't hear them, wrote Laurel's name on a note, the number six, and stuck it to a plate. "I hope we have enough," she said loudly.

"There's enough for everyone, plus your whole community here," Clara said dryly. "You have a plate for Theo, right?"

Kristen's heartbeat stuttered, and she finished writing out El's note before facing the women in the kitchen.

"Actually, Theo and I...we're not seeing each other anymore."

Jean froze, the piping bag of pink frosting hovering above a heart-shaped cookie. Clara gaped, her eyes blinking rapidly. "You're not seeing him anymore?" she asked.

"No." Kristen looked down at the plates. She *was* forgetting someone, but it wasn't Theo. "Who don't I have?"

Robin, Alice, El, AJ, Kelli, Laurel, Jean, Clara, Maddy...

"Oh, Julia and Tessa," she said, immediately going back to her Post-It pad.

"Mom." Clara left her decorating station and came over to the dining room table. "What happened?"

"Nothing," Kristen said. "We just...don't have the same goals." She glanced at her daughter. "He wants a companion, not another wife. I don't really see the point of just dating until I die. If I'm going to do that, there are plenty of other men here."

Clara's eyebrows shot up. "You don't want to be monogamous?"

"Of course I do," Kristen said, wishing this conversation had never happened. "I guess I still believe in marriage, even if you're as old as I am." She gave her daughter a smile she hoped would calm her down. "He doesn't. He's friendly with everyone, not just me. He just doesn't want to be alone."

"He introduced you to his kids," Jean said. "Is he doing that to everyone?"

"I don't really know." Kristen swallowed. "He has a neighbor who's husband was in the Coalition for sixty years."

"Mom." Clara's voice sounded like she'd pushed it off a cliff. "Did you talk to her?"

"No," Kristen said. "I have Alice doing everything."

Clara cleared her throat. "Uh, yeah, Jean and I wanted to talk to you about the lighthouse."

"*Clara* wanted to talk to you about the lighthouse," Jean said quickly. The two women exchanged a glance, and since Kristen had finished labeling the paper plates, she didn't have much else to distract her.

Clara looked back at her. "Yeah, I want to know what's going on with it. It's been weeks, and it feels like we're no closer to a solution."

"Alice is working on it," Kristen said.

"Yeah, but what's she *doing*?" Clara asked. "Because it feels like we've buried our heads in the sand, and we're hoping no one is ever going to raise the issue again."

"Maybe they won't," Kristen said.

"You have no legal documents saying you own the lighthouse, Mom." Clara put one hand on her hip, which would leave a white flour mark against her black pants.

"The display came down," Jean said. "No one seems to even know what the significance of it was."

Life had moved on, just as it always did. Kristen had cycled through enough seasons to know that each storm would blow over, another wave would come, and somehow, she'd still be standing there.

"*We* know," Clara said, shooting Jean another sharp look. "And we have to do something about it."

"What would you like me to do, dear?" Kristen asked. "Call her? Pester her?"

"I'm just saying," Clara said. "Maybe we should be a little more proactive on this."

"I trust Alice," Kristen said. "This isn't her only case, and she's working on it."

The doorbell rang at the same time someone knocked. All three of them turned toward the door, Kristen with a pounding heart. Then the door opened, and a tall, gorgeous brunette entered.

Alice.

"Hey," she said with a smile. "Look who I found lurking around outside." She moved out of the way as Robin entered, shaking her head.

"Oh, it smells good in here." Robin came forward, but she could read a room particularly well, and her footsteps faltered before she could cross the living room. "Oh." She looked at Jean, then Clara, and finally Kristen.

"What did we interrupt?"

Chapter Eighteen

Clara only semi-regretted bringing up the lighthouse. She and Jean had been discussing it to death, but everyone seemed afraid to approach her mother about it.

Clara wasn't afraid.

"Alice," she said. She still held the knife she'd been using to spread white frosting over sugar cookies. She dropped it at her decorating station and went into the living room. "We were actually just talking about you." She sent a swift look toward Robin. "And the lighthouse."

"Great." Alice didn't miss a beat. She also seemed far too smiley for Clara's liking. "Who wants to help me bring in the files?" She scanned the room, got no takers, and laughed. "All right. I'll get them myself."

She turned to leave the condo, and Clara got herself in gear. She hurried after Alice with, "I'll come."

"Clara," her mother said, but Clara ignored her.

"Put the cookies out," she said when she reached the door. "I'm just going to help her carry in some files." She might say a word or two, and everyone in the room knew it. Clara had lived large parts of her life with her opinions out in the open, and as she'd matured, she'd learned to contain the thoughts inside her head. Not everything had to come out of her mouth anymore, a level of maturity she prided herself on.

She caught up to Alice and said, "I can carry something."

"Things seemed a little intense in there." Alice didn't turn her head to look at Clara, but she felt her eyes on her all the same.

Clara didn't want to throw her mother under the bus. At the same time, she really liked Alice too, so she didn't want to sound accusatory toward the woman helping them. "Yeah." She sighed. "It's my fault. I get a little intense sometimes."

"You?" Alice grinned at her as she stepped off the curb and into the parking lot. "I can't imagine that, Clara." She laughed lightly and nudged Clara with her hip. "Was it about the lighthouse?"

"Yes," Clara said. "It's eating me alive, and Mom just goes about baking cookies." She stopped at the back of Alice's SUV. "And she broke up with Theo."

Alice sucked in a breath and stared at Clara while the liftgate lifted. "She did? When?"

"I don't know," Clara said. "She just told me and Jean."

Alice faced the condo building, then looked into the back of her car like she'd lost something important and had no idea where to start looking for it. "Her and Theo." She shook her head and pointed to a file box on Clara's side. "I need that."

"Is this full?" Clara reached for it, and with how easily it moved when she pulled it toward her, she reckoned it was not full.

"No," Alice said. "It just keeps things separated for me." She picked up a much smaller filing system—almost an accordion, with several slots for papers and packets—and stepped out of the range of the liftgate. "I could've gotten it all."

Clara didn't move so Alice could lower the back of her SUV. She met the other woman's eyes, familiar impatience burning within her. "Tell me out here," she said, her voice almost hoarse. "Are we going to lose the lighthouse?"

Alice's expression transformed into one with compassion and pity, and Clara's heart struck against her ribcage. "I don't think so," Alice said, which contradicted the look on her face.

"But..." Clara didn't know what to say.

"I think I've found the documents we need," she said.

"And now, we have to...well, it might be a bit tricky." She gestured Clara back, and she did move. Alice reached to press the button to lower the gate. "I'm essentially going to petition the Coalition to sign the documents."

"But they should own it."

"But they haven't been paying the keepers," she said. "The city has. If anyone should own it, it's the city of Five Island Cove, and that's against the county ordinances here in the cove. That's why your family owned the lighthouse in the first place."

"Then why was the city paying?"

Alice grinned, and Clara seriously wanted to slap the gesture from her face. "Can I explain it once, please?"

Clara pressed her teeth together, but she managed to nod. She went with Alice back toward her mother's condo, not enjoying the wind tunnel that the breezeway had become this winter. Her face felt like it would chap off before they reached her mom's door and Alice managed to get it open.

It operated on a spring, so they had to manhandle their way inside with the folders and files, and thankfully, Mom had cleared the table of the paper plates. Alice dropped her file on the table, where it made a loud clunking noise.

Clara bent and silently put the lighter box on the floor. All eyes turned to Alice. She didn't seem to notice as she started unpacking folders. "Can I have a cookie?"

"Alice," Robin hissed, and the dark-haired woman finally slowed. She still wore her coat, a puffy black thing that only told Clara how slim she was. She'd paired it with a pair of leggings, like perhaps she'd just finished an exercise class before popping by to ruin their lives.

She said she didn't think we'd lose the lighthouse, Clara told herself. She wasn't even sure why she included herself in the "we." She'd never wanted the lighthouse, and she still didn't want to live there, paint it every year, keep all the insane records, and deal with the stressful storms.

But Jean and Reuben did live there, and they both loved it. Clara did not want to find them tossed out on the street by the Cove Fisherman's Coalition, and she stole a glance at Robin, who wore her worry on her face.

She hadn't come from the same exercise class as Alice, as she wore a pair of blue jeans and a sweater in white, pink, and yellow. It almost complimented her honey-colored hair, which hung in straight layers to her shoulders. She pursed her lips and glared at Alice. "They're waiting for you."

"I need a cookie first." Alice went into the kitchen and plucked one of the decorated hearts from the tray. "These are adorable." She hugged Jean from the side, who did smile partway and hug Alice in return. "Okay, gather 'round, everyone."

"Should we call the others?" Kristen asked.

"I was just going to tell you," Alice said as she looked

over to Mom. Her eyes then darted to Robin. They'd had a close friendship growing up, and since returning to the cove, if Mom was to be believed. And Clara believed her mother. "Robin and I were—"

"You and Robin?" Clara interrupted, trying to watch both of them now. The human eyes were pretty amazing, because she caught movement from both Alice and Robin, including the way Robin reached up and tucked her hair behind her ears.

"We've been working on a few things together," Alice said coolly. "Come on. Come sit down, and let's go over a few things." She bit off one of the top humps of the heart and sank into a chair. As she chewed, she organized the folders with her free hand.

Clara saw no other choice than to sit. She wanted to hear everything anyway, and she was so glad she'd taken her one day off this week and come to her mother's to bake. It wasn't her favorite activity by any means, but she sure felt blessed to be here now.

Jean sat beside her, and she slipped her hand into Clara's. That about summed up their relationship; Clara felt very protective of Jean, and while she hadn't always treated her the best, she did love her like a sister.

"All right." Alice flipped open another folder. "I think I've found enough to establish your family as the owners of the lighthouse, Kristen." She produced photocopies of what looked like pay stubs. Three per page, and she had to have a stack of twenty, thirty, maybe more papers.

"These are paychecks to your grandmother, Rose." Alice pointed to the swirling, old-fashioned handwriting. "They start in 1962 and then get transferred to your father, Kenneth." She flipped over the stack to reveal a new one. "See? Then, when you and Joel take over the lighthouse duties, the checks change again."

Clara picked up one of the pages in this last stack, and sure enough, the copies here were checks from Five Island Cove made out to her mother. "I thought Dad was the primary keeper of the lighthouse," she said.

"I have both," Alice said. "These are your mother's. These are Joel's." She patted each stack as she said it. "It's proof that you were living and working at the lighthouse. No one can deny that."

No one said anything as the papers got examined and passed around. They made it back to Alice, and she put them in the proper piles, then stacked it all together and closed that folder. "It doesn't prove ownership, but the city isn't going to argue it."

"How do you know that?" Mom asked.

"Because I've met with their counsel," Alice said coolly. "They know they don't own the lighthouse. In their eyes, you do. They've been paying you or an ancestor of yours for a great many years. We can use them in court to show ownership."

"Why did they start paying?" Clara asked.

"Ah." Alice bent to open the file box. "The only record we could find was this." She extracted a single piece of paper that looked like someone had spilled black coffee on it and let it sit for a decade.

The paper was brown and almost brittle, but the writing was neat and legible. Clara wanted to swat her mother's hand out of the way so she could see what it said, but she waited quietly.

"I don't know what this is saying," Mom finally said. She passed it to Clara, who couldn't read fast enough.

"It's a document between the Coalition," Alice said. "And the city. For a time, in 1962, they operated without a President, because he'd fallen ill and couldn't perform his duties. His brother worked for the city, and he turned all affairs of the Coalition over to him."

Clara caught their names—Nathan and Collin Gant. They didn't ring any bells for her, and they didn't need to. The document looked like an agreement for Collin Gant, one city controller, to run the Coalition for a time while his brother, Nathan, recovered from an illness.

"He never did get better," Alice said. "I spoke to Collin's daughter. She lives in South Carolina now. She was maybe ten or fifteen when her uncle died, she thinks. Her dad took care of everything, even the Coalition, for a while."

"So that's when things got messed up?" Robin asked,

gently taking the paper from Clara. She let it go, because she didn't need to examine it letter by letter.

"I believe so, yes." Alice took another bite of her cookie. "These are so good, Kristen. I don't know how you make them so fluffy and moist. My sugar cookies are always burnt and brittle."

Mom smiled at Alice, her eyes glassy. "We're not going to lose it?"

"I think we have a strong case," Alice said. She glanced at Robin, who relinquished the paper to Jean. "Robin?"

She cleared her throat and pulled her hands off the table. Clara saw the way they trembled before she did. "Okay, so, confession," she said. "I thought maybe it would be...I don't know what I thought. Duke is the Vice President of the Coalition right now, so I told him about the lighthouse. I asked him if there would be any advantage to the Coalition owning it."

Clara stared openly at her. Robin had always been vocal and kind, which reminded Clara a lot of herself, actually. "You wanted it?"

Robin nodded as she cleared her throat. "I thought there might be an advantage to having it, yes."

"Is there?" Jean whispered.

"Duke doesn't think so. He also finds it very odd that the Coalition would've purchased the land or the lighthouse. He said that money would've had to come from the members, and he doesn't think they'd have been able to afford it."

"I went to the Coalition with Robin," Alice said. "She's been very helpful in introducing me to the right people there." Their eyes met, and so much was said between them. Alice still obviously trusted Robin, who likewise respected and trusted her. "We found no sales slip, no title, no evidence that extra money was collected from Coalition members in 1950. We interviewed anyone we could find, and no one recollects the Coalition purchasing the lighthouse."

"So...so, what?" Mom asked. "That newspaper article was a lie? Everyone who might know is dead?"

"We still have no title for the lighthouse," Jean reminded them.

Clara nodded emphatically, pointing past Robin to Jean. "We need a title."

Alice surveyed the group, and Clara just wanted her to spit out everything. Just tell them all. Now. "Robin?"

"I think it's the only explanation."

Alice sighed. "This isn't evidence," she said. "I don't know if the court will even care or allow us to enter it if they do ask or care."

"What is *this*?" Clara asked, her voice very nearly tripping over her pulse, which sat in the back of her throat.

"Based on the newspaper article, which I found in the archives and pulled—" Alice started fumbling through her accordion filing system, then gave up. "I have it in there. Rose Worthington didn't really *sell* the lighthouse. That was only the headline."

"Like clickbait," Robin said.

"Right," Alice agreed. "She was struggling financially after her husband died at war. No doubt about that. The bank here has gone through all of their non-digital records and preserved them digitally. We could see her account stretching back to the time when she and Clancy—Kristen's grandfather—bought the lighthouse. She was overdrawn a lot, and there were tiny notes in the margins of her statements. She'd trade things to pay bills, and that was pretty common back then."

"One of the things she traded was fish," Robin said.

"Fish?" Clara and her mother said at the same time. Clara wanted to look at her mom, but she didn't dare tear her eyes from Robin.

She nodded. "We spoke to a woman who kept the history of the Coalition—her husband was President three or four times—and she said that Rose was often at their meetings. She was a *member* of the Coalition."

Clara sat back in her chair, her lungs laboring to breathe. She wasn't even sure why, but the dots weren't all adding up to a complete picture for her. Yet. "I don't understand."

"Grandmother Rose," Jean said slowly. "Sold the

lighthouse to the Coalition..." She looked at Clara too. "I get lost there."

"I think Rose Worthington was a member of the Coalition," Alice said slowly. She took back the aged paper and slipped it back into the box. "Women couldn't be members, but we have a witness who says she came to meetings all the time. She was close with some of the leadership in the Sixties, before she turned the lighthouse duties over to her son."

"So are you saying she never sold it?" Mom asked.

Alice nodded. "I think it might've been a publicity stunt. I have a source who says Rose was close with the writer of the paper. She's seen at Coalition meetings." She let the words hang there. "And here's the real smoking gun."

She took out a folder that couldn't have more than a dozen pages in it. "She got one check per year from the Coalition. She didn't write the check *to* them. She got it *from* them."

"The Coalition doesn't pay its members," Robin said quickly. "You pay dues to belong to it."

"Okay," Clara said, eager to see the contents of the folder.

Alice finally opened it, and she handed each person a paper from it. Clara's had a copy of a check on it, made out to Rose Worthington, from the Coalition in 1955.

"One thousand dollars." She looked up, trying to make this piece fit in. "Alice?"

"She got paid from the Coalition," she said. "The only people who get paid from the Coalition are the officers."

"But women couldn't be officers." Jean looked up from her paper too.

"She was acting like one, even if she wasn't on the official records," Alice said. "Someone was paying her, and she attended the meetings."

"I think the title was burned in the fire," Robin said. "But if we still had it, it would have Rose's name on it. I don't think she ever sold the lighthouse."

"I agree with Robin."

Robin's face split into a grin. "Don't worry, I got her to say that while I was recording." The two of them laughed, but Clara had a hard time joining in.

"Okay." Her mother ran her hands through her hair. "So what do I do now?'

"Now, I'm going to file—with your permission—with the state of Massachusetts to get a replacement title, in Reuben's name, as we should be transferring titles when a new owner takes over the lighthouse, according to the Destroyed Public Records Act." She took back the papers and refiled them.

"I'll argue the case before the judge, and we'll see what happens." She sat back, then sprang to her feet. "I need another cookie."

"She went to yoga with Kelli this morning," Robin explained. "She's acting like it rejuvenated her metabolism."

"It was a metabolic class," Alice called from the kitchen. "I'm starving."

"Yeah," Robin said under her breath. "She's starving."

That finally coaxed a smile from Clara, and she looked over to her mother. She wiped at her eyes quickly, and Clara got up and went to hug her. They didn't say anything as they embraced, and Clara was so glad she'd returned to the cove to rebuild specifically this relationship.

"Thank you, Clara."

"I didn't do anything, Mom."

"You're here," she said, and that seemed to mean so much.

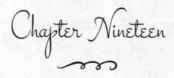

Chapter Nineteen

Maddy tapped on the tablet in the back of The Glass Dolphin, her shoulders feeling like someone had been winching them tighter and tighter all day long. She had been working a lot in the past few weeks, because she only had six more weeks until her wedding.

She'd be taking time off then—two full weeks—and she didn't want any of her employees to feel like she wasn't willing to pull her weight around the restaurant.

"Taylor," she said to her head waitress. "I'm off, but I'm having a meeting in the Sands, okay?"

"Sounds good, Maddy," the woman said. "I'll come get you if I need anything."

"Darren will be here in an hour." They'd reached the dead time of day, when hardly anyone came to eat. At The Glass Dolphin, that hour stretched from three to four p.m, as plenty of ladies came for a late lunch and lingered over cocktails.

She went back out into the front of the restaurant, unsurprised to catch her hostess taking Robin into the Sands. Maddy detoured to the restroom quickly, washed her hands thoroughly, and went to join her friend and wedding planner in the small conference room.

Robin stood at the windows, watching the water beyond, and she wore a pretty blue maxi dress and a white jean jacket. She turned when she heard Maddy enter the room. They smiled at one another, and Maddy gave her a quick squeeze before she turned her attention to the binder and textiles Robin had laid out on the table.

"Are these the linens?" she asked.

"For here," Robin said. "Thankfully, the manager gave me permission to bring in our own linens, so we can make the luncheon match the wedding."

"It's dinner," Maddy said.

"Yes, dinner." Robin didn't miss a beat. "You need to finalize the menu today too." She opened the binder, which had grown significantly in the past couple of months, and took out two laminated cards. "A or B."

Maddy still ran her fingers down the plum-colored fabric. "I like this apricot one." It felt very beachy to her. She'd gone with pastels for this wedding, and Robin had named the official colors plum, lilac, and apricot. Maddy's dress was a bit off-trend and non-traditional, but she didn't care one whit.

She and Ben were a bit off-trend and non-traditional, so she was simply fitting into her own theme. "I like the sandy one too." Maddy touched the cloth that reminded her more of burlap than something she'd spread over a table at a wedding dinner. It wasn't as dark as burlap, nor as scratchy, but it did have a bigger weave.

"Those are napkins," Robin said. "Since your dress is going to be beige, we don't want the linens competing with you. *You're* the star."

"You've made me feel like one, every step of the way." She smiled up at Robin. "I do like these for a napkin." She draped the lilac over the light sand-colored napkin, then the apricot one. The plum was deeper and darker, with more pink, and she didn't want pink draping her tables.

"I think apricot," she said. "The flowers will be blue and pink and white, so that'll bring in all the beach colors."

"Sun, sky, sand, clouds," Robin said. "Romance." She finally sat down, and she pulled the fabrics toward her and began filling out a form. "Check the menu, if you would. They wouldn't put the steak on the same menu with the kabobs without charging an astronomical amount. I had them do beef, chicken, and veggie for each one."

Maddy picked up the first card and looked at it. She and Ben had talked about the wedding a lot in the past three months since he'd asked her to marry him. His transfer to the Coast Guard station here was complete, and he knew when he could retire. Not for five more years, but Maddy didn't mind.

They wouldn't have kids together, and she just wanted him.

He wanted her—and steak at the wedding dinner. The man adored red meat, and Maddy didn't have to look past the top item on the menu to pick one. "A." She handed the card back to Robin. "Ben wants the Wellington."

Robin tucked the card into her binder. "Then Ben gets the Wellington." She smiled at Maddy. "Your dress is supposed to be ready by next Monday. Terralyn from the shop should be calling you. If she doesn't, text me, and I'll find out what's going on with it."

Maddy nodded. "What do you think about the venue?"

Robin looked out the windows again. "I think it's been a very strange winter and spring."

Maddy could agree with that, though her heart didn't like it. "I feel like it's not going to be an outdoor wedding." The calendar had just flipped to March, so they had time for the ground to warm, the leaves to blossom and bud, and the sun to come out. But the wedding sat only six weeks away, and Maddy just had a gut feeling.

"I have the Rock House on standby." Robin lifted her

eyebrows. "We will have to tell them in the next couple of weeks, and if you book it, they'll want their deposit."

Maddy got up and wandered over to the windows too. "The ocean never quits, does it?"

"She does not," Robin said quietly.

Mother Nature couldn't be tamed either, and her will asserted itself in the relentless roll of the waves, the unyielding growth of a tree's roots through solid rock, and the fierce dance of a storm, a wild symphony that whispered of her freedom in every note.

Maddy wanted that same freedom, and she smiled to her partial reflection in the glass. "I think we should book Rock House," she said as she turned around. "I just have this feeling that a beach wedding isn't going to happen until June."

"El and Aaron got married on the beach in April," Robin said.

Maddy had heard the stories, and she smiled as she slipped back into her seat. "Rock House. We can get married there, and then perhaps walk down the beach before we pick up RideShares for dinner here."

"It is right on the beach," she said, reaching for her phone. "Let me see if they have the option of indoor-outdoor on your date..." She started typing and swiping, and a few moments later, she lifted her phone to her ear.

She jumped to her feet and said, "Yes, Willow, hi. It's Robin Grover. I need to talk to Therice, please. She's still over scheduling, isn't she?" She paced to the windows, said, "Yes," and faced Maddy again.

"There's a paper on Rock House in the venue section," she said. "Grab it for me, would you?"

Maddy started flipping through the binder, awed at how detailed and organized Robin was. She found the right section and pulled out the paper with the beautiful insignia at the top alongside the words *Rock House: Where Dreams are Cemented in Stone.*

She didn't mind if the slogan was cheesy or not. No one ever married thinking they'd get divorced, did they? Maddy hadn't the first time, and she didn't this time either. Life could warp reality sometimes, and sometimes people did that to themselves. Everyone handled stress and bad luck and depressing times in different ways, and no two brains functioned the same.

Maddy had two children, and they'd both taught her how different people could be, even when they came from the same tree of DNA.

She handed the paper to Robin, then returned to the table when her phone started to ring. Ben's name sat there, and her pulse thumped out an excited beat as she swiped on the call. "Hey," she said.

"Hey, yourself," he drawled. "Where are you? I thought I'd find you at the ferry station."

"I'm meeting with Robin today," she said. "I'm in the Sands."

"Hmm." Something buzzed on his end of the line and the wind whipped across his receiver.

"Are you on the boat?"

"I'm on a boat," he said. The man loved boats and water and the ocean. He'd taken every training possible for him to take in the Coast Guard, and he'd been a captain for a few years now. Julia had dubbed him Captain Gorgeous the first time they'd met, and Maddy still thought of him that way sometimes.

Like right now.

"Will you marry me in your uniform?" she asked, suddenly thinking of it.

"Of course," he said matter-of-factly.

"You'll be the only one wearing white then," she teased, because she would not show him her wedding dress. She'd gone shopping with Julia, Alice, Robin, and Laurel, and she'd put a picture of it on the group text for all the women to see.

Now that Alice had filed for a new title for the lighthouse, and everything had been explained there, Maddy didn't have to feel guilty filling the thread with frivolous wedding plans. They weren't frivolous to her.

Ben growled and said, "I found a dock near The Glass Dolphin. Will you stay and have dinner with me?"

"Only if we can stargaze from your boat afterward."

"Honey, that's implied."

She laughed lightly, even when Ben did not. He could

joke with her, but he definitely had a more stoic and serious personality. He called her his sunshine, because she was blonde and bright and personable. He was more like the storm cloud—he claimed.

She didn't mind, because he was good to her, kind to her, and doted on her endlessly. He loved her, and she loved him, and as Maddy hung up, she sure hoped this marriage would never end.

Her teeth pressed together as she worried, and she turned back to Robin, who'd also just ended her call. "Well?"

"The outdoor beach is already reserved for that day," she said. "But I got you the London Hall there, and it's gorgeous. They'll fly in plants and flowers, even if they haven't bloomed here yet." She smiled at Maddy. "What did Ben want?"

"I think he's coming here on his boat," she said, once again twisting to look out the windows. "I don't know where he's going to park that thing, but..." She trusted him, so she didn't worry too much about it.

"Meal A," Robin mused. "Apricot and potato skin napkins." She tucked things back into the box she'd brought. "Dinner here, venue secure both indoor and outdoor. Dresses. Flowers." She flipped to another tab. "Oh, the cake."

Maddy sighed as she sat down. "How have you and Duke made things work for so long?"

Robin blinked at her, then she too sank back into her chair. "I...don't know. He's just...perfect for me. I'm like, this ball of energy." She sighed, and Maddy simply watched her as she looked over to the art hanging on the wall across from them. It depicted a big, blue whale under the water, with so much life and energy beneath the surface, and plenty above it too.

The perfect cross-section of land, air, and water.

"He calms me down," she said. "He listens to me when I need to rant about something. He helps me see things I don't even consider."

"He never cheated on you?"

"No," Robin said, shaking her head slowly. She looked back over to Maddy. "I don't know why men do that, Maddy, but I really don't think Ben will. You walk on water for him."

"But how do you *know*?"

"I can see it with you two," she said kindly. "With me and Duke..." She didn't shrug. She didn't blow Maddy off. "I guess I'm not sure I knew when we first got married. I loved him, and he loved me. We'd known each other for a while and had been dating. We'd talked about everything under the sun, and I felt like we were on the same page."

Maddy had spent some time with Duke and Robin, and they did seem to operate from the same page a lot. "It can be hard to get on the same page."

"It sure can."

"He says he doesn't care about having kids, but with AJ, and Kelli, and El…" She trailed off, but Maddy couldn't have another baby. Not only did she not want to, she actually couldn't carry one. "He's younger than me," she whispered.

"Which only makes him hotter," Robin said with a grin.

Maddy allowed herself to laugh with her. "He's really good to me." She met Robin's eye, hoping the other woman knew that Maddy didn't just mean he was nice to her. Or that he was good in bed. He was nice to her, and he was good in bed, but what she meant was something much…deeper.

Robin took her hand and clasped it tightly in her own. "I'm not the expert on divorce," she said. "Alice has been through it. Kelli too. Laurel, even. But having listened to them over the years, I do know one thing—when he stops being *good* to you, then you know there's a problem."

Maddy nodded, and she drew in a long, energizing breath. "Okay, the cake."

"Yes," Robin said, immediately focusing back on her binder. "Let's go over the cake. Now, I know you said you didn't want anything outlandish…"

* * *

Later that evening, Ben held her hand steady as Maddy climbed the last rungs of the ladder. "Whew," she said, her breath almost steaming in front of her. "That was harder than I thought."

Ben wrapped her up tightly in his arms and swayed with her. Or maybe that was just the boat swaying where he'd tied it to a private dock. When she'd seen his boat there—not a Coast Guard boat, but just one of his smaller, personal vessels, she'd freaked out.

You drove that on the ocean?

It was nice today, he'd said.

It's nighttime.

He had an answer for everything. *I'm not planning on driving it at night.*

Whose dock is this?

I got permission.

Maddy had given him the evil eye for a solid minute before he'd started laughing. *Let's go eat dinner,* he'd said, and they'd come back up the path to The Glass Dolphin. She'd lingered there, the idea of staying on his boat with him until tomorrow morning almost too much for her stomach to handle.

Even now, she considered only staying for a few minutes, then calling a ride and catching the last ferry back to Rocky Ridge. She could see the twinkling lights of The Glass Dolphin up the beach and on the overhanging rocks. She wondered if anyone could see them.

"It's so dark out here," she murmured.

"Yeah." He backed up and let go of her. "Stay here, and I'll go get the blankets." He jogged across the boat a few steps and went down the narrow set of stairs. He had to turn his shoulders sideways to do it, and Maddy wrapped her arms around herself, suddenly feeling very small and very alone beneath the vastness of the sky.

The ocean didn't have street lamps on it, and when she turned her back on Diamond Island, all she could see for miles and miles and miles was darkness. Pitch-black, pure darkness.

Ben's footsteps came back up, and she turned toward him. He carried a mountain of blankets, and she went to relieve him of some of them. "I got it," he said, but he dropped them unceremoniously in the middle of the deck.

Then he reached down and spread out a thick, fluffy blanket. He dropped to his knees and puffed up the others around the edges, then dragged a couple of pillows into the nest. Ben looked up at her, and the soft light from the land shone on his face. "Come on, sweetheart," he said softly.

Maddy lay down with him, feeling instantly warm and safe and secure in his arms. "There's no moon tonight," she whispered.

"Which is why I'm here with the boat," he whispered back. She couldn't feel the hardness of the deck beneath her, and the wind had died too, cutting above them as the sides of the boat shielded them.

She gazed up into the drape of darkness overhead, finding the stars easily as they pricked the night with their light. Ben nuzzled her neck and kissed his way across her collarbone, his eyes nowhere near the stars.

Maddy didn't mind, because she wanted to match the rhythm of their love-making to the soft undulation of the water rocking the boat. Ben obviously had the same idea, and she finally gave up on getting any stargazing done and turned to meet his hungry lips.

"I love you, Madeline," he whispered against hers. "Do you still want to marry me?"

"Yes," she whispered back.

"You're sure?"

She put enough space between them to get a good look at him, his normally vibrant blue eyes like deep, dark pools she wanted to dive into. "Are *you* sure?"

"I've never wanted to get married all that much," he said. "Until I met you. Now, I swear, it's all I think about." He smiled at her, a soft, slow, sensual smile that made Maddy's bones melt. "I worry I won't make you happy."

"You can't make another person happy," she said, gently pressing her lips to his. She didn't let him take control and kiss her breathless the way she had in the past. "I'm happy by myself, but I'm happier with you. I'm happier when I get to talk to you, when I get to hold you, when you whisper how much you love me, and when you do little things that tell me you've been thinking of me."

"Yeah? What do I do?" he asked.

"You pack your boat full of warm, fuzzy blankets, take me to dinner at the nicest restaurant in town, and plan a stargazing night with me," she whispered.

"We really can stargaze," he murmured, his lips already seeking the soft skin along her neck. "After, okay?"

"Mm, okay," she said, enjoying the heat the two of them put off into the night, and the way he absolutely took her current happiness and multiplied it.

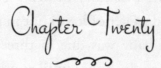

Chapter Twenty

Kelli walked through the silent yoga studio she owned, so much peace and contentment filling her. She'd grown up in this house, and it had often been a place of contention. Of bad memories. She'd wanted to escape it more often than not, but now?

Now, she loved this house with the stained glass windows and the creaky hardwood floors. Dozens of women came here every day to find their purpose, a good workout, a friend, and their health.

She'd played a huge part in their lives, and she could feel their life energy in the very walls around her.

Kelli had stopped teaching yoga five or six weeks ago. She attended classes every day, but she couldn't always do the routines that had become so second-nature for her.

She didn't mind so much, because any sacrifice was worth it for her baby girl.

With the clipboard resting on her very pregnant belly, she finished up the inventory in her yoga studio, Whole Soul, and retreated to her office to put in the order for the next month. Her baby was due in three days, and Kelli wouldn't be back to the house until another order needed to be placed. At least not to work.

Her teachers and the woman she'd hired to run Whole Soul while she was out on maternity leave had thrown her a baby shower, and they'd made her promise to bring in the little girl as soon as they could both make it. Kelli had promised, and she always kept her promises.

Somewhere in the house, a door opened, but Kelli wasn't alarmed. She offered two evening classes, one in each of the big spaces out front, and they'd be starting in about a half-hour. Shad had been dropping by every evening on his way back from Diamond Island too, as he didn't want Kelli on a ferry by herself at this stage of her pregnancy.

"Just me," Robby said as he poked his head into her office. "I saw the new steps. Thanks, Kelli." He grinned at her, and she smiled back.

"Oh," she said as he started to turn to go get his room ready. He taught aerobics and tension strength training twice a week, and she'd been lucky to get him. "Another review for your class came in." She moved around the mess of papers on her desk. "I had it here…" She found the blue paper and struggled to get to her feet. "Here you go."

He simply pinched the paper between his thumb and fingers. "Do I want to read this?"

"It's a good one," Kelli assured him.

Robby swallowed and looked at the paper. "From the moment I walked into the pulsing energy of this step aerobics class, I knew I had stumbled upon something special." He looked at her, his green eyes dancing. "The choreography is a vibrant blend of cardio and rhythm that never fails to get my blood pumping. The sequences are challenging yet accessible, accommodating both beginners and fitness enthusiasts with a fiery workout that leaves you both drenched and craving for more.

"But the real heartbeat of the class is our instructor, Robby. His charisma and enthusiasm reverberate throughout the room, infecting us all with a contagion of positivity that makes every session feel like a party. His warm, encouraging smile sets the tone for each class, and his clear, concise instructions ensure no one gets lost in the rhythm.

"More than his fitness expertise, what sets Robby apart is his genuine care for each of his students. He fosters an environment of camaraderie and inclusivity where everyone feels seen and supported. Whether you're mastering a complex sequence or catching your breath, Robby is right there, cheering you on.

"And, let's be honest ladies, the sight of Robby, all energetic strides and sculpted muscles, definitely doesn't hurt. His passion for fitness is reflected in his well-toned physique, a sight that often serves as motivation on those challenging days."

He finished and looked up. "Let's be honest, ladies?"

Kelli laughed, because she'd take reviews any way she could get them, and if "TinaF" wanted to say how sculpted Robby's muscles were, she wasn't going to say no. "Hey, you're motivational," she said.

He looked down at himself. "I feel like maybe I should wear more clothes to the class." He wore a pair of sweats and a tank top right now, and Kelli had seen him teach in gym shorts and bicycle shorts too. Those might be a little tight, but he was *working out*. What was he supposed to wear? Jeans?

She shook her head. "You're fine. It's a good review." She sat back down, her feet aching as she'd definitely neared the end of her day. "Tammy should like it." She grinned at Robby, who folded up the blue paper and stuck it in his pocket.

"Maybe I can get her to go out with me again because of it."

"She won't go out with you? Why not?"

Robby's jaw jumped. "It's just a thing. I'll figure it out." He turned to leave as he said, "Thanks for showing me this." He left, and Kelli looked at her desk. She really should clean it off before she left. She couldn't just leave a jumble of papers for Selma to deal with.

She set about filing and shredding, then she put the ordering clipboard back on the shelf. She'd just finished when the loud music from Robby's class began, so she expected Shad would show up at any moment.

Just as soon as Robby's class had started, the music stopped. Shouting came from the front of the house, and bells did clang in Kelli's head this time.

It took her a few long moments to get to her feet, and by the time she managed it and made it to her office door, the yelling had intensified and was getting closer.

"...ask her myself!" a man yelled.

"Sir," Robby called, and they both came striding around the corner. "She's pregnant, and—" He cut off when he saw Kelli standing just outside her office door. Thankfully, he didn't stop moving, and he caught up to the other man just as he arrived in front of Kelli.

Her heartbeat screamed through her whole body, beating wildly against its normal rhythm. She had two heartbeats inside her, and her little girl kicked as the adrenaline flowed freely between them.

"Do you own this place?" the man growled. He had wild, curly, black hair but he wasn't unkempt. He didn't smell of alcohol or body odor. He wore normal street clothes, not the type of gym attire Kelli's clients usually wore.

"Yes," she managed to say. "I'm Kelli Webb, and I've owned Whole Soul for a couple of years now."

"This is a residential home," he barked. "You can't just make it into a business."

Kelli wasn't sure what to think. Was this guy just going around checking every home in the area? On Bell Island? On all of the islands in Five Island Cove?

She so wasn't good at confrontation, and more people had crowded into the hallway. Robby's class-goers, and probably Moxie's too. She taught a relax and unwind yoga class against Robby's aerobics.

Her throat felt like old glue as she tried to swallow. "I grew up in this house," she said. "I'm married to the Finance Director for Five Island Cove. I know the laws, and I have a permit to have a yoga studio here."

"I'd like to see it," he demanded.

"Well," Kelli said calmly, not really sure where this well of nerves had come from. "You can call the Building Permit office and ask to see it. It's a public record. But I don't have to show it to you just because you say so."

He took a step forward, and Robby jumped in front of him. "Sir, you have to leave. Now."

"She's pregnant," a woman called from down the hall. "I'm calling the cops. He's threatening a pregnant woman!"

Kelli held her head high as she continued to gaze at the dark-haired man. He didn't budge either, but at least he didn't come any closer. "Unless you're a paying member of one of our two classes tonight, you're trespassing."

"Time to go," Robby said, and he put one hand against the man's chest. He swatted it away, which caused a ripple among the class members down the hall. Another man came through the women, and Kelli almost sagged against the wall when she saw her husband.

"Kel?" he asked. "What's going on here?"

"He's trespassing," someone said.

"He hit Robby."

"The police are on their way."

The voices started to blur all together, and Kelli's face grew hotter and hotter. Shad arrived and he wrapped one arm around her and steered her back into her office. He closed the door and the noise out, and Kelli tried to find a strong piece of ground to stand on.

"Kelli," Shad said, and she blinked until she could focus on him. It looked like he'd just entered the office. "He's gone. It's okay."

"I have the right permit," she said.

Shad didn't smile at her as he approached. "Of course you do. And it's not his job to come in here and badger you if you don't."

"Did the police come?"

Shad guided her around the desk and to her seat. "I don't know. I just know Robby got him to leave."

Kelli collapsed into her desk chair, and her back

spasmed at the same time a gushing, warm, wet feeling drenched the front of her pants. She yelped, and then froze. She breathed in very deeply, sure she'd just imagined the wetness. Or perhaps she'd had an accident.

"Are you okay?" Shad knelt down in front of her, pure concern on his handsome features. "Kelli, you're not talking."

As she exhaled, she looked down, but her belly was so big, she couldn't see if she'd wet herself or not. Then, all at once, a stretching, slicing, agonizing pain tore from one side of her abdomen to the other.

She cried out, doubled over, and groaned.

"Kelli!" Shad cradled her face in his hands and forced her to look up at him.

"My water broke," she said, the words laced with air, fear, and pain. "I'm going into labor."

Shad held very still for one, two, three long beats of time. Then he jumped to his feet and frantically tapped on his phone. "I'll get us a ride."

"We have to get to the hospital," she said, trying to get to her feet. Whole Soul sat right around the corner from the ferry station, and she'd walked the distance many times. Tonight, she wouldn't be.

"A car is one minute away," he said, and he grabbed her arm and helped her stand. "Lean on me. Tell me what to do."

Kelli didn't know what to do. "Get me to the hospital," she said, and then she and Shad exited her office and headed for the front exit.

She had to walk by both classes to get out of the house, and the people closest to the doorways saw her lumber by. "Kelli," someone called. "Are you okay?"

"I'm having the baby!" she yelled back.

"Her water broke," Shad added.

That caused everyone to flood into the hallway and doorways, and they all called well wishes to her. Kelli's eyes burned with tears, and not because she was wearing wet clothes and another contraction would steal her breath and shock her with pain at any moment.

But because her customers—her friends—were cheering her out of the building. Cheering her on as she had this baby.

In her wildest dreams, Kelli would've never put herself in this situation, and yet, she'd never felt so loved and so cared for. She waved to everyone as she reached the door, and thankfully, their car waited at the end of the sidewalk.

"Get us a ride on Diamond," she panted as she went down the steps, her hand gripping the railing. They couldn't normally schedule a RideShare at a ferry station during peak travel times, but Kelli knew Shad would find a way to make an exception.

In the car, he said, "My wife is in labor. How do I make sure we have a car to get us to the hospital the moment we arrive on Diamond?"

The RideShare driver turned around, took one look at Kelli, and said, "I'll call right now, sir." He called and drove, and Kelli leaned into Shad, both hands supporting her belly, as if she could keep her baby inside for just a little longer that way.

Shad pressed a kiss to her temple and whispered, "You are strong. You are brave. This is so exciting."

Kelli grinned, because she wanted to be strong, and brave, and yes, she was extremely excited to meet their little girl. "And it's not March fifteenth."

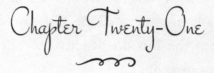

Chapter Twenty-One

Robin didn't carry anything with her as he navigated up to the maternity ward at the hospital. Kelli had not alerted anyone to her baby being born until this morning, and by the time Robin saw the little girl, she'd be twenty-four hours old.

Kelli would be fed and well-cared for, and Robin wouldn't have wanted flowers or gifts brought in that she then had to cart home with her brand-new daughter.

She wasn't surprised to find AJ and Asher in the waiting room outside the double-wide door that led back to the patient rooms. "Hey," she said to her friend, and AJ rose from the couch where she held a toy for her almost two-year-old.

"Robin." She smiled and stepped into Robin's hug. "How are you?"

"Cold." Robin enjoyed the embrace from AJ, and then she stepped back. "You're here alone?"

"Alice, Laurel, Kristen, and Jean went down to the cafeteria." AJ looked past Robin as if they'd come around the corner at any moment. "Eloise, Clara, and Julia are on their way from the inn on Sanctuary." She smiled and focused on Robin again.

"Is she taking visitors?" Robin looked to the big door she'd have to be buzzed through.

"Yeah. Oh, they're back." AJ moved past Robin as if she were less important, and Robin's eyes widened as she followed AJ's movement toward the other women. Something pinched in her chest, and she wasn't sure why.

She ran a wedding planning business, and she couldn't come to everything—but AJ didn't go to everything either.

"Did you see they're hiring nurses here?" Jean asked. Robin had seen the signs on the way in, but she hadn't paid them any attention. She wasn't a nurse, and she didn't know anyone in the field who didn't already work here or at a doctor's office.

"I heard the airport is short-staffed too," Kristen said.

A hint of worry suddenly entered the group. They'd congregated several paces from the couches, and Robin took Jean's little girl from her. Heidi smiled at her and waved her arms, and Robin let herself feel the magic that a baby always brought.

"This is why we need more people here," AJ said with pure conviction in her voice.

Kristen and Jean exchanged a glance, and Robin quickly averted her eyes back to baby Heidi's face.

"I think if there were less people," Alice said carefully. "We wouldn't have the needs here at the hospital or at the airport."

"Are you saying you agree with the likes of Weston Bent?" AJ demanded. Behind her, her son squabbled, but she didn't move a muscle.

"Of course not," Alice said, holding her own with AJ. If any of them could go toe to toe, it was the two of them. Robin usually didn't have any problem expressing her opinions either, but she stepped away from the huddle to go sit with Asher.

The group came with her, and Alice added, "I just think things should be done systematically. Carefully."

"There *is* a system in place," AJ said.

Alice stared at her, her dark eyes burning. "It's been exploited."

AJ sputtered as she stood at the edge of the couch. Everyone else had taken a seat, but AJ planted her hands on her hips. "If El was here, she'd agree with me. We need people to come to the cove to support our businesses."

"I'm fine with summer tourism," Alice said.

"We need local people living here to be able to support the tourism," AJ said.

Silence draped over the group for a moment, and Robin met Alice's eyes. She clearly told Robin to chime in, but Robin didn't quite know what to say. "We haven't had a problem supporting the tourism in the past," she said carefully. "But it's not tourist season yet. We shouldn't have problems supporting our population in March."

AJ glared at her, and Robin nodded to the other half of the uncomfortable couch. "Sit down, AvaJane."

"You're not my mother," she barked. But she sat. "You need people to plan weddings for, don't you?"

"Yes," Robin murmured. "But I'm not getting hired by people coming here to get married. Five Island Cove isn't a destination wedding locale."

"What if it was?" AJ challenged.

Robin shook her head, hoping the conversation would change as El, Julia, and Clara came around the corner. El looked like she'd been crying, and Robin got to her feet. "Alice."

Alice sat with her back to the hallway, but she twisted and then got to her feet. El said something to Julia, and then made a detour into the bathroom before Robin or Alice could say anything to her.

"What's going on?" Alice asked as Julia and Clara approached.

"She's just stressed about the inn," Julia said.

"You guys want the cove to keep growing, don't you?" AJ asked.

Clara blinked past Alice to the couch where AJ sat. Robin took her seat again, her chest vibrating with tension. Apparently, AJ wasn't going to let this go.

"AJ," Kristen said.

"No, I want to know," she said. "We need to take a vote."

"A vote?" Alice asked. "AJ, come on."

"This isn't going to accomplish anything," Robin said.

"I want to know." AJ put a determined look on her face. "My poll for the op-ed piece was simple. Two choices. Yes, the cove needs to keep growing at its current pace to support our livelihood and to ensure our communities don't die. No, the cove government needs to slow down the rate of building to control the businesses and people who move here." She lifted her chin, daring everyone there to defy her.

No one said anything, so Robin handed Heidi back to Jean, who immediately busied herself with the baby, her eyes down.

"AJ," she said. "It's not that simple. For anyone. Not even for you."

"It is," AJ insisted.

"I read your piece," Robin said. "It was really good, AJ. You're an amazing writer, but you addressed the middle ground over and over. You thought you were making a point for yes, or even no, but there's *so* much middle ground."

"Duke would literally not have a job if people didn't need fish," AJ said. "He sells to the restaurants here. What if there weren't restaurants here?"

"What if we overfish the oceans?" Robin countered. "Why does it have to be all or nothing?"

A pause filled the waiting room, and then Alice said, "I agree...with Robin."

AJ pulled in a breath, but Julia said, "I wouldn't be here if the cove didn't allow expansion. Maddy either."

"See?" AJ gestured to her. "One of our friends. You'd kick her out?"

Robin shook her head, a sigh moving through her whole body. "Come on, AJ. You're making things so black and white." She knew that was never the case. She'd lived a lot of her life trying to fit into the black box or the white box. Her mother insisted there was one right way to do things.

But even she'd started to change. Even she'd started to admit there were an infinite number of gray boxes between the black one and the white one.

"I think the City Council needs to slow the heck down," Alice said. "There's a lot to consider, and that's literally their job to consider it. So I actually think I'm in favor of moving slower than Robin is."

"I'm about where Robin is," Laurel said.

"I'd love to see our small-town atmosphere preserved," Kristen said.

"You live in a new development," AJ pointed out.

Kristen didn't cower away from her, despite the disgust in AJ's voice. "I'm aware of where I live, AvaJane. I know what I see washing up on the beaches where I walk. I know about the traffic I encounter just to go to the grocery store. I think there need to be some measures to preserve our way of life."

Jean nodded and nodded, and that told Robin where she stood. "Kelli doesn't want a ton of growth either," she said without actually vocalizing her own opinion.

"I agree with you, AJ," Julia said.

Clara, who'd said nothing, met Robin's eye. They hadn't always been the best of friends, nor had they hit everything off right at the beginning. But Robin loved Clara, and she'd come to understand more about how she operated.

Several seconds of silence filled the waiting room, and Robin played nervously with the hem of her blouse.

"I think I'm in the middle," Clara said. "I see both sides—and AJ, you have to admit there are a lot of sides."

"Sides to what?" Eloise asked, and Robin startled at the introduction of her voice to the conversation. She hadn't seen or heard her approach. Her face had been washed and all evidence of distress and tears scrubbed away.

"El and Aaron agree with me," AJ said.

El looked at her, then glanced to Robin, her eyebrows raised. Robin didn't see a way out of this conversation, because AJ had forced it on them. "You want the growth to continue in the cove," Robin supplied for her.

"Oh," El said. "Yeah. I do. We do. Aaron needs good cops to come here, and it's hard to get them here without amenities. Parks, shops, things to do for them and their families."

"And some of you work with locals," AJ said. "But you have to see our side."

"I said I did," Robin said at the same time Clara said, "I literally just said I see both sides." They both glared at AJ, who apparently could only hear what she wanted to hear.

"Robin's right," Alice said above a couple of other voices. "There's so much more to this than *yes* or *no*."

"I have to go." AJ scooped her son and started away from the group without waiting for a hug or a good-bye. She had long legs and pure determination and she'd put quite a bit of distance between herself and the group in only a few seconds.

"You left your bag," Jean said, but AJ obviously didn't hear her.

Awkward silence descended on the group, and then El

said, "I don't want to be here either." She left as quickly as she'd come, and Robin had no idea what to make of that. She'd been very close with Eloise since she'd come back to the cove, and she blinked in surprise at the sudden departure.

"I came to see the baby," Robin said, her eyebrows lifted. "Have you guys all seen her?"

"Yes." Alice got to her feet. "I have to get back to work." She looked at Jean, who nodded. She picked up AJ's bag, but Kristen shouldered it. The three of them left —again, without a good-bye—and Robin didn't know what to make of the splintering happening literally in front of her face.

"She's my ride," Clara said quietly. "I'll call you later, Robin."

"Okay," she said numbly as one more of their party departed. Julia and Laurel looked at Robin like she'd know what to do, but she didn't. She cleared her throat and got to her feet. "I'm going to go see little Daphne."

She looked from Julia to Laurel. "Will you come with me?"

Laurel's smile appeared, but it stayed small. She lifted her baby boy, and Robin took him so she could stand. "I'll come in with you."

"Me too," Julia said in a quiet voice. "Maddy wants the growth too, because it's our jobs..."

"I know that," Robin said. "I'm not for or against. I

think there's a lot of middle ground to cover." She turned away from the conversation and headed for the big door. She pressed a button, gave Kelli's name, and prayed she'd be let back into the patient rooms.

She had to get away from this place, where so much tension had lived. Where she could barely breathe.

Thankfully, the door swung open, and she led the way back to Kelli's room. She lay in the bed with the most perfect baby asleep in her arms, and all of the negativity flowed right out of Robin.

"Oh," fell from her lips as her friend looked up. She wore exhaustion in her eyes, but the pure joy masked it perfectly.

"I'll take James," Laurel murmured, and Robin barely turned to give the little boy back to his mother.

"Can I?" she whispered as she approached Kelli. She transferred the baby to Robin, who gazed at her like she'd hung the moon. "She's perfect."

"We named her Daphne," Kelli said, apparently thinking that Robin didn't read the group texts. She did, almost obsessively.

"You did great," Robin said, finally looking away from the little girl. Her heart filled with love for Kelli, who'd had such a long, twisted road to get to where she was. They all had, but Robin just knew more of Kelli's hairpins and potholes. "You're the best, Kel."

Kelli smiled and reached out to touch Robin's forearm. "Thanks for coming, Robin."

She didn't tell her that everyone else had left, and she exchanged a glance with Laurel and then Julia before focusing back on the baby again. She couldn't ignore the rift between her friends forever, but for right now...she could.

Chapter Twenty-Two

Eloise simply didn't have mental energy to debate opinions. She left the hospital behind AJ, the other woman's blonde hair flowing behind her as she strode with purpose toward the exit. El walked with the same clip, but she had no purpose.

She'd come to see Kelli's baby, and she hadn't even done that. As she pushed out into the wind, the sky the color of steel and the ocean waves crashing angrily from down the block, El realized what she'd said.

I don't want to be here either.

She couldn't remember a time in the past few years since they'd all returned to Five Island Cove that she didn't want to see any of them. Of course they hadn't agreed on everything. They'd had a pretty big split when

Laurel had been investigating a drug case. She'd had to look at everyone as suspects, and that included El herself.

She had, in fact, almost been a victim of the drug network moving their wares through her inn. "We survived that," she muttered to herself.

But could they weather this?

Eloise felt like she was splitting apart at the seams. It boggled her mind that she could experience so much happiness, so much good, enjoy so many things in her life, and then also have to endure the opposite. Life, she'd been learning, was like an intricate piece of music, a symphony composed of soaring crescendos and dissonant chords, punctuated by silent moments of quiet introspection. Each note, no matter how sweet or jarring, contributed to the exquisite complexity of the melody, a testament to the beauty found in contrast and the enduring resonance of the human spirit.

She didn't want the dissonant chords. She didn't want to go through the devastating loss of a miscarriage. And yet, her body was bleeding.

A sob broke free from her throat, and Eloise looked around the parking lot outside the hospital, completely lost. She didn't have her car here, as she'd taken a Ride-Share with Julia and Clara.

She needed a name for the feelings streaming through her, and they weren't necessarily sadness or horror, though she was both. She could still recall yesterday morning when she'd first seen the spotting. She'd stared, horror snaking through her like a frozen snake, ready to strike with venomous fangs.

Her phone buzzed, but she didn't check it. She didn't want to talk to anyone, not even Aaron. He'd wanted to go to the hospital, but Eloise honestly couldn't see the point. What were they going to do? They couldn't give her the hormones her body needed to keep the baby.

"It's already lost," she said. She had to deal with the pain of that on so many levels, and she didn't even realize Alice stood in front of her until the brunette drew her into a hug.

Then, all Eloise had to do was hang on. Alice smelled like cotton and a slow, summer day where no one would ever have to face such heartache. Life was easy inside the circle of Alice's arms, and Eloise clung to her and sobbed, and sobbed, and sobbed.

Alice said nothing, and Eloise would never be able to tell anyone about the roiling, boiling turmoil inside her. She hadn't told her friends she was pregnant yet. She and Aaron hadn't told the girls either.

She hadn't meant to keep secrets; she'd simply wanted to be sure.

As she finally quieted, Alice asked, "Do you need a ride home?"

Eloise nodded, and Alice lovingly led her to her car. Kristen and Jean waited in the back seat, but no one asked her any questions. She'd wrung herself dry, but when she cried that hard, she sniffled and hiccuped for a while afterward.

Alice got behind the wheel and started the car, going about everything perfectly normally. She buckled her seat-belt and adjusted the volume on the radio. In the back seat, Jean's baby babbled, and that only made a hot streak of tears silently flow down Eloise's face.

In that moment, she realized that Jean had been in situations like this. She hadn't been able to have any children either, and she'd suffered miscarriages. Eloise could potentially talk to her.

But she didn't want to, not right now. She didn't want to talk this through, not with as raw and as immediate as it was.

"Clara said she'll get a RideShare," Kristen said quietly from the back seat.

"I can go," Eloise said.

Alice reached over and punched the door locks. "No," she said firmly. "Clara can get another ride." She looked at Eloise. "You don't have to talk to us. Just let me take you home and make sure Aaron's there to take care of you. Or I'll stay until he gets home."

"The girls," Eloise said. "I have to pick up the girls." She loved Billie and Grace, and they'd given her so much purpose. She couldn't fall to pieces in front of them. They'd go through so much pain and heartache in their lives, and Eloise had to show them a good example of how to deal with it.

"I'll get them," Alice said. "Kristen, you and Jean are going to the lighthouse?"

"Yes, please," Kristen said, and Alice maneuvered out of the parking space. Eloise didn't even remember walking over to the car.

The radio played merrily in the car as Alice drove, and she even sang along with the lyrics. Eloise kept her eyes out the window, everything blurring into one smear of color. Alice stopped; Kristen and Jean got out of the car, and Eloise watched Jean labor under the weight of the car seat that held her baby as they walked up the sidewalk to the dark blue door of the lighthouse.

Alice backed out and the ride continued. Eloise and Aaron lived up the beach from the lighthouse, and she watched the cliffs roll away into the flatter grasses and sand dunes. She thought about the first time she'd met Aaron when she'd first come back to the cove. It had happened on this beach that ran behind his house. He'd been running with his dog, Prince, and the canine had knocked her right into the waves.

"I still have Aaron," she whispered to the glass. She turned toward Alice. "I..."

Alice cut her a look out of the corner of her eye and said, "El, I don't know why you're upset, but it hurts my heart. I don't need to know right now." She gripped the steering wheel. "I've been there, whatever it is."

Eloise nodded, her emotions quivering through her whole body. They shook her chin, and she said, "I don't want anyone else to know right now."

"I would never tell them anything," Alice said.

"I lost..." Eloise couldn't even say it. Alice made the turn off the highway that circumnavigated Diamond Island, the car slowing as she entered the neighborhood. A few moments later, she pulled into Eloise's driveway.

With the car in park, Alice faced Eloise fully. "What time are the girls done?"

"Billie's done at the high school at two-fifteen," Eloise said. "Grace at the junior high at—"

"Two forty-five," they said together. Alice nodded. "I'll get them and bring them home."

Eloise suddenly didn't want to be in the house alone. She didn't want Alice to show up and pick up the girls. Then they'd know something was so wrong that Eloise couldn't do it herself. They'd worry, and the fact that Eloise might cause a problem for Billie and Grace tormented her.

She shook her head. "You know what?" A long drag of oxygen cleared the cobwebs that had come into her mind. "I can do it."

"El."

She started to crack again, and she still didn't want to

be alone. "Will you come inside with me? We can have some tea, and just…I don't want to be here alone."

"Have you talked to Aaron today?"

Eloise nodded, but she reached for the door handle and pulled it open. Aaron struggled in his own way, and she'd never seen the strong, capable, smart cop cry about anything except his girls. He maintained a level head during a crisis, and Eloise had relied on him so much over the past few years.

She could lean on him during this, but she had to be a pillar of support for him too. "He had to testify in court today," she said. "For that drug case, if you can believe that."

Alice's jaw jumped, and a fierce look of defiance entered her face. "You missed a lot of the conversation, but AJ is pretty upset we don't all want the cove to burst at the seams in the next year."

Eloise didn't have mental space or energy for the small-town island politics swirling through the cove. "Will we survive this?"

"I don't know," Alice murmured. She rose from the car in the fluid, perfectly poised way she always moved, and Eloise lumbered to her feet too. "She attacked Robin and some of the others pretty harshly."

Eloise nodded, and then Alice met her at the front corner of the hood and hooked her arm through Eloise's. "Come on," she said. "Tea and a fluffy blanket and your favorite movie will help." She sounded so confident as she said it that Eloise simply let herself believe it.

Then she entered the house she wouldn't be welcoming a baby to in September, trying to be as strong as she could be.

* * *

Later, Eloise smiled at Billie as she sank into the front seat of the car with a sigh. "Hey," she said. "How was school?"

Billie gave her a look that said she'd rather go anywhere tomorrow but back to the high school. "I'm so ready for summer." She pulled her seatbelt across her body and faced the front.

They made the drive over to the junior high, and Billie usually spent the time on her phone. Eloise did too, catching up on emails or answering texts from her managers. Today, Eloise joined the pick-up line in the drive-through and turned to face Billie.

"Bills," she said, her voice already breaking. That got the teen to look up from her phone, her blue eyes wide and perfectly clear with concern. Eloise wasn't sure if she should tell her without Aaron. Or at all.

She'd learned to go with her gut when dealing with the girls, and something told her to just tell Billie. She drew in a breath and thought a small prayer as she exhaled.

She couldn't look at the beautiful blonde girl in the passenger seat while she spoke.

"Your dad and I were expecting a baby," she whispered. "But not anymore."

Billie's shocked intake of air felt like a slap to Eloise's lungs. Her voice made a sound, but not an intelligible English word, and Eloise ducked her head.

Billie's hand landed tentatively on Eloise's, which still rested on the steering wheel. "El," she whispered. "I'm so sorry."

Eloise nodded and looked up at her step-daughter. "I love you so much," she said.

Billie's eyes brimmed with tears. "You are an amazing mother." She swiped at her eyes, because she'd been wearing makeup for a while and likely didn't want black smudges across her face. "I am so lucky you're *my* mom."

Eloise wept, and the best part was that Billie did too. She leaned over the console between them and hugged her. "Can we just lay in my bed and watch movies this afternoon?"

"And maybe skip school tomorrow?" Billie whispered, her grip on Eloise tight, tight, tight.

"Yes," Eloise asked, though she'd have to get that story later. "We work hard, and we put up with a lot, and it's okay to take one day and not get out of bed."

Billie half-laughed as she settled back into her seat. "And we'll order all of our meals, and we'll make Dad stay home with us, and he'll get us whatever we want—all—day—long." She grinned and blinked rapidly against her fingers. "Okay?"

"Yes," Eloise said again. Something settled into her stomach, and while it still hurt slightly, she didn't feel like she'd swallowed wet cement against her will. She'd give herself the rest of today and all day tomorrow, and she wouldn't let Aaron go to work. "Maybe we should text your dad and make sure he knows he's going to be a butler tomorrow."

Billie retrieved her phone from beneath her thigh. "On it."

A swell of love filled Eloise, and while she'd desperately wanted a baby she shared with Aaron, she did have so much with him already. They weren't a consolation prize; they were her daughters, and armed with that knowledge, Eloise wiped her tears and asked, "What movie do you want to start with this afternoon?"

Chapter Twenty-Three

Alice entered the house where she'd grown up, only the good memories in her mind. "Della," she called, looking for her step-mother.

"On the back deck," echoed to her from the rear of the house. Her dad had remarried many years ago, and Alice had been making more of an effort with her family here in the cove. For so long, she'd relied on herself and the twins and her ex to be all the family she needed. Then there was the PTA moms, the neighbors in her swanky neighborhood in the Hamptons, and all of the fake relationships she had.

When she'd moved back here and given up everything, Alice had been reconnecting with her high school friends. With Kristen—and truth be told, with herself.

Now that she felt more secure in her life, with the twins off at college and her relationship with Arthur actually good, she'd set up a pedicure with her step-mother. *We need to get our summer toes ready*, she'd told Della, and since Della loved the spa, she'd readily agreed.

Alice went past the living room, which held a nice brown leather couch and a matching recliner, and through the kitchen. The back sliding door stood open, and Alice stepped down to the deck her father had rebuilt only last summer.

She breathed a sigh of pure pleasure as she stepped back into the sunshine. March had been full of thunderstorms and dark skies by three p.m. Alice swore it had rained every afternoon, but now that April had bloomed, so had the trees around Five Island Cove. The sun shone more and more, and Alice didn't think there was a better month on Rocky Ridge.

"Ahh," she said as she exhaled. "I love this black sand." The beaches here didn't glow golden like some other places. They shone with black gold. Alice had grown up with this view, and she'd never loved another beach more than the one that only took her seventy steps to descend to from this back deck.

"Hey, you." Her dad wrapped her in a hug, obviously pleased with the effort Alice had been making in the past several months since the twins had gone off to college.

"Hey, Dad." Alice hugged him right back, her smile

real and genuine as it filled her face. "Guess what?" She pulled away in a jerk. "I wanted to tell you and Della in person." She felt like she'd swallowed a lantern, the electric light beaming from her the way they did in lighthouses.

"Arthur and I got roles in *Kiss Me, Kate*."

Della whipped out her phone. "What dates will you be performing?"

"It's not until July," Alice said. "The second week, after the Fourth."

"That's great news," her father said, and Alice hadn't even told him what roles they'd gotten.

She couldn't stop smiling, though there was plenty to turn her grin into a frown. She'd tried to shelve the things that troubled her, and she'd already spent a lot of today worrying over Kristen and Jean and the lighthouse.

She'd filed the paperwork with the county court-house to get a duplicate title, but she hadn't heard anything about it in ages. The only two people she'd spoken to since the incident at the hospital were Robin and Eloise, and she knew hardly anyone was talking to each other.

The group text had been very quiet in the past three weeks, and Alice actually found that she missed it. The last time they'd gone silent, it had taken a strong person and personality to get them all back in the same room.

Alice wondered if that was her role this time. Last time, it had been Robin with the sharp words and lecturing texts. It had been El, with her insistent messages that they didn't have to let Laurel's case break them up.

With a jolt, Alice realized that she was talking to both El and Robin. Eloise definitely didn't have the mental fortitude to do much right now. Alice still wasn't sure what had caused her to completely come apart just outside the hospital's sliding doors. Honestly, with Eloise, it could be something with Aaron, one of the girls, or the inn. Or something else entirely.

Robin wouldn't allow conversations to die, and Alice had her phone out before she realized her father had asked her what roles she and Arthur had gotten in *Kiss Me, Kate.*

He currently looked at her with quizzes in his eyes, and Alice gave herself a little shake. "I'm sorry," she said. "I have so much on my mind." She tried to laugh lightly, but it didn't last long and certainly didn't sound happy. "Arthur is playing Baptista, who's got some speaking parts. I'm playing Hattie, who's the assistant to the lead actress in the show." She grinned. "It's like a show within a show."

"We can't wait to come," Della said, her smile wide.

"Paul said he'd be there too," she said. "Oh, did I tell you? He got a citation for his participation in that pro-growth group."

"Yeah," her dad said with a sigh. "Of course he doesn't want the cove to make it harder for him to sell houses."

"The ones that are already here shouldn't be a problem," Alice said.

"Well, he sells more than that, doesn't he?" He dad raised his eyebrows, and Alice supposed her brother did do more than just sell existing homes on Five Island Cove.

"Ready?" Della asked, clearly trying to break up this conversation before it grew too many teeth.

Alice wanted that too, so she said, "Yes. You?"

Della smiled her back into the house, and Alice led the way away from the black sand beach and through the house. "I ordered a ride," her step-mom said from behind her. "They're waiting."

Sure enough, a gray sedan waited in front of the house, and Alice slid into the back seat. She'd often wished for a mother to chit-chat with while she picked up her house or did her dishes. Her mother had died when she was a teenager, and she'd never invited Della into the role.

She still hadn't quite done it, but today, she looked over to her. "My friends and I are kind of in the middle of a thing," she said. "It's because of the building permits, the speed the cove has been growing, all of that."

Della blinked at her, her dark eyes wide and completely interested. "It seems to be all anyone can talk about."

Alice nodded, her throat so narrow it almost seemed like air couldn't get down it. She somehow managed to keep breathing as the car navigated toward the only nail salon on Rocky Ridge. This outlying island didn't have as many amenities. Only one park, which was right next to the ferry station, and a small corner market that sold gas and groceries and hardware items and anything else they could cram onto the shelves. It was enough for people coming to their expensive second homes—one of which Alice had used to own—and anyone coming to spend a couple of hours on the black sand beach.

Right next to the gas station sat a strip mall that had been there for as long as Alice could remember, though the shops it hosted had changed a lot over the years. A nail salon sat there, and it only took five minutes to get there.

Alice had not unraveled her thoughts before then, but as she went inside with Della, she said, "I need to get everyone in the same room, so we can talk."

They'd done that at AJ's before Kelli's wedding. They'd been forced to talk through things in Kristen's cottage. At the lighthouse. At their semi-regular lunches.

Alice could do this. She wasn't going to let the cove swallow her friendships, and she wasn't going to let anyone slip through the cracks.

Not this time. Not her.

"I'm a lawyer," she said. "Contention doesn't bother me as much as some people. But...we had a heated discussion at the hospital a few weeks ago, and now it's like everyone has...moved on."

As she spoke, she realized that was what bothered her

the most. AJ had said her piece and now she was just going to march forward in her life. She was headstrong enough to do it, but Alice also knew once she cooled off, she could be reasonable.

She's probably embarrassed, Alice thought. AJ had pushed the conversation hard at the hospital, going so far as to force them to vote their opinions. The problem was, Alice agreed with Robin. The op-ed piece had been too black and white. AJ's opinion had been far too obvious. It wasn't a fair and balanced report of the issues—Alice doubted she'd even seen such a thing.

"How do I get them back together?" she asked.

Della reached over and patted her hand. "Sometimes you can't."

Alice wasn't going to accept that. She'd text them all individually if she had to, the way others had done for her when she just couldn't be on the group text.

She picked a color for her summery toes—Sunset Sorbet—which reminded her of the cold, sweet treats summer would bring, along with the glorious sunsets she could look forward to. She sat next to Della. They chatted about this and that, the conversation moving to something less stressful and totally neutral.

As Alice's legs got massaged, she picked up her phone and texted Robin. *We need a plan to get everyone back on the same page.*

Is that possible? Robin asked.

We don't have to agree, Alice said. *We just have to talk.*

Lunch? Robin suggested, but Alice shook her head. This had to be more than lunch. It had to be more than just getting all twelve of them in a room and expecting everyone to magically come to an agreement.

Her mind worked and worked, but the solution didn't come easily or quickly. She needed to talk to Robin face-to-face, and she texted, *Let's you and I go to lunch and discuss some ideas.*

I'm in, Robin said. *I'm also dying to know what you and Arthur got for the play. Why haven't you told us?*

Alice knew why, and she quickly thumbed out, *Because I didn't want to get on after days of silence like nothing big has happened between us. It feels cheap, and then all the responses will be Yay, Alice! or Can't wait! and then we'll fall into the abyss again.*

You don't know that, Robin sent back, and Alice almost rolled her eyes.

"Fine," she muttered, and she left Robin's solo text string to navigate over to the group one. She told everyone what parts she and Arthur had gotten in *Kiss Me, Kate* and when the dates were. *I'll have a link to buy tickets later*, she ended, and then she sat back, ready to prove her point to Robin.

Sure enough, the texts started coming in. One from Laurel, whom Alice had spoken to a few times. Then Eloise, then Clara, then Julia. A minute passed before

Robin responded, and that meant she'd deliberately waited so she wouldn't be first, or even second.

Kristen and Jean and Maddy all said the exact same things—*Congrats! Can't wait!!*—right down to the exact number of exclamation points, and that shot annoyance straight through Alice.

Kelli responded, and so did Tessa, whom Alice would've sworn had dropped off the face of the planet in the past few months. Apparently, her boyfriend hadn't been able to retire as much as he'd like, and he still spent a lot of time in Nantucket. Therefore, Tessa did too.

"That leaves AJ," Alice said, staring at her phone, almost willing AJ to respond.

She didn't, and no one else picked up another topic. They had no news. Nothing to share with the group, when normally, Alice had two dozen messages from the time she stepped into her home office at nine a.m. until she broke for lunch at noon.

She didn't need to go back to the private string with Robin and point out the fact that she was right. Robin texted and said, *Lunch tomorrow. The Glass Dolphin? Eleven-thirty.*

I'll come pick you up. Then Alice sighed, leaned her head back, and closed her eyes. She hoped together, she and Robin would be able to come up with something that would rebuild the bridges that had been swept away.

Something sharp and needled poked at the back of her mind, saying, *Sometimes bridges are irrevocably damaged.*

A chilling gust of realization swept over her as she suddenly understood the truth of that thought, echoing like a prophecy in the caverns of her mind. But what bridge was she about to cross, or perhaps already had, that could never be mended?

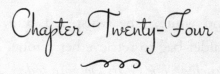

Chapter Twenty-Four

Julia leaned into the railing that marked the edge of the outdoor waiting area at the north Diamond Island ferry station. Her eyes drifted closed all by themselves, the sunshine glorious and warm against her bare skin.

Maddy would be thrilled that the weather had turned from stormy to something better, and Julia prayed it would hold for another couple of weeks until the wedding had been gloriously beautiful, bright, and absolutely unforgettable.

A smile graced her face, because with the current breeze, and the sound of the lapping waves, and this lazy day where Julia wasn't working at the Cliffside Inn, pure happiness had found a place inside her.

Once upon a time, she didn't think this feeling would ever belong to her again. After raising three boys and being married for twenty-five years, Julia should've known that feelings and emotions were fleeting and quick. There were good times and bad, and they each only stayed for a season.

"Black and white," she whispered, and she reached into her shoulder bag to retrieve her phone. *I'm meeting Maddy for lunch at The Glass Dolphin today. Do you want to join us? Her ferry should be here in about ten minutes.*

She sent the message to Robin, wondering if she should invite Laurel or Alice. They both lived right here on Diamond Island, and she'd enjoyed spending time with Alice in a smaller group. They'd even gone to lunch together—just the two of them—a few times since Julia had moved here.

Alice just picked me up, and we're headed to the Dolphin for lunch too. Do you want to join us?

Julia's first inclination was to say yes, of course. She and Maddy would love to join Robin and Alice for lunch. But hesitation pulled through her, because there had been no friend luncheons since Kelli had her baby.

The conversation at the hospital had played through Julia's head every day since it had happened. The texts had been slow and nothing important. Julia missed the closeness she'd been developing with the women here, and so, yes, she wanted to go to lunch with Robin and Alice.

Then, the fact that Robin and Alice were going to lunch, just the two of them, without inviting anyone else told Julia that clearly, some relationships were continuing around her. She just wasn't part of them.

So that hollow space inside her shouted at her to definitely deny the invitation to lunch. She'd only been told about the lunch because she reached out first and they'd end up in the same place.

So what? she thought. Before she could let the pinch in her stomach rise through her throat, she tapped out a response. *I'll talk to Maddy, but I can't imagine she'll say no.*

A sense of longing pulled through her, and she added. *I miss you guys.*

Julia didn't care if she'd revealed too much. She should've said things throughout her marriage that she hadn't. She wasn't going to hold back important things anymore, and her thoughts wandered to Liam.

Their relationship had been progressing along just fine. Julia sensed he was a little frustrated with her, but he hadn't said so. She'd talked to Maddy about him, and Maddy had questioned why she was holding back.

It was a good question, one Julia didn't have an answer to. With Maddy getting married soon, Julia wondered why she was dragging her feet with Liam. She didn't want to break-up with him. She sure enjoyed spending time with him, whether they cuddled together on her couch or they went out for the best lobster rolls in Five Island Cove.

JESSIE NEWTON

She looked down at her phone and realized she hadn't sent the text to Robin. She quickly tapped to send it, the express ferry from Rocky Ridge appearing on the horizon. *We'll be there in about twenty minutes.*

Perfect, Robin said. Julia hugged herself against the weather, a little shiver working its way through her body. Before she knew it Maddy had arrived, and she took one look at Julia's face and said, "What's going on?" Her footsteps slowed and she approached, and Julia wished she knew what her expression said.

"Robin texted," Julia said. "She and Alice are going to lunch at the Dolphin too. They invited us to eat with them."

Maddy's perfectly sculpted eyebrows rose a little higher with every word Julia spoke. "Okay," she said.

"I said we probably could," Julia said, her heart pounding a little harder now. "But if you don't want—"

"I do," Maddy said. "I'm just surprised."

"I was too," Julia said as she turned to head out to the RideShare line with Maddy. She didn't know what else to say, at least about this fractured group of friends she and Maddy had somehow found.

"When are the kids coming in?" she asked instead.

Maddy brightened. "Bea and Kyle will be here on Friday. Chelsea isn't coming until Saturday, because her relationship with Robert is getting serious, and she has a date with him that, in her words, is very important."

298

Maddy grinned and grinned as she spoke, and Julia should probably check in with her sons more often. They could go weeks without talking over the phone, as none of them really liked to discuss their lives in great detail.

She'd text, and get a line or two, but nothing like Maddy got from Chelsea. Men and women were different, and all Julia could do was work on her own relationships with her children, no comparison necessary.

"Why doesn't she bring him to the wedding?"

"I guess he has an important meeting on Monday morning, and she doesn't want to leave the cove right after the wedding."

"She knows you and Ben are leaving the cove right after the wedding, right?" Julia asked.

Maddy's smile faltered, slipping away like a faded sunset swallowed by the encroaching indigo of night. "She does," she said, immediately clearing her throat. "She might be staying at the house on Rocky Ridge for a few days."

Julia opened the door of the car that pulled up to the curb. She sank into the sedan and then slid across the seat to make room for Maddy. Once they were settled, with the doors closed and the car on the way to The Glass Dolphin, she looked over to Maddy, clearly telling her to finish the story.

"She lost her apartment," Maddy said, her throat bobbing as she swallowed. "Uh, Chris won't pay for it anymore, and I'm not exactly in a position to help with an apartment in Boston. She's got some options she's working on, and she's going to be staying at the house while Ben and I are gone."

Julia nodded, something inside her wanting to help. "I'll check on her while you're gone."

"Thank you." Maddy breathed in deeply, and then blew her breath out. "So lunch with Alice and Robin?"

"I had the thought I should ask Robin, and she said they were already going." Julia looked out her window at the few trees they whizzed by. The island had started to bloom, though there were still lots of trees that still only bore bare branches.

Julia loved springtime, and she'd never experienced one here in Five Island Cove. The true green season hadn't arrived yet, and she couldn't wait to see the islands come blaring back to life. She loved the renewal which reminded her that even when she felt beige and bare, she could look forward to a rebirth.

They arrived at The Glass Dolphin, and Julia's stomach tightened as she stood from the car. She faced the restaurant, seeing so many things at once. Her memory threw scenes through her mind, and she smiled at the other times she'd met Maddy here. She'd had lunch with Alice here, and she'd met the larger group a few times too.

Liam had brought her here for a romantic dinner on Saturday evening, and their popular Sunday brunch.

She could see the windows after they'd been smashed in, and she remembered holding Maddy's hand on the sidewalk as the general contractor went through the damage.

"Julia," Maddy said, and she startled.

"Yeah," she said, turning away from her memories. "I'm coming."

They went into the Dolphin, and Maddy smiled and hugged her hostess. "We're here with a couple of others," she said. "So you can mark us off." She scanned the restaurant, and Julia did too.

"They're on the porch," the hostess said, and she turned to lead them into the restaurant. Maddy knew the porch, but Julia didn't, so she walked a couple of steps behind everyone else, finding Robin and Alice at a table for four which faced the ocean.

Every muscle inside Julia relaxed as both women stood, smiles etched on their faces. "Hey," Robin said, stepping into Julia for a hug. "I'm so glad you texted."

"I hope we're not imposing," Julia murmured. She pulled back and looked Robin right in the eye. Hers held anxiety and concern, and it moved through Julia like lightning. "I didn't realize people were still meeting up."

"They're not," Robin said. "Alice wants to stage an intervention to get everyone together."

"We've done it before," Alice said. "We just need to..." She sighed as she sank back into her seat. She and Robin had taken the two chairs in the middle, leaving Maddy to take an end chair almost across from Julia.

"I don't know how to get everyone together without causing another fight like we had at the hospital." Alice lifted her water glass and took a sip. Their menus sat closed over their chargers, and Julia didn't pick up her menu either.

No one said anything, and Julia was glad they'd arrived before her, so she had a glass of water too. She took a drink, wishing she could order something stronger. Without a waitress nearby, Julia met Maddy's eyes.

Then Alice's. She raised her eyebrows, as if Julia had called this luncheon and had all the ideas needed to bring a dozen opinions together into a cohesive whole. She wasn't even sure that was possible, but she didn't want to say so.

"Okay," Robin said at the same time Maddy did. They looked at one another, the tension strong enough to blow the windows out.

Julia cleared her throat. "Okay," she said, and all three sets of eyes came to her. "I know Clara and El are on the same page." She looked around nervously, but Maddy gave her a small smile big enough to instill some confidence in her. "Even though Eloise wants tourism to grow, and Clara is fine with the cove how it is. They don't let it get between them."

"Good," Robin said. "So we can pull them into our plan pretty easily."

"Well," Alice said, and she shifted in her seat. "El has... something going on." She squeezed her wrapped silverware. "She didn't tell me what, but I found her sobbing outside the hospital."

"When?" Robin asked.

Alice cut her a look. "That day."

That day seemed to have marked history, and while Julia hadn't seen El sobbing, she did know something was a bit off. Aaron had come to the inn with her several times in the past couple of weeks, something Julia had never known him to do.

"El spends a lot of time in her office, when she's normally out with the guests, checking on the kitchen, all of that." Julia didn't want to gossip either. "Something's going on, but I don't quite know what."

A beat of silence went by. "She'll still come," Robin said. "She was instrumental in getting us all together for Laurel's wedding."

Julia hadn't been here for that, but she'd been through plenty of evolutions in her own relationships, namely a key one with Maddy, who sat right across the table from her.

"Could that be the reason again?" she asked. "My wedding is in ten days."

"I don't want to wait that long," Alice said. "I'm dying." Her voice broke, and she clamped her lips shut. Robin reached over and covered Alice's already fisted hand around the silverware. "I can't keep going on like this," she said through her tight throat.

"A party," Julia said, the idea coming out of nowhere. "We need to have a party, like we did for Thanksgiving." She leaned forward, balancing into her elbows on the table. "Because I know Jean isn't going walking with AJ and Laurel anymore either. In fact, Laurel's been getting her exercise in by doing yard work."

"She does like yard work," Robin murmured.

"Don't be ridiculous," Alice said. "No one likes yard work." They glared at one another for a moment, and then everyone at the table burst out laughing. Julia had never heard such a glorious sound, and as she settled back into silence, her party idea continued to grow and grow.

Maddy sighed and looked at Julia. "How do you know Jean and Laurel aren't walking together anymore?"

"Clara's been complaining about walking with Jean." Julia shrugged. "I inferred, and I've been to the nursery to price things for the inn and El, and I saw Laurel there with one of those flatbed carts."

"Kelli's disappeared," Alice said.

"Kristen broke up with Theo," Robin said. "So I bet she's lonely."

"I think she still talks to Jean and Clara," Julia said. "If I had to guess."

"I don't have to guess," Maddy said. "I saw their names down for a reservation for the other night.

Dinner." She glanced around, her blue eyes full of worry. "I think their husbands came, but still. They're getting together. They're talking."

"Can't stop talking," Robin murmured.

Julia dug her phone out of her purse and started tapping and typing and swiping. The conversation mused around her, but she broke into Robin's explanation about Kristen's break-up with, "I've got it." She turned her phone so the others could see it. "I'm going to rent this boat, and we're going to have a party on it."

No one said anything immediately, but then Alice plucked Julia's phone from her fingers. She studied it. Even swiped a little.

When she looked up, a spark resided in her dark eyes. "What will we call it?" she asked.

Once again, no one said anything. Julia looked at Robin. "You're the wedding planner."

"We don't name weddings," she said. "They're just weddings." She looked at Alice. "You surely had a monthly thing like this in the Hamptons."

"Yes," Alice said and nothing more. She looked at Maddy. "You were a congressman's wife."

"Yeah, and everything they did was formal and stuffy, with gold-embossed invitations." She rolled her eyes, then focused on Julia again. So did everyone else.

Her mind spun. "Fine," she said. "What about— something—uh—Springtime Sips and Dips?" The words just flowed out of her. "We can have drinks and food. Come as you are clothes. We set sail at three o'clock, and we'll mix and mingle and then eat dinner at five. Back on dry land by six."

She raised her eyebrows, looking for objections. When Alice handed her phone back, Julia took that as her approval. She looked at the boat on the screen. "All right," she said. She drew a deep breath. "All right."

"Don't rent that," Robin said. "I can get you an in for something far cheaper."

"And we'll all pitch in," Alice said.

Everyone looked at her again, and Maddy nodded. "You'll issue the invite."

Julia wanted to protest, to ask *why her?* But she didn't. "Okay," she said. "But I'm inviting everyone. Spouses and partners and kids too. This shindig is going to include everyone."

By the time she stepped down of her proverbial soap-box, Alice was grinning and Robin dabbed at her eyes. Maddy only smiled, and their waitress arrived, out of breath and red-faced.

"Shawna." Maddy got to her feet. "What's wrong?"

"Nothing, ma'am," she said. "I just." She swallowed and glanced nervously around the table. "I didn't realize your whole party was here, and Justina says you've been sitting here for ten minutes." She gulped down another breath of air, then pasted on a smile. "What can I get you ladies to drink?"

Julia put in her margarita order and then focused on her phone again. After all, she had to word this invitation for the Springtime Sips and Dips just right...

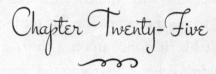

Chapter Twenty-Five

Clara tossed a can of sunscreen into her beach bag and called, "Lena! We have to get going."

The boat that Julia had rented for an event she was calling Springtime Sips and Dips would be leaving the dock in a couple of hours. She was taking her daughter to the ferry terminal, where they'd pick up Scott, her husband.

Then, Clara had to stop by her mother's and get her too. Finally, her last stop would be the lighthouse, where she was collecting Jean and Heidi. Reuben wouldn't be able to come out on the boat today, but he said he'd keep an eye on them as they meandered around the west side of the islands.

She still couldn't believe Julia had done something like

this. Clara had gotten a personal, in-person invite as they worked at the same place. Only five days ago.

"But it's not like we have anything going on," Clara muttered to herself. With the cove coming back to life, Clara wanted to do the same. She felt restless and caged, and she didn't like it. Once upon a time, she'd been so busy, she couldn't get to everything the women here put together.

She missed that vibe, that atmosphere of coming together and sharing her life with others. She couldn't believe she did, but she was mature enough to admit she did.

"Lena," she called again, this time leaving the island which held her packed and ready bag, and moving toward the mouth of the hallway.

"I'm coming." Her daughter came out of the first door on the right, and she wore a bright sundress that shouted flowers in pink and purple and white. Clara couldn't help smiling at it, though she'd never drape her body in something like that.

"You look beautiful," she told her daughter, who glowed like she'd just been crowned a princess. "Get your shoes, okay?"

As Lena went to do that, Clara pulled out her phone. *All set?* she sent to Kelli. She'd not been present for the showdown that had happened in the hospital lobby outside of maternity, but Clara had caught her up on all of it.

She'd spoken to Julia about the true purpose of this Sips and Dips activity, and she knew it was to bring them all back together again. Her heart ached for such a reunion, and her fingers tightened around the plastic case of her phone as she willed Kelli to respond faster.

She hadn't been a mother of a baby in over two decades, and Clara couldn't even begin to imagine what Kelli's days looked like. A certain exhaustion pulled through her, and she jerked her head up at the sound of the garage door slamming shut.

"Lena?" Clara went past the steps to the garage door exit. Sure enough, her daughter was just getting in the front seat of the minivan, and Clara quickly turned to get her beach bag. She usually had to prod Lena out of the house, so there was no need to dawdle otherwise.

Her phone chimed as she left the house again, beach bag slung over her shoulder, and she prayed it'd be Kelli. Once behind the steering wheel, she checked her phone, and Kelli had said, *I'm almost to Diamond. AJ still hasn't committed.*

Clara's heart fell, but she pressed her teeth together. Alice and Robin, Julia and Maddy, Eloise, Jean, her, and her mother had all committed to this afternoon's ocean soiree.

Laurel was up in the air, and AJ hadn't responded to anything that Clara knew of—besides Kelli's texts.

Alice and Robin had said they'd get Laurel there, and Clara had tasked herself with getting Jean and her mother on the boat. Part of her had enjoyed the past couple of weeks of quiet, but it had brought unrest to her soul as well.

She still saw her mother and sister-in-law often. Those relationships seemed a bit strained, but nothing Clara hadn't managed in the past. She worked with El and Julia, and they both wanted Five Island Cove to continue to grow at its current pace. Clara didn't, but she still got along with them just fine.

She figured she could voice her displeasure at the polls. She could show up to City Council meetings and stand behind the mic to express her opinion. She'd never throw tagged buckets through windows, but some people obviously thought that was an option.

A group of real estate agents on the two southern islands had done a march on City Hall a couple of weeks ago. There were plenty of options for voicing an opinion. Heck, AJ had done it by writing an op-ed piece for the Cove Chronicles.

Truth be told, Clara didn't really have an opinion on this growth issue. She'd seen how the community had flocked to City Hall when Aaron had announced the discovery of a "time capsule." People here were invested in their community, and Clara could admire that. She didn't feel the same roots to the cove as others, but she had started cultivating and fertilizing them again.

"Just get them there," she said as she backed out of the garage. She had a mission, and she was going to accomplish it.

* * *

By the time she got to the lighthouse, Clara felt like she'd run two marathons back-to-back. No rest. No food. Her mother had not been ready on time, and Clara had to stand right beside her and coach her on what to do and what to bring.

"All right." She sighed as she pulled into the parking lot. "Mom, do you want to text her?"

Her mother looked over from the passenger seat. Lena had gotten into the back when Clara had finally made it out to the van with her mom. "I'm thinking maybe I'll just sit with Reuben."

"Mom." Clara didn't have the patience for this. "You can't do that."

"I don't want to listen to them fight." She looked out her window toward the lighthouse. "I never thought the cove would be the thing that would break up the girls."

"It's not," Clara said. She didn't know how to say this without being rude, but she'd sort of earned the title of

Being Blunt. "Mom, there's only one person who's causing a problem."

Mom nodded. "AvaJane."

"She just needs to accept the fact that not everyone thinks like her. It doesn't make her wrong, or them wrong. It's not mutually exclusive." As Robin had said, the issues were never black and white.

"Is she coming?"

"Kelli is doing her best to get her there, yes."

"I'll text Jean," Mom whispered, and she turned her attention back to her phone. Clara watched the oh-so-familiar door of the lighthouse, but Jean did not come out. She was bringing Heidi, and she'd need a few minutes to put in the car seat, situate her diaper bag in the back with Lena, and get comfortable.

"We're late," Clara muttered. Jean didn't normally run late, and she should've been standing on the sidewalk, ready and waiting.

"She's coming," Mom said. "She said the last batch of cookies weren't quite done."

"Why is she baking cookies?" Clara griped. "Julia said all of the food would be catered."

"Clara." Mom sounded beyond tired, but Clara wanted to tell her to join the club. Jean didn't need to be baking. "It might not even be for this. The Seafaring Girls are starting up again soon."

"Okay, sure," Clara said, and relief punched through

her when the dark blue door opened and Jean stepped out. She struggled with the bag and the baby, even with Parker exiting the lighthouse behind her, and Clara launched herself out of the car to go help.

"Sorry," Jean said when Clara still had several paces to go. "I'm sorry." She seemed near tears, and Clara certainly didn't want that. When she'd lived in Vermont and came to the cove—completely against her will—she hadn't treated Jean and Reuben very well. They'd been nothing but kind and accepting to her, and Clara let all of her irritation seep away.

"You're fine," she said. "I don't think we'll be the last ones there." Clara glanced over to Parker, who gave her a small smile. "Hey, bud." She focused on Jean again. "They're not going to set sail without us."

A gust of wind kicked up and over the cliffs, and as Jean relinquished the hold on her baby carrier, she shivered. "I can't believe we're going out on the water at all."

"It won't be bad," Clara said. "We're not in a clipper or anything. We'll barely be moving." She gave her sister-in-law a smile and faced the minivan. "I'll put Heidi in the way-back. Parker, you can ride back there with her?"

"Yep," he said.

Clara thought it a pretty genius move for Kelli to give her son to Jean. Now, no matter what, Kelli had to come to collect her son. Surely AJ wouldn't make her do that alone.

Twenty minutes later, Clara pulled up to the appointed dock on the west side of Diamond Island, her nerves fraying more and more by the second. She recognized Alice's car, and she sure hoped there'd be others here as well.

"That's it right there," she said, eyeing the yacht. "It's a legit yacht."

"We are definitely helping her pay for this," Mom said with great conviction in her voice. Clara had offered, and Julia hadn't said no.

She got out of the van and collected her beach bag as she said, "Lena, help Aunt Jean with her bag."

Thankfully, her daughter didn't argue, and the five of them—six with the baby—made their way toward dock three. Before they arrived, Robin, Alice, and Laurel—praise the stars; Laurel was on-board—waved to them from the boat.

Yacht. This was way more than a boat, and it certainly wasn't like the fishing boats that went out every morning from the many docks around the cove. Clara smiled and waved back, glad she'd brought sunscreen and her sunglasses. She paused on the cusp of the gangway and let her mother go first, followed by Parker.

Jean followed him, and Lena hesitated for a moment. She met Clara's eye, and she nodded at her daughter. She didn't super-love boats, but she took the first step, and then Clara did the same.

"Wo-ow," Jean said, really drawing out the word as she stepped on-board. "This is incredible."

The breeze up on deck somehow smelled sweeter and didn't seem as cold, and Clara smiled around at everything too. Plenty of places to sit, some in the shade of the over-hanging deck and some under umbrellas. Some seats sat in full sun, and Clara could imagine herself there, a fruity drink in her hand, her face tipped back into the golden sunshine.

It was a picture of perfection.

She hugged Alice, then Robin, then Laurel, holding onto the last woman for several long moments. "It's so good to see you, Laurel," she whispered, and Laurel nodded as they separated.

"You too, Clara." She looked past her to Jean, and Clara sensed...something there.

"Jean," she called, ever the bull in a china shop.

"Clara," Laurel muttered, but Jean turned toward them. Her smile wavered, but only for a moment. Then she rushed at Laurel, colliding hard enough with her to push her back against the railing.

"Oh." Clara reached out and steadied Laurel, though she was strong enough to withstand Jean. They started whispering, and Clara moved away from them and to her mother's side. She watched Laurel and Jean too, and Clara took the opportunity to throw her arm around her mom's shoulders.

"I love you, Mom," she said. "Even if we don't agree on everything." This issue of small island growth wasn't actually an issue for Clara at all, but her mother smiled at her.

"I love you, too, dear."

Alice joined them and handed Clara a beautiful glass of pink champagne. "Oh, wow." She grinned at Alice and took the drink.

"Now." She faced the gangway entrance. "Now we just have to see if Kelli and AJ make it."

"Everyone else is here?" Clara asked.

"Maddy and Julia are inside setting up the food," Robin said as she joined them. "Wait until you see the dining cabin. It's *incredible*."

"Boats should never have chandeliers," Alice commented in a dry voice, and Clara turned to look over her shoulder. A chandelier? On a boat?

"I can't wait to see it," she said.

"El isn't here either," Robin said, and she took what looked like a casual sip of her champagne.

"She said she would be." Julia grinned at Clara. "You accomplished your mission." They embraced, and Clara sure did like these ladies she'd become part of.

"It was touch and go," she admitted.

"Alice," Laurel called. "Julia. Robin. They're here." She faced them briefly, and then spun back to the parking lot. Clara moved with the tide of women, and after she'd found a spot at the railing, she found El and Aaron unloading from his police cruiser, their girls getting out of the back seat.

Love filled her for all of them, because they worked incredibly hard for the people of Five Island Cove, and they'd both been so accepting of her and Scott when they'd come to the cove after a financial disaster that had almost landed her husband in jail.

A handful of spaces down, Kelli straightened and shaded her eyes as she looked toward the boat. Clara couldn't read her expression from this far away, and her heartbeat shrank to a mere murmur.

Then AJ came around the back of the car, a bundle of a baby in her arms. Clara took in a sharp, salty breath and reached for the woman closest to her. "She came," she breathed to Robin, who squeezed her fingers hard.

"All right," Julia said in a decidedly authoritative voice. "This isn't a big deal, okay? She's our friend, and of course she was always going to come."

Clara knew that wasn't true, but she also saw AJ pass the baby to Kelli and then reach for her husband's hand. He carried their toddler, and as Shad joined them, they made quite the sight as they advanced toward the yacht.

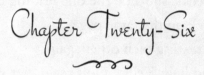

Chapter Twenty-Six

Kelli didn't like the entourage of eyes on her as she walked toward one of the nicest boats she'd ever seen. She'd never super-appreciated the spotlight, though in this moment, she did feel like she'd worked a miracle.

Without Matt, she wouldn't have been able to get AJ to come. Kelli wasn't even sure why AJ was so resistant to this reconciliation. She'd fully admitted to Kelli that the fight at the hospital the day after Daphne had been born was her fault.

But only to Kelli. She hadn't told anyone else that, and AJ didn't like groveling. Who did? But apologies had to be made, because none of them were running from the cove this time. They lived here, together, and they had to figure out how to get along.

I'm sure it's not the only thing you've disagreed on over

the years. Kelli thought of her mother's words, and she'd been right. Kelli had been through a lot with these women, and if she hadn't been dealing with a newborn for the past few weeks, she'd be the one leading this charge to get them all back on the same page.

Or at least texting each other again.

"Go on and help Kelli," Eloise said, her voice carrying over the space between them. Grace skipped toward her, and she received the girl with a smile. Kelli hadn't meant to retreat from her friends.

She'd had a baby at age forty-eight. Her pregnancy had drained her mentally, emotionally, and physically. She hadn't been sleeping through the night, because Daphne wasn't doing that yet. She hadn't been back to the yoga studio, and most days, she could barely consider herself dressed.

Shad had taken the past three and a half weeks off, but he'd have to go back to work come Monday. The day after Maddy's wedding.

Kelli had raised a baby before, and she grinned up at her son, who waved to her from the deck of the yacht. She waved back, so pleased with what her family had become. A strong, handsome man at her side. Someone who loved and adored her, Parker, and their new baby girl.

Her son, who yes, sometimes gave her attitude, but who loved her no matter what. She loved spoiling him too, and she loved that he had a myriad of people around him to show him what it looked like to be a good friend, forgive one another, and work hard.

And her new daughter, who depended on her for everything.

Her eyes jumped to Jean, who stood next to Parker, and she'd definitely become part of Kelli's family too. Alice, Robin, Eloise, and AJ had always been her rock solid foundation, and they'd become so close in the past few years since they'd all returned to the cove.

She passed her purse to Grace to carry, as Shad already shouldered the diaper bag. Anxiety at being trapped on a boat—no matter how nice—for the next few hours coated the back of her throat. She'd brought extra clothes, loads of diapers, and plenty of formula. Daphne would be fine, even if she soiled her clothes.

They arrived at the gangway first, and of course, everyone paused and waited for her to go ahead of them. Kelli wanted AJ to start up the ramp first, but she took the initial steps, saying, "Come on, Ava. Let's get this over with."

Kristen met her at the top of the gangway, already reaching for Daphne. Kelli had been sharing her with anyone who came to visit her and Shad at the townhome on Pearl Island, but not very many had done that. Her mother, and his, and Kelli's sister had come for a weekend. Alice, Robin, Julia, and Jean had come.

When she'd heard about the argument just down the

hall from her hospital bed, Kelli had been beyond irritated. She'd heard multiple versions of the same story, but none of them had come from AJ until Kelli had called her and confronted her.

AJ had brought Asher out to Pearl after that, and they'd had their own tearful reunion. *She's just proud*, Kelli thought as she passed her baby off to Kristen. Without the infant in her arms, Kelli didn't quite know what to do with her hands. So she turned back to the gangway and took her purse from Grace and her bag from Shad.

"I'm going to find a place for these," she said, and then she headed for the couches and chairs across the deck and toward the interior of the yacht.

"Where are you going?" Robin demanded, and Kelli thought she could take her bite down a couple of notches.

She gave her a glare and said, "I'm just going to put these down." Robin fell into step beside her, the tension radiating from her brushing Kelli's skin. "You need to calm down," she muttered.

"I know." Robin didn't bother to keep her voice low. "I'm so nervous."

"So is she," Kelli said as she found a puddle of shade for her bags. "Don't forget that, Robin." Their eyes met, and Kelli pulled her into a fierce hug. "She's so worried too."

She turned back to the open front of the yacht, and AJ and Matt were just stepping on. Asher squirmed in his daddy's arms, and Matt set him on his feet with the warning to, "Stay where I can see you, buddy." He immediately ran off toward Jean and Parker, which didn't surprise Kelli that much.

AJ claimed not to be talking to anyone but her, and the way everyone watched her testified of that. She wore a look on her perfectly painted face that screamed "back off," and Kelli couldn't see her eyes behind the large pair of designer sunglasses.

She wore an all-white dress with white sandals, and she could be a beauty queen though she was just as close to fifty as Kelli. Thankfully, the people already on-board the yacht had somewhere else to look as Eloise and Aaron arrived.

"All right," Duke said loudly. "Is everyone here?" He came out from the shadows of the interior and scanned everyone standing near the railing and those who'd just come aboard as they spread out across the deck.

"We have drinks," Alice called.

"Pink champagne," Arthur said, but Kelli wouldn't be drinking. At least not alcohol. "We've also got fruit juices for the kids," he added. "And this gorgeous sparking blush." He held up a bottle that shone with glorious light pink liquid. "It's apple with a hint of raspberry." Arthur raised his eyebrows at Kelli, and she gave him a nod and a smile. She could hold a champagne flute with that pretty apple cider in it while her friends sipped something harder.

"Sips and dips," Julia called. "Come on, we're doing drink orders first."

Everyone started to move away from the gangway and railing and into the seating areas. Kelli didn't want to stand out in the sun though she hadn't worn anything sleeveless or strappy. She wasn't exactly someone who spent a ton of time outside.

In the shade, she found the bar, and she helped Parker get some Sprite with his orange juice. Grace and Billie wanted Diet Coke, and Kelli helped them with their sodas as well. El stood very near to Aaron, and neither of them had made it much further than the first couch, still out in the sunshine.

"We're putting out," Julia called. "Might be a slight bump."

They'd all been on plenty of boats, and Kelli barely felt the movement as they got untied from the dock and the yacht eased out into the restless water. "This is an incredible yacht," she said to Alice.

"One of Duke's friends owns it," she said. "We got it for really cheap."

"Julia is going to send out bills, right?" Kelli shot a glance over to the woman, who poured champagne for Matt and handed him the glass before starting on one for

AJ. The fact that they'd come so deep into the yacht told Kelli something, and she tried to catch AJ's eye.

Her very best friend in the whole world would not look at her, and that only made Kelli step over to her. "AJ," she said.

She finished her sip of champagne. "This is great, right?" She'd always liked the expensive things in life. Kelli couldn't fault her for that, but she didn't want to talk about the beauty of the yacht.

A couple of people laughed, and everywhere around them, people chattered. Kelli didn't want to ruin the party. Quite the opposite. She wanted to enjoy it, and she couldn't do that—no one truly could—until everything had been said that needed to be said.

"New Truth," she shouted into the fray of people lingering in the seating area, indoor and out. "I'm calling a New Truth. Let's circle up."

"Right now?" Kristen asked, looking up from baby Daphne.

"Right now," Kelli confirmed. She searched for an ally and found Alice setting down her glass. Kelli took a long breath as Shad came to her side. "This is how the New Truth works."

"I don't want to do a New Truth," Robin said, shooting a look at Duke.

"Too bad," Kelli said. "Everyone was invited here, and

this is important. It involves everyone." She looked at her husband. "Right, baby?"

He nodded, though he wore plenty of worry in his eyes too.

Alice joined Kelli. "How about the men can pass if they want to? Would that keep the integrity of the New Truth?"

"All the women have to say something," Kelli said.

Robin folded her arms, but she didn't argue again. Kelli wasn't sure why she didn't want to do the New Truth. Had she been expecting to send Duke away to some corner while they all talked?

"It's a lot of people for New Truth," Alice said. "But I think it's probably the best thing we've got. Let's just try to keep it brief, ladies? Trust me, you're going to want to get to the dessert dips. There's this monster cookie dough dip that I can't stop eating." She beamed around at everyone, nodded like her word was as good as gold, and looked at Kelli.

Kelli never started anything. She sat back and listened. She inserted her voice when it came her turn, but she never went on very long. Being brief wouldn't be hard.

"New truth," she said. "Being a mom to a newborn is really hard." Her bottom lip quivered with unexpected emotion, but Kelli pushed through. "It's been astronomically harder without all of you there beside me." She met AJ's eyes, and she'd already started to tear up. "I need you.

All of you. I need us to be together—strong. So my New Truth is that I will do whatever I need to do in order to fix us."

"You can't fix us," AJ said, stepping out of the shade of an umbrella. "I have to do that." She slid her arm around Kelli and squeezed her. "I didn't mean to be quite so polarizing." She looked around at Alice, Robin, Julia, and Maddy, who stood closest to the bar.

Duke, Arthur, Ben, and Liam—their male counterparts manned the other end of the bar, and they too stood and watched AJ. Matt came to her side, as did Kristen. AJ had always prided herself on being smart and strong, but even she needed her family in times like these.

"My New Truth is that I was a huge jerk at the hospital. I let my temper dictate what I said, and I've regretted it every day since." She reached up and swiped at her eyes. "I still have my opinions about the growth here in the cove, but Matt's reminded me that there are better avenues for expressing them."

"And that we can still be friends with you guys, even if you don't agree with us," Matt said.

"More than that," AJ said, her voice breaking. "I can love you, even if I want the cove to keep expanding and you don't." She leaned into Kristen, then turned and hugged her. She wasn't the only one sniffling, but Kelli could only feel joy and the miracle of forgiveness moving through her.

"New Truth," Robin said. "Getting us all in the same place is the hardest thing we do." She smiled at Alice. "Isn't it?"

"It is," Alice said. "We sure seem to know how to do it in style, though." She grinned at Julia, and all eyes looked at her.

"New Truth," Jean said. "Reuben and I aren't going to adopt again. We love Heidi to death, but I've got my Seafaring Girls, and—" She looked around at everyone, her big brown eyes like that of a deer who's run out in front of a fast-moving truck. "It just feels like my family is already big enough." She indicated all of them, and Kelli reached up and pressed her hand to her heart.

She loved Jean so much, because Jean loved her first. She loved Parker unequivocally, and that meant so much to Kelli.

"New Truth," Clara said. "I have missed the group texting more than I thought I would." A slow smile crawled across her face. "I never thought I'd say that, but well, there you go." Several people twittered with light laughter, and it was enough of a mood breaker for Kelli to actually feel the rifts between them start to close.

"New Truth," Laurel said as she cleared her throat. She leaned into her cop husband and Kelli felt a flash of gratitude for the man who'd been there for Laurel in times when she'd needed him so desperately. "I am toying with the idea of starting a landscaping company." She beamed up at Paul, who swept a kiss along her forehead.

"That's incredible, Laurel," Jean said.

"It's seasonal," she said. "So I won't have to work all the time. Paul and I are still working through a lot of the logistics." She looked across the seating area, and Kelli started searching for someone who hadn't spoken yet.

Eloise stood next to Aaron, but she made no move to say anything. Kristen hadn't spoken, and she still stood beside AJ. Alice hadn't said anything either, and neither Julia nor Maddy had divulged a new truth.

"I'll go," Julia said. "Wait. I have to say New Truth?" She glanced at Alice, who nodded. Julia pushed her hair over her shoulder. "New Truth." She looked over to Liam, her smile warming to the temperature of the sun that shone down on them. "Things are going really well with Liam Coldwater. I think I'm falling in love with him, which is ultra confusing and scary, and while he thinks we're going too slow, it's because I just..." She paused, and Kelli's eyes shot over to Liam.

He wore a devilish smile, but he said nothing.

"You just need to be sure," Maddy said as she linked her arm through Julia's. "You just take your time to be sure, and that's okay."

Julia nodded, and Kelli's heart warmed at these two new women in their group. She hadn't had a lot of experiences with Julia and Maddy, but enough to know she wanted all the happiness in the world for both of them.

"New Truth," a man said, and Kelli's gaze flew to Liam Coldwater's. He didn't look away from Julia at all. "I'm falling in love with Julia Harper, and it's fast and confusing and I'm trying to do what's right for me, her, and my son."

"New Truth," Alice said at the same time as Maddy. They looked at each other and giggles broke out. "You go first." Alice actually took a step back.

Maddy walked over to Ben and said, "New Truth. I'm so excited to marry Ben in only five more days."

He pulled her in for a kiss, and Kelli whooped and cheered along with everyone else as Maddy kissed her fiancé.

"All right, all right," Alice called as the kissing died down. "New Truth, I am so nervous for you guys to see me in *Kiss Me, Kate*."

"Come on," Robin said with a scoff. "You're going to steal the show, and you know it."

"And don't think we all don't know that you didn't even do a New Truth," Alice shot back at her.

Robin's mouth fished and her eyes widened, but she didn't get anything out before several people started laughing—including her husband. Kelli joined in, because while she loved Robin, she could rarely be found speechless.

She scanned the group, and said, "Kristen? El?"

Eloise wore pure determination on her face as she took a little step forward. But it was Aaron who said, "New Truth. El and I were expecting a baby this fall, but—" He looked at her as he stepped to her side. "We lost it a few weeks ago."

Kelli could only stare at the pair of them, standing there side-by-side. No one said anything, and even the wind and waves went dormant.

A few weeks ago… Kelli had had Daphne a few weeks ago, and everything clicked together in her head. It had taken El a few days to come visit Kelli and Daphne in the hospital, and looking back, she *had* seemed uncomfortable.

Kelli had thought it was because of the fight, which she'd heard about at that point. El had been building and building the Cliffside Inn for years now. She looked tired right now, but she leaned into Aaron, and they seemed absolutely unified. That scene touched her heart, and Kelli closed her eyes and committed their sweet devotion to each other.

"New Truth," Kristen said. "I was worried this would be the thing that finally broke us apart. We're large enough now to splinter into smaller groups, and well, I'm ashamed to admit I thought this would be the thing that did it." She wiped her eyes and ducked her head.

"Kristen," Robin murmured, but she didn't add anything else.

Kelli saw her friends as teenagers as they all gathered at the lighthouse with a much younger Kristen for their Seafaring Girls lessons. She saw them sitting together at a funeral, and lining the aisle as El walked down it to marry Aaron.

She saw AJ going into labor on the beach, and she saw herself opening her yoga studio in her newly renovated childhood home. She saw Alice and Robin standing in a pavilion after a tsunami, all of them wondering how they were going to pay for the things that had been damaged and needed to be restored.

She saw herself out in a storm, on a boat, saving teenagers. Saving Jean.

Kelli blinked, and she only saw Eloise. She moved away from Shad and the others she stood with and hurried toward her. "I'm so sorry," she whispered as she wrapped her arms around Eloise.

El hugged her back, and the next thing Kelli knew, she found herself in the middle of a group huddle hug, with Kristen's arms around her, and Jean's, and Laurel's. The group moved as Alice, Robin, and AJ piled around them.

Then Maddy, then Julia, then Clara. Kelli pressed her eyes closed as condolences got whispered through the group, and then someone said, "I love you guys," and Kelli echoed that back to them all too.

Life changed, rapidly sometimes. Nine months for her to grow a human in her body and then become a mother later in life. A single conversation to make them retreat to themselves, to silence their communication with each other.

But love took a lot longer to change, to warp, and to experience. It moved like a mighty glacier, carving its path with an indomitable will and persistent strength. Even as seasons ebbed and flowed around it, love retained its essence, immutable and enduring, forever leaving a deep imprint on the landscape of human hearts.

And Kelli loved these women, their very friendships imprinting on her heart and soul, as they stood together on the deck of that yacht.

"Okay," Alice finally said. "You guys *have* to come see this dips bar. It's *incredible*."

Chapter Twenty-Seven

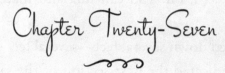

Kristen stood with Clara and Jean, staring at the spread of food in front of her. "This is incredible," she said.

"It's from Dip'n Dive," Julia said as she joined them. "It's this new place perched right on the north beach of Diamond." She beamed at the table covered with regular, ridged potato chips, corn chips—white and blue—pretzel sticks and twists, pita chips, baguette chips, ginger snaps, graham crackers, and vanilla wafers.

And more. The platters and trays and bowls of dips crowded in the front half of the table, with their vessels behind them.

"Okay, everyone," Julia called. "Gather round, so I can explain this." She carried such a light, and Kristen really wanted to get to know her better. "Down on this end, we have the typical appetizer dips. Chips and pineapple-mango salsa, guacamole, loaded ranch dip for veggies and chips, corn and bacon dip. There's veggies, chips, and crackers. They've paired up their dips with the things you use behind them, but you can mix and match whatever you want."

She moved down several feet—several feet of appetizer dips—and indicated the next section of the table. "These are the main dish dips. There's a Margherita pizza dip. It's incredible with the pitas or naan." Julia's grin stretched across her whole face. "There's warm crab dip, buffalo chicken dip—you use veggies on this or you can use the Ritz crackers. I couldn't stop myself from eating this when Maddy and I sampled the dips the other day."

Julia trilled out a light laugh, and Maddy stepped to her side. "My favorite is the Reuben dip," she said. "It's got the corned beef, the cheese, and the sauerkraut. It's to die for with the rye bread, but the pumpernickel chips or the pretzels are good with it too." She indicated another bowl. "There's queso and chorizo, and the classic artichoke dip, but this has chicken, so it's a bit more substantial."

Julia went by her and indicated the last little bit of the table. "This is the dessert dip section. You can eat in any order, but we got the four-dip platter, and it features a peanut butter cup cheesecake dip—excellent with vanilla wafers—monster cookie dough, which I liked the best with pretzels. Then we've got your classic fruit dip for those of you who think fruit is dessert." She grinned at everyone, and Kristen's smile broke onto her face.

"And lastly," Maddy said. "The pumpkin pie dip. It's mind-blowing with ginger snaps, but if you want to just dip a toe in, try it with the graham crackers first."

They both beamed out at everyone, and then Alice said, "Well, I'm not waiting. This looks absolutely incredible."

"Dips," Clara said. "A whole restaurant that only does dips." She wore a delighted look on her face. "Who thinks of this stuff?"

"I want the pizza one," Kelli said. "Baby? You want me to get you something?"

"No," Shad said as he cradled their little girl in his arms. "You get what you want, and I'll get something when you're finished."

"I can hold her," Kristen offered.

Shad shook his head, a kind smile on his face and radiating in his eyes. "Thanks, but I know I'll be in trouble if I keep you from eating with your girls."

"Come on," Robin said, hooking her arm through Kristen's. "You're not hiding out behind a baby today. Come get some food."

"The crab dip is *fantastic*," Alice said in a loud voice, her words slightly marred by the food in her mouth.

"I went for dessert first," AJ said. "Definitely get the ginger snaps with this pumpkin pie dip." Chatter continued as most of them stood at the table and spooned dips onto their plates or simply feasted on the dips to taste them all.

Kristen wanted to do that, and she dunked a blue corn chip into the guacamole, which happened to be one of her favorite foods. Lemon and garlic and creamy avocado exploded in her mouth, and she moaned.

"I knew you'd like that," Alice said as she leaned into Kristen slightly. "This is so amazing, right?"

Kristen often felt a little removed from this group. She wasn't the same age as any of the women here, as she came from another generation. But she loved her girls with everything inside her, and tears pressed behind her eyes as she leaned into Alice too.

"Thank you for including me," she whispered.

"We wouldn't be here without you," Alice said, and Kristen nodded her acceptance. As she tried the corn and bacon dip, she settled into herself, and into her place here in the group. She absolutely did belong here, just as every songbird finds its tune, so too had she found her harmony among this diverse, beautiful medley of women. She was a note in their shared symphony, her presence contributing to the melody that was uniquely and collectively theirs.

A couple of days later, Kristen stood up on her tiptoes and waved to the couple glancing around. "Kyle," she called. "Bea."

She heard her, and she indicated to her husband where Kristen stood. She'd met the couple briefly when they'd gotten married last summer, but they all wore smiles as they approached with their luggage and their baby.

"Kristen," Kyle said. "Thank you for coming to get us."

"Of course." She took the little boy from Kyle. "Look how big you've gotten." She grinned at the baby, who had to be close to a year old now. "Your momma wanted to be here, but she's working her last shift for a while, and it just didn't work out."

Kristen had been honored that Maddy had called her to help with her son and daughter-in-law today. RideShare had recently put limits on the number of cars that would be available at the airport and ferry stations, because they were short-staffed. That didn't bode well as the summer months—the largest tourist months—approached, but Kristen didn't know what to do about it.

The cove could only support so many cars and so many people. RideShare was working with city officials to make sure they expanded responsibly, and that meant long lines in key places like the airport.

So Kristen had come to help Kyle and Bea get from

the airport on the south east side of Diamond to the ferry terminal on the north end of the island.

"Are you hungry?" she asked.

"Starved," Bea said at the same time Kyle said, "We're okay." They looked at each other, and Bea grinned. "I want one of those lobster rolls from Mort's." She turned her sunny personality on Kristen. "Can we stop and get one?"

"We absolutely can," she said with her own smile. "I never say no to lobster rolls." She turned toward the exit, and Kyle and Bea followed her. "Are you guys excited for the wedding?"

"Yeah," Bea said enthusiastically, but Kristen noted that Maddy's son said nothing. "Maddy is so amazing. She deserves to be so happy."

"I agree," Kristen said as they went past the travelers waiting for their RideShare vehicle. Usually, she saw a line of cars just waiting, but today, there were only people with an officer there to maintain the front of the line.

As Kyle bent to put Knox, his son, in the car seat that Kristen had borrowed from Jean, her phone rang. "Oh, it's my son." She took a couple of steps away from the car and swiped on the call. "Hey, Reuben."

"Mom, you'll never believe what I'm holding in my hand."

Kristen's pulse bounded through her veins. "What?" whooshed out of her mouth.

Reuben started to laugh, and from someone on his end of the line, Jean yelled, "It's the title to the lighthouse!" She laughed too, and Kristen almost sank to her knees.

She reached out and placed her hand on the roof of the car she stood by, quickly pulling it back when the heat registered. "Oh, thank goodness." Relief ran through her so swiftly, her fingers trembled and trembled.

"It's got my name on it," Reuben said.

"Alice," Kristen whispered, pure gratitude overwhelming her now. She drew in a long breath. "We should celebrate. I just picked up Maddy's kids, and we're headed to Mort's."

"We'll join you," Reuben said. "I could really use that cole slaw from Mort's." He laughed again, and it sounded so good in Kristen's ears. Her son was so good and so hardworking, and he deserved to own the lighthouse.

She turned back to her car, her happiness filling her over and over again. "We'll see you there." She ended the call and lowered her phone. "Is it okay if my son and daughter-in-law meet us? We just got good news."

"Of course." Bea grinned and wrapped her arms around Kyle's waist. "Maybe we can meet your mom on the ferry if we stay here long enough."

Kyle seemed to resign himself to whatever his wife wanted. "Sure," he said. "I'm fine with whatever."

Kristen smiled, wondering who would be able to come

to Mort's on zero notice. She got behind the wheel and started the car so the air conditioning would start to blow. She tapped to open her group text, but Jean had already sent the news. In all caps.

She just laughed and then added, *We're celebrating at Mort's with Maddy's kids. Anyone and everyone is welcome to come.*

Of course, not everyone would be able to come. Kelli and Eloise, Jean and Clara, all lived or worked off-Diamond. Maddy hadn't been able to pick up her son, because she had to work. Alice and Robin had jobs they couldn't always just walk away from.

Congratulations started to come in, and AJ said she'd stop by Mort's, because she was already out and about and could.

Kristen told Kyle and Bea the good news as she pulled out of the parking spot, and pure joy filled her the same way the rays of sunlight spanned the entire breadth and width of the sky.

The lighthouse was hers, and that history had been such a huge part of her life. The lighthouse had defined her for so long, and now she didn't have to abandon it and try to find something else to establish her history.

Now, it was time to celebrate with good friends and good food.

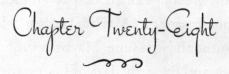

Chapter Twenty-Eight

Maddy stood at the window in her master bedroom in her house on Rocky Ridge, the morning of her wedding dawning. The sky moved from dark gray to light, then to sky blue which would deepen throughout the day.

She'd once thought she would not be able to have her outdoor beach wedding. She'd booked the Rock House on Diamond Island, and she had to decide in the next thirty minutes where to say her vows.

Still, she didn't move from the windows, and instead, lifted her coffee mug to her lips. After taking a sip of her lukewarm tea, she sighed and turned to her nightstand. She and Ben had texted a lot last night, as he had returned to his barracks at the Coast Guard station.

He'd moved into her house already, so everything would be set and ready once they returned from their honeymoon. But she didn't want to wake up next to him this morning—but tomorrow.

The first full day of her second marriage. She wasn't sure why, but Maddy wanted to pay attention to every detail of this marriage. Maybe because she'd gotten married so young the first time. Maybe because her memories of the day, and the early days of her marriage with her first husband, were fuzzy and hazy.

She didn't want to forget anything about her relationship with Ben, though she realistically knew everything faded.

Inside or out? she sent to Ben. *What are your thoughts?*

Despite the early hour, Ben started typing immediately. The man didn't sleep much, or maybe he was nervous and couldn't sleep.

I don't care, honey.

But I need you to vote, she said. He'd left so much of the wedding up to her, which Maddy appreciated. But at this moment, her decision fatigue overwhelmed her, and she just wanted someone to tell her where to have the wedding.

No matter what, she'd lose a deposit.

You love the beach, he said. *But honey, just because it's warm doesn't mean it won't be windy. Think of your dress and your hair. I think you'll be happier at Rock House, and I just want you to be happy.*

Maddy nodded as she read his text, and instead of

answering him, she quickly fired off a text to Robin. She felt like she was being a pain in the neck for her friend and wedding planner, but Robin came back with, *Perfect, Maddy. I'll get it done, and I'll see you there at two.*

"Two." Maddy took a deep breath and looked up from her phone. She went to shower, and when she stepped out, the scent of frying bacon met her nose. Chelsea.

She got dressed in her wedding day sweats—and outfit she'd gone shopping with Julia to buy—and she went into the kitchen. Her daughter had made herself right at home, and she stood at the stove, moving something around in a pan.

"Smells good," Maddy said.

"Bacon and eggs wedding day breakfast," Chelsea chirped. She'd shown up yesterday afternoon, all smiles, and Maddy hadn't asked her any questions about Robert, because she didn't want Chelsea to shut down.

Maddy hummed and sat at the kitchen counter. She let her daughter serve her, and when Chelsea sat down with her own plate of food, Maddy casually took a bite of scrambled egg and looked at her daughter. "How was meeting Rob's parents?"

A smile bloomed instantly on Chelsea's face, and oh, Maddy knew that look. "It actually went really great, Mom."

"Mm." Maddy picked up a piece of perfectly crisp

bacon. Chelsea liked it well-done, and that was fine with Maddy. Ben would think it overdone, but he got to like his bacon how he liked it.

"Don't just hum," Chelsea said, her smile slipping and her frustration leaking into her voice. "Tell me what to do."

"You haven't told me anything about him," Maddy said.

"That is not true." Chelsea rolled her eyes. "We've been dating for months now. Maybe eight or nine? His parents are really nice. Still married." She started rattling off facts about them, about Rob's life in Boston, where he'd grown up in Wellesley.

"This is all great," Maddy finally said, their breakfast long gone now. "But Chels, how do you feel about him? Do you really know him? Does he know you?"

"We're working on it," Chelsea said.

"That doesn't actually answer my questions." Maddy stood and picked up her plate, then her daughter's. "I'm not going to tell you what to do if you can't even tell me how you feel about him." She moved over to the sink and started rinsing their dishes. She loaded them in the dishwasher, waiting for Chelsea to speak.

Once she'd completed the chore, she looked pointedly at her daughter. Chelsea ran both hands down her face. "I don't know, Mom."

"I don't know is not good."

"It's good," she said slowly. "I like him far more than anyone else I've been out with in college. I'm almost done, and then..." She let the words hang there. "I know I'll still be able to meet men once I'm not in college, but it kind of feels like I won't."

"Rob's not in college."

"Yeah." Chelsea didn't expand on that, and Maddy wished she could take all of her worries and iron them flat. "He's great." She stared at something only she could see. "I like him a whole lot."

"You've said that twice now," Maddy teased.

Her daughter blinked and focused on Maddy, who raised her eyebrows. "I'm not going to move in with him."

"I didn't know that was on the table."

"He offered last night," she said. "But I know that brownstone is going to come through."

"Eloise's?"

She shook her head. "No, she said it's rented already. Had she known I needed somewhere, but...she didn't."

"You found somewhere else?"

"Yeah, I think so." Chelsea sounded confident enough, but Maddy moved over to stand in front of her.

"Listen," she said. "I don't want this to be one of those things where you try to pretend everything is going to be fine when it's not."

"Mom, I don't do that."

"Yes, you do." Maddy cradled her face in one palm. "I

know you, Chels, and you do." Her daughter didn't argue with her again. "If you don't have somewhere to stay, you tell me. Right away. Up front. I don't want you living in a dangerous situation. We have options."

"Like what?"

"A long-term hotel," she said. "A vacation rental. There are places that aren't your friend's couch or your car. Promise me right now you will not get yourself into a bad situation. You just have to say something."

Tears filled Chelsea's eyes, and she nodded. "Okay," she whispered.

"Okay," Maddy said fiercely. "Now, come on. Come help me gather up all of my stuff. Let's practice my makeup one last time. You can tell me about Rob and why you think you're falling in love with him."

"I didn't say that."

"You didn't need to." Maddy smiled softly at her daughter and tucked her hair behind her ear. "He must be something special to have caught you for so long."

"Yeah." Chelsea sighed. "I guess I do really like him enough to admit that maybe I'm falling in love with him. Maybe."

Maddy giggled with her daughter as they returned to the master suite. "Sweetheart, falling in love isn't weakness. It's wonderful and exhilarating, and you love adventure."

"Falling can hurt," she said simply. She got out

Maddy's makeup bag, and Maddy sat in front of the vanity, and then moved back so Chelsea would have room too.

"It can," she admitted. "But you don't really know until you take that leap."

Chelsea met her eye, nodded bravely, and then said, "I think we should go easy on the dark makeup today. Everything is pink, blue, and apricot, and you should be too."

"Make me beautiful," Maddy said as she closed her eyes. The conversation turned easy after that. Bea came in with Knox, and they chitchatted about Kyle's job in the city, and when they could come back to the cove.

Before Maddy knew it, it was time to leave for the ferry station, and it took all of them to get her clothes, makeup, and hair supplies to Rock House. When she entered the bridal room, Robin turned from where she spoke with another woman.

"And there's our bride," she gushed as she strode toward her. She wore a beautiful dress in the most cornflower of blues, which really accented her eyes. Her makeup sat flawlessly on her face, and her step was sure and strong.

She moved right into Maddy and hugged her. "You've got everything?"

"We've got it all," Maddy confirmed. "Ben texted when he got on the ferry, and we timed it so he was taking the one right after me. He should be here in twenty minutes."

"Perfect." Robin's smiled dazzled Maddy, and she thanked all the stars in heaven that she'd found this woman. Not only for Bea and Kyle's wedding, which had been moved last-minute last year, but for herself.

Robin exhaled and turned. "Okay, we have an hour. You ladies help your mother into her dress, and I'm going to go check on a few things." She left the room, and Maddy faced Bea and Chelsea. They both looked like they came from her, as Bea had blonde hair and blue eyes too.

"Your makeup just needs a few touchups," Chelsea said.

"Who's doing your hair?" Bea asked.

"Julia." Maddy put down her hair kit just as the door opened again. This time, Julia, in all her dark-haired glory, walked in. "There she is." She took a few steps until she reached her, and she gripped her tightly in a hug.

"You're ready for this," Julia whispered in her ear. "It's going to be so amazing."

Maddy had lost Julia when she'd been married the first time. She hadn't had a truly close, trusted friend in the bridal room, not like she did now. She clung to her, the way she wanted to cling to the memories of the two of them and how far they'd come in the past couple of years.

"Mom, don't cry," Chelsea said.

Maddy laughed, or she might burst into tears. She

released Julia and they separated. "It takes ten minutes for me to get zipped and laced into my dress," she said. "That gives you forty-five minutes for my hair. Chelsea can do the touch-ups on my makeup at the same time."

Julia nodded, her battle face slipping into position. "Let's get this done." She plugged in the curling iron and started setting out the jars and bottles of hair products that would transform Maddy's normally semi-wavy, long hair into a curly up-do. Classic and elegant and totally befitting a woman her age.

"Are Ben's parents in town?"

"Yes," Maddy said. "He entertained them all day yesterday, and we only saw him for a few minutes in the evening."

She sat and she let Chelsea, Bea, and Julia talk and work around her. She loved going to the salon and spa, and she loved being taken care of. Every women should have that on their wedding day, and with only about fifteen minutes before the ceremony would begin, the door opened again.

Maddy expected Robin, and she got her—along with several others. Alice entered, and she'd chosen a pink bridesmaid dress. Maddy had simply texted out the colors, asked them all to walk in her bridal party, and said they could wear whatever they wanted.

Slacks, skirts, dresses, she didn't care. Each of them came in wearing something flowy and pastel, and

Maddy felt like she'd missed out on a shopping party. She probably had. She worked a lot compared to some of the ladies in the group, but she smiled at each of them.

"Wow," she said to Laurel about her peachy, barely-there dress. "That's stunning on you."

"I don't normally like dresses the same color as my skin," she said. "But this one called to me."

Eloise and Clara wore blue too, like Robin, and Jean, Kristen, and Alice wore pink. AJ and Kelli had chosen a lighter plum-purple. Julia wore apricot too, and as the last couple of women entered, Maddy felt like they'd pretty evenly distributed the colors.

"Tessa," she said warmly. "How are you, my friend?"

"I made it," she said breathlessly. "Nothing would've kept me away, though." She hugged Maddy too, and Maddy was glad she'd made it. Things in Tessa's life had not quite worked out the way she'd anticipated, and as a result, she hadn't been around the cove as often.

She smiled and faded out of the way, the way she normally did. She wore a lovely lavender dress that flowed all the way to the ground, her silver heels just peeking out of the bottom.

"Helen," Maddy said to the older woman. "Thank you so much for coming."

The white-haired woman smiled, her face wrinkly but absolutely gorgeous. "Of course, my dear. I can't miss out on this." She wore a blue dress that wasn't as long and flowy as the others, but she still somehow fit perfectly.

"Ladies," Robin called as Maddy stepped out of the hug with Helen. "Ladies!" She clapped her hands together three sharp times, and that finally got everyone to quiet down a little bit. Maddy stepped into her shoes, pulling the back strap up and over her ankle on her right foot.

"We need to get Maddy into her dress, and she needs to be ready in fifteen minutes." She clapped again. "I have it on good authority that Ben is already pacing in his suite, so let's not keep him—or the guests—waiting. Okay?"

Maddy stood and cocked her hip. "Do you think I can walk down the aisle in this?" She currently wore a slip and her wedding heels, and she grinned down to her toes which peeped through the ends of her shoes.

Robin blinked like Maddy would really walk down the aisle in her slip and heels. Alice pressed one palm to her heart, and then voices broke out. Chelsea unzipped the bag holding Maddy's wedding gown, and Maddy took Julia's hand to balance herself as she stepped into it.

Her daughter and daughter-in-law shimmied up over her hips, and the zipping and lacing commenced. Maddy stood still and let Alice weave one more piece of ribbon through her hair.

"Almost...done," Chelsea said, and she pulled one more string tight. She stepped back, and Robin stepped in front of Maddy.

"One look in the mirror. Then we have to go." She took Maddy by the shoulders and turned her. Maddy pulled in a breath as she took in herself in the reflective glass. Robin fell to her side, as did Chelsea and Bea. All of the other women crowded around her, and the moment paused as they all gazed at each other in the mirror.

A couple of people sniffled, and Maddy's own emotions stormed and marched and surged through her body. She linked one arm through Julia's and lifted the other out in front of her. Alice almost immediately covered it with hers, and then Clara lifted her hand and placed it on top of Alice's.

One by one, each woman reached and touched the arms or hands of the woman next to her, until they had formed a link, a bond, forged through contact. Maddy felt her heart knitting with the others too, and she sniffled as tears filled her eyes.

"Don't cry, Mom," Chelsea whispered from right over Maddy's shoulder. But she definitely wore water in her eyes.

Maddy took a big breath, which broke the moment. It didn't matter. She'd committed it to her memory, and she turned into Julia to hug her. Around she went, giving every woman a hug until Robin stood near the door, tapping her toe.

"It's time, right?" Maddy asked as she reached the woman.

"It is."

Maddy drew her into a hug and said, "You have already made today perfect. Thank you."

"He is going to tear me apart if you don't get out there soon," she whispered back. "Like right now."

Maddy giggled as she pulled back. "Okay. Where's my son?" Her parents had come to the wedding, but she hadn't wanted her father to walk her down the aisle. That felt so...twenty-five years ago, for a wedding she'd thought would initiate a marriage that would last forever.

"He's standing right outside the door." Chelsea smiled as she opened it, and she joined her brother in the hall. Kyle wore a black suit, his tie the color of bright blueberry skins, and his smile showing off the bright white, straight teeth his teenage braces had given him.

"Mom, you look amazing." He hugged her, then offered her his arm. She slipped her hand through the crook, then kissed her daughter's cheek as women started to flow out of the room in pairs. They'd all walk down the aisle ahead of her and Kyle, and then finally, Maddy would come face-to-face with her husband-to-be.

The hallway in front of them emptied, everyone taking a left at the end of it. Maddy's heart pounded faster and faster until her son said, "Ready, Mom?"

"Yes," she said, raising her chin. "Yes, I'm ready."

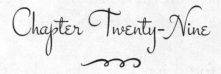

Chapter Twenty-Nine

Julia could absolutely not stop smiling. She carried her bouquet of flowers down the aisle, her eyes on Ben Downs —aka Captain Gorgeous—for the first few steps. She walked next to Laurel, as instructed by Robin, and the moment she caught a view of Liam, she couldn't look away.

He wore a gorgeous black suit, his smile as contagious as his kisses, and his hands clasped in front of him like a perfect gentleman. Julia went all the way to the altar, where Ben stood, and he took her flowers from her, the faintest of smiles touching his lips for the briefest of moments.

She turned and went to stand next to Liam, who received her with joy, those big hands sliding along her waist, and his lips landing on her temple. "Who's the most gorgeous woman in the world?" he murmured.

"Today, it's Maddy," she whispered back. The last of the wedding party arrived at Ben, and he stood there with Maddy's pink, blue, and white bouquet. "Here she comes."

Her best friend appeared at the end of the aisle, her son stepping with her, his smile as bright as hers. They moved slowly down the aisle, past the men and women Maddy worked with at The Glass Dolphin. Past all the women and their families who had so easily folded her and Maddy into their midst.

The crowd wasn't large by any means, but the hall held them all easily. The vines and flowers overflowed in the hall, the big stones comprising the walls and pillars complimenting the greenery perfectly. The air smelled of roses, and a faint seabreeze wafted down from the open windows near the double-high ceilings.

Maddy reached Julia, and though they'd already hugged, Julia reached out and squeezed her hand as she went by. Her son hugged her at the altar, then fell back to his wife's side. She took the bouquet from Ben as she made eyes at him, her head ducked. She looked utterly ravishing, from that beige dress that clung to her upper half and swelled along the top ridge of her hips.

The skirt flared slightly from there and fell down to

her feet in wave upon wave of what looked like structured feathers. Her left strap over her shoulder lifted up toward her ear, the lace stiff and starched and utterly unique. The train poofed and puffed down the back, and Maddy looked like she'd taken handfuls of clouds and fashioned a ballgown out of them.

Her hair had been curled and looped and pinned up in a seam along the back of her head. Silver and diamonds dangled from her earlobes and circled her neck. Every single piece of Madeleine Lancaster sat precisely in place.

She'd lived a lot of that life as a senator's wife, and Julia knew she loathed it. Ben stood there in his Coast Guard Captain dress uniform, which was pressed and starched and the most blinding white. It bore stripes and medals that Julia didn't understand, but the most drastic change for him came in the harsh lines of his jaw.

When he looked at Maddy, everything dissolved away. His tension. His irritation. His grumpy attitude. He obviously adored her, and the feeling she had only grew as he leaned toward her, kissed her just under her chin but high enough on her neck to stay respectable, his eyes falling closed.

Pure adoration, Julia thought, and she sigh-sagged into Liam at her side. She'd once thought she had a love like that, but it had leaked through her fingers while she wasn't paying attention.

She held her head high, the last dregs of resentment finally flowing out of her. She hadn't even realized she'd been hanging onto the hurt and the betrayal for this long, when she'd thought she'd moved past her ex-husband and started afresh.

The wedding ceremony began, and Maddy and Ben wanted something simple and elegant. Classy but not traditional. The pastor didn't go on for too long, and Maddy turned to Ben and said, "I have lived almost a half a century on this Earth." She smiled at him, her eyes never leaving his. "I have loved, lost, and learned. But standing here with you today, I know that the best is yet to come. I promise to cherish every moment we have together, to love you deeper with each passing day, and to hold you close in both joy and sorrow."

She nodded, her words simple but ringing with truth. Ben cleared his throat, the very first time Julia had ever seen the tough, stoic show any signs of nerves. "Today, I join my life with yours. Not as a beginning or an end, but as a continuation of the journey we have chosen to embark upon together. You have taught me that love doesn't have an expiration date and that it's never too late to find the person you're meant to share your life with. I vow to love, honor, and respect you for all the days of my life."

"Oh," Julia said before she could stop herself. That

was simply so sweet. Cheering brought her back to the present, and she found Ben kissing Maddy while they both laughed. They faced the crowd and lifted their joined hands, and Julia burst into tears.

She mobbed Maddy, feeling a sense of loss and unending happiness at the same time. Funny how the positive and the negative could co-exist inside her, but she'd learned that such things were a symptom of being human—and she wanted all the experiences she could get.

Later that night, Julia sighed as she finally stepped into her beach bungalow, at least four toes pinching from the shoes she'd been wearing for hours. A long sigh escaped from her mouth as she touched the light switch and yellow light bloomed to life in her house.

Behind her, Liam closed the door, and she turned to face him. "You didn't have to accompany me all the way home."

"I certainly did," he said. "What kind of cop would I be if I let a woman like you go home alone, on the last ferry to Sanctuary?" He gave her a sultry look that made her blood heat all the way through.

She stepped into him, pressing both palms against his chest. "I'm exhausted."

"It was a beautiful wedding, though."

"The best." She smiled up at him, warmth moving through her. "Do you have to go?"

Liam gazed down at her, his blue eyes sparking with lightning. She'd seen this heat in his eyes before, and she hadn't known what to think of it. She did now.

"I need to get out of this dress," she whispered when he simply watched her.

His right eyebrow went up, which made her smile. "Do you want my help with that?"

"I do," she said.

He leaned down and kissed her, and a rush of new energy filled Julia. She matched him stroke for stroke, wondering if she was going too fast. She didn't think so, as the quivering feeling in her stomach didn't hit her this time.

"Your son," she gasped as Liam's lips moved to her earlobe, and then trailed kisses down her neck.

"He's with my parents," Liam said gruffly. "I wasn't planning on getting him tonight, because I wasn't sure how late I'd be out."

Julia pulled away and laced both hands around the back of his neck. For whatever reason, she couldn't quite look him in the eye. "Then you don't have to go."

"That's up to you, Jules." He kneaded her closer, his lips seeking a spot somewhere against her skin but never settling.

She only had to say a couple of words to him to get him to stay, and she closed her eyes and imagined herself saying them. The electricity between them sizzled as his breath drifted over her shoulder, and Julia whispered, "Don't go."

Chapter Thirty

Eloise stood in the back of the crowded room, knowing full-well that the City Council meeting would go late. Aaron already looked exhausted, but he stayed alert through every question. He didn't have to answer very often, because everyone who'd gathered for this May meeting wanted to know if the tourist season was going to be as easy as it had been in past years.

Those business owners and others who made the bulk of their money in the summer months—like Eloise—had organized and congregated tonight. The Council had already listened to their presentation, and they'd been able to put in their proposal to hire more workers, employ more ferries and cars while the islands were full, and expand outdoor seating at restaurants.

The Mayor's Safer, Cleaner Beach Initiative would go

into full effect this year, and Aaron had been hiring as many men and women as he could. Even those without complete police training, simply to wear a special polo and be on the watch for dangerous situations. "Almost like a neighborhood watch," he'd told her.

Eloise was booked at Cliffside, and she had the employees she needed for now. But she wanted more Ride-Share vehicles in the pool, because her guests couldn't fly straight to Sanctuary. They had to come to Diamond, and then they needed rides from the airport to the ferry terminal, and then from there to the inn.

She'd even thought of hiring her own driver to go to the ferry terminal and back to the inn on Sanctuary, to eliminate waiting for one leg of the trip. She'd brought a car with her from Boston; she could get it to the inn, put a sticker with the inn's logo on the side, and then find someone to make the ten-minute drive.

She'd listened to the presentation. She heard the protestor's side, and the woman currently at the mic asked something that had already been answered. Eloise marveled at the patience of the City Council members, many of whom she knew and had known for a while now.

Aaron spoke highly of all of them except one woman, and even then, he didn't say anything negative.

Councilman Hayes answered the woman's question and then held up his hand. "Folks, we could go on and on about this. We have." He gestured to the Council members to his left and to his right. "We've been out in the community. We've seen all of the discussions online. We bring our own experiences and opinions to the Council."

The man only had hair on the sides and back of his head, but he wore a full beard. He'd obviously not been sleeping as much as he should, if the exhaustion lines around his eyes told Eloise anything. He cleared his throat, and she stood up straight. This was it. The moment everyone in the cove had been waiting to hear.

She feared there might be protests no matter which way the Council went. They'd already suspended the approval of building permits for the past couple of months, and they'd been discussing the growth and how to handle it for the past five months' of meetings.

"Five Island Cove is a premier vacation destination in the summer," Councilman Hayes said. "Many of us rely on this season to pay our bills and feed our families for the rest of the year. Our City Manager and the City Planner have been working hard to improve roads and walkways so there are ways for everyone to get around the cove as the population of it expands this summer." He looked down the line. "Shad?"

"We've pooled all the budget we have, and the roads will be done in two weeks," he said. "We do have the capability to have the tourists here, with the cars on the road. We have invested in two hundred new e-bikes for the walkways we've been improving over the past two or three years. That project is done too." He stood and leaned into the table in front of him, and Eloise smiled. Kelli sure did love Shad, and Eloise had never known him to handle things with anything but grace and professionalism.

"We can handle the traffic coming to the cove this year," he said. "Chief Sherman says we have the police force. We have the support staff, some of whom come to the cove to work only in the summer."

"Those people need housing," someone yelled from the crowd.

"They have housing," Councilman Hayes said. "It's almost eleven o'clock. It's time to vote."

Eloise stifled a yawn, the proceedings in front of her interesting enough to keep her awake long past her bedtime. She quickly pulled out her phone and sent a couple of messages as Councilman Hayes read through the proposal of seasonal expansion in the cove.

Almost done, she sent to Billie.

Full report tomorrow at lunch, she sent to her friends' group. Then she focused up front, ready for this to be behind them, at least for a little while.

Eloise pressed forward to get on the ferry, because she couldn't take the next one. She'd stand for the twenty-minute ride to Diamond if she had to, but she was going on this ferry. Everyone would be waiting at The Glass Dolphin as it was, because Eloise should've been on the previous ferry.

Sure enough, about the time the ferry pulled in at Diamond, her phone started chiming. *We're here*, Alice had said.

I put us in the Sands, Maddy said. *I'll be there in ten.*

Mom and I are five minutes out, Clara said.

The ferry is just pulling in, Eloise said. *I'm ten minutes out.*

They hadn't all gotten together for a Wednesday lunch in a while, because schedules made getting a dozen women together somewhat difficult. She silenced her phone as the others updated where they were and when they'd arrive. Eloise knew she'd be one of the last there, and she was used to running late and showing up last.

She had found more balance in the past six months, and the fact that she could attend a Wednesday lunch spoke of that. She smiled to herself and then up into the sunshine as the ferry bumped against the dock and got secured.

She'd parked at the terminal this morning, so she didn't have to wait for a ride. She'd have to find parking at the Dolphin, but she put the worry out of her mind. Her fingers squeezed around the steering wheel as she drove, mimicking the tension in her stomach.

Yes, they'd all be talking about the City Council's decision from last night. Only she and Aaron had attended it, though Matt Hymas had been there for the first hour or so. Of course, everyone could read about the whole meeting online, as Eloise had seen the headlines that morning as she rode the ferry to work.

Eloise knew she had more to say than just the fact that tourist season was upon them. While some companies and public service facilities were still hiring summer help, the cove would be burgeoning with people, and even those who'd rather keep the small-town feel of Five Island Cove agreed that tourist season was an outlier in their discussions.

When she finally entered the Sands, a conference room big enough to seat their party at an oblong table, with stunning views of the ocean beyond the floor-to-ceiling windows, Eloise found a couple of seats still empty.

Robin met her eyes, and she'd obviously saved a seat for Eloise. She even said, "El," and indicated the seat. Alice sat on the other side of the empty seat, and Eloise went around the end of the table to get to it.

Kristen stood, and Eloise paused to give her a hug. Conversations went on, and Eloise sank into the chair. "Who's still not here?"

"Heidi threw up right when Jean was leaving," Clara said from across the table. "She had to run back inside to change her. So she's running late."

"And Laurel just stepped out to take a call." Alice raised her glass to her lips. It looked like innocent water, and Eloise's throat suddenly turned dry.

Laurel ducked back into the room with the words, "Look who I found."

A harried-looking Jean entered too, her pudgy baby balanced on her hip. Julia swooped in and took the little girl, who shrieked and flapped her hands. Several of them laughed, and Eloise at least didn't feel like running.

She could even smile at Julia and Heidi as others assured Jean they hadn't started yet. Two waitresses entered, and Maddy clapped her hands. "Guys," she said. "They're ready to take our drink orders and appetizers."

"There's a paper here," Robin said, moving Eloise's plate out of the way. Most of the chatter stopped as orders got put in, and Eloise ordered the crab rangoons and a Diet Coke. "Easy on the ice, please."

With that done, everyone looked around at everyone else, most of the eyes coming to Eloise. She cleared her throat. "First, I think most of us are okay with the Council's decision to more thoughtfully plan out communities and building, put commercial restrictions in place, all while still allowing for our tourism industry to take center stage."

Murmurs of assent went through the group, with AJ particularly smiley about last night's meeting. "I really have no complaints," Alice said. "It's a few months of the year, and I recognize how important it is to a lot of people here."

"I agree," Kristen said, as Kelli nodded. They'd been the ones to vocally say they didn't want a lot of growth.

"Plus, our roads on Pearl are finally getting the attention they need," Kelli said. "And they've approved the build of a legit grocery down south for us." She beamed around at everyone, and Eloise did often forget that the outer islands had far less amenities. She lived on Diamond, the largest of the islands, and Sanctuary had been well-kept for years too.

"Oh," she added. "I displayed my commercial permit in the house on Seabreeze Shore. I do have permission to have a commercial business there, and I always have."

"Of course you have," AJ said as she covered Kelli's hand. "Our tee times are full through June and part of July already—at both locations. So Matt and I aren't going to complain."

The drinks arrived, and the conversation paused. Once Eloise had her cola, she took a long drink, enjoying the burn of the carbonation as it slid down her throat.

"Let's order," Alice said, and small side conversations broke out. Beside her, Robin said nothing, and Eloise leaned closer to her.

"When is Duke leaving?"

"A couple more weeks," she said, and Eloise could've imagined the way Robin's chin went up, but she didn't think she had. She lived the summer alone, and Eloise put her hand over Robin's and squeezed.

"We can have so many beach days and movie nights," she assured her.

Robin nodded, barely flicking her eyes over to Eloise. "Mandie's coming home for the summer this weekend. I'll survive."

"We always do, don't we?" Eloise asked.

Robin looked fully at her then. But the waitress reached her, and they had to put in their lunch orders. "I'll take the avocado garden salad," Eloise said. "With salmon, please."

Once the ladies had left to put in their orders, Eloise couldn't believe all the eyes had come straight back to her. At the same time, she'd told them all via text she had something to say, and they were obviously not going to settle into lunch until she did.

"Yes," she said. "Aaron and I were hoping for a baby this past winter. It's something I'd given up completely." Her eyes landed on AJ, then Kelli. "Until I saw you guys having babies. So I allowed myself to hope. I even got pregnant. But." She shook her head, that tight pinch in her chest flying into its familiar position right behind her lungs.

She'd practiced this speech, and it was still so, so hard to say. "My doctor says we can try again, but at my age..." She shook her head. "We've decided not to try. I have Billie and Grace, a very busy inn to run, the sexiest husband ever, and—"

Tears pressed into her eyes, and she couldn't hold them back. "All of you."

Robin reached over and squeezed her hand while Alice put her arm around her. She wouldn't know what she'd do without these good women at her side, even if she hadn't confided all in them quite the way they wanted her to.

"I love you guys," Eloise said.

"I do too," Robin said.

"I just have a problem with one thing you said," AJ said, and Eloise sucked in a tight breath as she looked over to AJ.

She wore a very serious line to her mouth, but her eyes sparkled. "*Your* husband is the sexiest husband ever?" She scoffed and that was when her smile broke onto her face. "Alice? You agree with that?"

"I mean...the Chief is pretty sexy, yeah."

Eloise's gaze flew to Alice. "Alice."

"What?" Alice laughed. "He's good-looking. Doesn't mean *I'm* attracted to him."

"I think I agree..." Laurel paused thoughtfully. "With AJ. I mean, have you guys seen Paul without his shirt off?"

"Okay, okay," Robin said, throwing her arms up, but even she grinned like a fool. She even got to her feet as others started claiming their husband was definitely the sexiest one in the bunch. She laughed as she said, "Maybe El spoke a little too firmly about Aaron. But that's no reason for us to argue."

She put her hand out in the middle of the table. "Come on. Hands in. Everyone stand up."

"We're not cheerleaders," Alice said, but she got to her feet and put her hand over Robin's.

"I liked this when we did it at Maddy's wedding," Julia said. She put her hand in too, and Eloise didn't need further invitation.

They all put their hands in, and once they'd done that, Robin said, "We've weathered storms and soaked in sunshine, argued and laughed, cried and celebrated together."

"We're more than friends," Alice said. "We're family."

"We're a constellation," Kelli said, her smile beautiful and bright. "Each of us is a star, shining brighter for the others."

Eloise's throat closed up, because they were so right. She wanted to add something to what they'd said, but her mind had turned blank.

"Here's to us," AJ said as she pulled her hand out of the group. She lifted her drink, and everyone hastened to do that. "To resilience, to love, and to the future."

"To family," Eloise said.

"To family," several of them chorused.

"No matter where life takes us," Robin said. "Let's

promise to always lift each other up, to always be each other's..." She looked over to Alice and grinned. "To always be each other's cheerleaders."

"Hear, hear," Eloise said, and she plunged her glass out into the middle. Clinking filled the room, as did laughter and other pledges of love and friendship. Eloise's heart warmed at every murmur of every voice in the room.

She looked down to Kristen, then to Jean. Over to Robin and Alice. Across to Clara, Laurel, and over to the curved corner where Julia and Maddy stood beaming.

Finally, down to Kelli and AJ, both leaning in to reach the core of the table. She realized they each carried some part of the core of this friendship, even her, and she tucked that knowledge away, ready to call on it whenever she might need to.

* * *

Read on for the first couple chapters of **THE BICYCLE BOOK CLUB, the next book in the Five Island Cove Friendship Saga.**

Preorder it by scanning this code with your phone!

Sneak Peek — The Bicycle Book Club Chapter One:

Tessa Simmons wished she could smile as the express ferry from Nantucket pulled up to the northwest dock on Diamond Island. She lived on Sanctuary, so she'd still have another boat ride to make before she could return home.

But the express ferry only went to Diamond Island, and Tessa had to work today anyway. She'd grab lunch somewhere—alone—and then walk herself over to the library.

She finally turned her face toward the early summer sunshine, a tickle of a smile touching her lips. She loved the island life far more than living in New Jersey, but she didn't want to stay on Nantucket.

Rather, she couldn't.

The brief life she'd led there had been borne in hope, but quickly marred by mystery and death. Memories of the horrors she'd lived through—waking up from a drugged state, the sound of gunshots, the red-blue of police lights... She suddenly felt cold despite the warm temperatures and the frilly sunshine.

Just as quickly as she remembered, the images, the sights, the sounds, they all faded. Tessa contained them behind a wall in her mind, the way her therapist had been teaching her.

A sigh filled her lungs and leaked out of her mouth as the ferry docked and people moved toward the steps that would lead them to dry land. As if on auto-pilot, Tessa's legs moved too, and she joined the small swell of people who'd come to Five Island Cove from Diamond Island today.

Tessa didn't think many of them were tourists. Most likely, they were like her. They had business on Nantucket, but they'd come home. Or, they had business here, and would return to Nantucket and their homes later that day.

A particular weariness accompanied her as she disembarked and faced the row of shops that lined the street opposite the ferry station. She could get something to eat there, as she had many times before. She adored seafood, and the cove had no shortage of it.

Sometimes, Tessa just wanted a burger, or maybe a salad, but today, she honestly didn't know what she wanted to eat. Her stomach felt hollow, and she knew she had to have a little something before she started her shift at the library.

She only worked a few days a week, but that meant the shifts were longer, and she'd be closing tonight.

Her fingers tightened around the strap of her purse, which she wore across her body, as she thought about getting out her phone and texting someone to ask if they wanted to eat lunch with her.

She hadn't quite integrated herself into the friendships here in the cove the way Maddy had, but everyone still welcomed Tessa with open arms. To anything she could get to, that was.

"You need to get to more," she muttered to herself, bypassing the taco truck and deciding then and there to get a ride downtown. She'd be closer to the library, and she could spend the next couple of hours in the sunshine, sipping tea and enjoying a slow, carefree meal at her favorite bistro here in the cove.

As she backtracked to join the RideShare line, which only had a couple of people waiting, Tessa did text Maddy. *I'm on Diamond for the next few days. Lunch?*

The power blonde she'd met in Nantucket had gotten married about a month ago, and Tessa had been there in her flowing lavender gown, which now hung in her boyfriend's closet in Nantucket.

The closet Abraham Sanders was nowhere near cleaning out, packing up, and moving here. He'd claimed to be passing his deli on Nantucket to his son once fall came, then the New Year, but that had been almost six months ago, and Abe still went into his meat shop every day.

Tessa had been splitting her time between working at the library here in the cove, riding the ferry back to Nantucket, and walking the beaches there while she waited for Abe to finish up working.

She had a house there, but Tessa couldn't stay in it. Her sister lived in Nantucket too, but Tessa had a love-hate relationship with her. She loved her, because they had the same blood flowing in their veins. But Tessa didn't particularly love spending time with Janey.

As she sank into the back seat of the sedan which had just pulled up to the curb, Tessa said, "The Harbor Bistro, please."

"You got it." The man smiled at her in the rear-view mirror, and Tessa guessed his age to be close to hers. She leaned back and closed her eyes, wondering what to do about Abe.

They'd been doing for almost two years now. Two years, and while she loved him, and he'd said he loved her, actions always spoke louder than words.

He had not moved here, despite claiming to want to be here with her full-time. She'd started going to Nantucket more and more, and he hadn't been to the cove in a couple of months now.

Maybe it's over, she thought. At the very least, they were horribly stalled, and one of them would have to say or do something to get things moving again. Tessa wasn't sure if she wanted to be that person or not.

Thoughts of AvaJane Hymas ran through her mind. She didn't know the woman all that well, but what she did know was almost enough. She'd waited and waited for men who never truly wanted her.

Was Tessa doing the same thing?

"Ma'am," the man said, and she jerked her eyes open.

"Sorry," she said a bit groggily. "I think I fell asleep." A hint of embarrassment tugged through her, and Tessa hastened to get her purse and get out of the car.

"Are you okay?" the man asked, and Tessa paused at the question. He twisted and looked at her, concern in his blue eyes.

"Do I not look okay?"

"I don't know," he said. "It's just a...feeling I have. I see a lot of people with the driving." A smile flickered across his face, there for a moment, and then gone.

Tessa wished she knew what her face looked like or what vibe she gave off to alert someone like him that she wasn't okay. "I'm okay," she said as firmly as she could, and she tapped her card to the RideShare pad to pay for her ride. "Thank you."

"Sure thing," he said. "Enjoy your lunch." He re-positioned his ball cap on his head as the pad beeped. Tessa got out of the car and slammed the door, then stood on the sidewalk and watched it drive away.

Seconds seemed to slow, and she wasn't even sure why. Her phone beeped and buzzed, and she startled back to the present. Back to reality. She looked at her phone and found Maddy had returned her text.

Lunch sounds amazing! Tomorrow? Should I invite Julia?

If you can tear her away from Liam, Tessa said, smiling to her screen. She lifted her face, feeling better with plans with her friends. That alone gave her enough courage and stamina to face the bistro, knowing she'd be dining alone.

"Tessa?"

She turned away from the shelf where she'd just inserted a hardcover book to find her boss, Bonnie, standing there. "Hey, Bonnie."

"Do you have a minute?" She nodded back toward the offices and check-out desk in the small library. Bonnie was at least fifteen years younger than Tessa, and she'd been hired as the new library director only two months ago.

Tessa liked her a lot, because she had good ideas for the small island community library, and she was willing to work to get the programs, the funding, and the concepts in her head out into the public.

"Sure." Tessa took the few books she had in her arms with her as she walked down the aisle between bookshelves behind Bonnie. She'd worked or volunteered in a library for many years, and there was nowhere she'd rather be than around books, books, and more books—except maybe flowers, as Tessa adored gardening too.

Bonnie led her into her office, which was lined with books, and held carts of books, and had stacks of books on her desk. "Close the door, would you?"

Tessa did, and she balanced her few books on her lap as she took the only chair across from Bonnie. The room smelled like oranges, and Tessa wasn't at all surprised to watch a gray cat leap lightly onto the librarian's desk and meow.

"Not now, Dusky," Bonnie said briskly. She'd inherited the cat with the library, as it lived here. The first librarian who showed up in the morning fed her, and there were no less than three beds for the feline around the library, all of them on top of bookshelves, so the cat could look down condescendingly on all the patrons who dared to look for something to read.

Dusky meowed again, then sat down and looked at Tessa. She smiled at the cat, as she owned two of her own. She'd adopted them from the local shelter here, and her neighbor took care of them while she went to Nantucket.

"All right." Bonnie sighed like an older woman and folded her arms in front of her. She looked past the cat and all the books and beamed at Tessa. "We need an assistant library director to help run all the programs starting up this summer."

Tessa's heart began to pound. An assistant library director was a full-time position. She wouldn't be resolving books from the return cart, and she'd be expected to work every day.

"I want to offer it to you," Bonnie said, her smile growing. "I think you're perfect for it, because we have programs I want to get off the ground for men and women your age. It's not just summer reading for kids and teens anymore."

"I know." The words scratched on the way out of Tessa's mouth. She attended all staff meetings, and she'd heard and seen all of Bonnie's ideas. She'd voted on some of them, and she liked how the director didn't take offense when her ideas got shot down.

She simply moved onto the next one, or she went back to the drawing board to refine the idea before she brought it up again.

"The Book Club," Tessa said, her voice only slightly stronger.

"For young moms, moms of teens, and those beyond."

Tessa smiled, because she knew she was in the "those

beyond" category, and no one wanted to label people her age as *old*. Bonnie had never used the word, and she gently corrected anyone who said anything like, "older generation."

The truth was, Tessa *was* part of the older generation who didn't think of the library when it came to their hobbies or how to spend their afternoons. Tessa worked here, so it was completely different for her.

"It's a full-time position," Bonnie said, plucking a yellow file folder from somewhere on the other side of the stack of books between her and the library director. "Monday through Friday, with some Saturday work. I want you to work on all of our adult programming, including the Book Clubs, because you're perfect for it. Everyone here respects you, and—"

She stopped when Tessa held up her hand. "You don't have to flatter me." She smiled at Bonnie. "I'm honored that you thought of me."

Bonnie's eyebrows went up, and she casually pushed her strawberry blonde hair over her shoulder. "But?"

Tessa paused, because she didn't know what came behind that word. If she lived here full-time, she could go to lunch with her friends any time she wanted. She could become better friends with Robin, Alice, and Eloise. Heck, she might even learn the whole story behind AJ, Kelli, Jean, and Clara's lives.

She wanted relationship with those women, but she'd

been choosing Abe over and over...when he hadn't been choosing her.

Her throat narrowed, the walls of it nearly sticking together as she weighed her options in mere nanoseconds. The human mind was so amazing, and Tessa blinked, the answer to this job offer right in front of her.

"I'd be honored," she said, her own smile finally reaching way down deep inside her and touching a hidden spot of happiness.

Bonnie squealed and clapped her hands together. "Perfect. I still want you to take this." She got to her feet and rounded the desk. "It goes over your salary and your benefits. Ask me or the city lawyer any questions. I had to work hard to get this position."

She grinned and ran the last few steps to Tessa. "I'm so happy you said yes."

Tessa hugged Bonnie back, a bit awkwardly because she still sat and Bonnie stood. She even managed to laugh a little. She stood and took the yellow folder from her boss, looking at it with eyes that felt like they could see for the first time.

"Thank you," she said again.

"If you accept everything," Bonnie said. "You could start as early as June first."

"June first," Tessa echoed. "That's next week."

"Yes," Bonnie said. "And I'd love to sit down with you as soon as possible to talk about a focus group for your age group, to find out what would get them to utilize the library more."

"My age," Tessa said, her mind starting to work again. "I know just the women."

Bonnie hadn't stopped grinning, but her smile sure seemed to somehow get brighter and bigger. "I knew you would."

Tessa looked up from the folder, so much to suddenly do before then.

And the top item on her list: Talk to Abe and find out if he was ever going to leave Nantucket...or if things between them should just be done.

Sneak Peek — The Bicycle Book Club Chapter Two:

Robin Grover took the box Arthur handed her and turned. Mandie stood there, still talking, and Robin waited for her daughter.

"I need more than just a few hours in the soda shop," Mandie said. "Have you heard of any other part-time jobs?" She'd been home from college for about a month now, and the job hunt had not been going well. "Or do you have anything for me to do?"

Mandie took her box from Arthur and joined Robin on the sidewalk. Clara and Scott had found a house they could afford to buy, and they'd moved on it quickly. Thus, they were moving again today. Thankfully, they'd already made the big move from Vermont to the cove last year, and Clara had really pared down the things they owned.

"I'm sure I could have you do a few things," Robin

mused, though she didn't want to employ her daughter. Mandie thrived when on her own, and Robin liked being home alone in her office.

Of course, school would be out for the summer in a couple of weeks, and then her youngest daughter would be home too. Jamie was fifteen this year, and Robin thought a job would be beneficial for her too.

"I can help you look," Robin said.

"Look for what?" Alice asked as she passed them going the opposite way. Her face held a flush from the exertion of carrying boxes up and down steps, as Scott and Clara's new house had ten of them just going up to the porch.

Robin could admit she'd been trying to take boxes and items that would then go on the main level, so she didn't have to climb another flight of stairs to the second floor. Right now, her box had been labeled *kitchen*, and a few items clanged around in there to suggest as much.

"A job," Mandie said. "Charlie got so lucky at the golf course."

Robin only caught the whiff of Alice's smile as they passed. Her twins had split themselves in half for the first time in their lives, with Charlie returning to the cove to work for the summer, and Ginny staying in New York City.

She was living with her father, something that Robin knew troubled Alice greatly. They'd talked about it a couple of times, but Robin always let her best friend bring it up.

She suspected that Charlie's decision to come back to the cove had a lot to do with her daughter, though Mandie had not indicated that they were any more serious in their relationship now than they'd been during the school year.

"I've got to find something soon," Mandie said, her breathing turning to panting as they ascended the steps. "I hate looking for a job."

"You need a job?" Tessa Simmons asked from the top of the steps.

Robin took the last two and paused on the porch, mostly to hear what Tessa had to say but also to catch her breath. Moving really was the worst activity on the planet —maybe right behind looking for a job.

"I'm working at Soda Spectacular," Mandie said, moving further onto the porch and out of the way of others entering and leaving the house. "But it's only about twenty hours per week—and that's with the extra shifts I pick up."

Tessa had the luxury of standing in the shade without a heavy, bulky box in her arms, and she smiled prettily. "I wanted to ask you about doing a focus group at the library, Robin," she said. "Maybe you should come too, Mandie. I have a few things I need to work out, but I'm anticipating needing to hire more people."

"Full-time?" Mandie asked.

Matt came out onto the porch too, and Robin slid her box into his arms, relief filling her tired limbs. The first pod had gone quickly, but she felt like the things in this second packing pod would never end.

"No," Tessa said, shaking her head. "It would be part-time."

"That's perfect," Robin said. "You don't need full-time."

"Two part-time jobs is what I want." Mandie wore such hope in her eyes. "I'll only be here through the end of summer."

"This is for our Summer Reading programs," Tessa said, her face brightening with every word. Her dark eyes sparkled, and Robin had seen a look like this before. Maybe not on Tessa's face, as she was still very new to their friend group.

Robin watched her for a moment, sensing something. "You have news," she said slowly.

"Yes," Tessa said. "I was going to wait until the pods were empty, because Maddy said she had an announcement to make then too."

Robin looked down the steps to the stream of people still coming into the house with boxes and then going back for more. Mandie passed her box to Shad as Kelli joined them, her baby in her arms.

Robin smiled at her and Daphne, wanting to reach for

the infant. She didn't, because she'd come to work, and Kelli shouldn't be lugging heavy items up and down steps.

Maddy and Julia came outside, chatting back and forth, but they quieted as they joined the group. "What's happening over here?"

"Nothing," Robin said quickly, exchanging a glance with Tessa.

"I just have some news too," Tessa said, her voice much quieter than Robin's. "I thought, when the dough-nuts come, and the moving-in is finished, I'd tell every-one." She nodded at Maddy. "Like you will."

"Am I missing something?" Alice asked as she reached the porch, two plastic bins stacked on top of one another in her arms.

"No," Robin said, taking Mandie by the elbow. "We'll wait until announcements." She steered her daughter toward the steps. "Go on. There's more to bring in."

Mandie glared at her, but Robin was used to that look on her face. She complied and went back to the pod, where Arthur handed them each another box to carry in. Robin went back and forth three more times before she ran out of things to carry.

Reuben, Shad, and Aaron wrestled with an enormous dresser, finally getting it to submit and enter the house. They still had tons of work to do to get unpacked enough to live in the house—get beds set up, put dishes in cupboards, and fill the fridge with something to eat—but

Robin stood in the shade and accepted the water bottle Eloise handed to her.

"Doughnuts are here," Clara called from the street, and that caused a commotion. She carried a long, wide white box that probably had fifty doughnuts in it, and Aaron's girls cheered as she neared.

"Let's go inside," she said. "The AC works, and we can get the doors closed and see if we can't cool off."

"Let me take that," Matt said, relieving Kristen of the pastry box.

One more trip up the steps, and then Robin entered the house and let someone else close the door behind them. Scott and Clara had bought an older home, southern corner of Diamond Island. It was two levels, with a bedroom and a bathroom on each one.

The kitchen sat straight back through a living room that held a side-den off to the right. Robin would use it for an office, as she ran her wedding planning business from home, but she had no idea what Clara and Scott would do with it.

Boxes had been piled there. And in the living room. And in the kitchen.

Still, Matt found enough space for the doughnuts, and the kids weren't the only ones to descend on the box and get a treat. They'd all come to help with the move this morning, and Robin smiled at Jamie as she came to her side.

"Were you helping out in here?"

"We got Lena's bed set up," she said as she gathered her hair off her neck and held it in a ponytail. She let it drop, her smile finally appearing.

Others had started to chat as they ate, but Robin really wanted to know what the news was. She'd kissed her husband good-bye for the summer fishing season in Alaska only two days ago, and she wanted a weekend at home to normalize herself back to being a single mom—at least for a few months until Duke returned.

"All right," Eloise said, which sent a bolt of surprise through Robin. El wasn't usually the one to quiet everyone and start spilling secrets. Today, however, she beamed at Aaron and the girls and lifted one hand until the conversations waned.

"We want to invite everyone to a beach bonfire at our place," El said. "Next Sunday."

"Tomorrow?" AJ asked from somewhere in the recesses of the room. A small dining room added to the kitchen, with another pass-through to a sunroom at the back of the house.

"No," El said. "Next Sunday."

"Tomorrow *is* the next Sunday," AJ said.

"Then the next one," El said, and she turned to look at Robin, her expression conveying all of her annoyance. Robin wanted to burst out laughing, but she thankfully controlled herself.

Alice twittered a little and then said, "We'll be there. Well, maybe not Charlie. I'll check with him." He worked full-time at the golf course, and that included weekends. According to Mandie, he made good tips when he worked with patrons, and he liked being outside when he didn't.

"We are having a tasting menu at The Glass Dolphin," Maddy said next. "It's a private event, and we're asking those who come to provide feedback for a possible new menu item."

"I want to come," Robin said immediately. Her mouth watered right now over the food at The Glass Dolphin, and lately, it had become *the* place they met for lunch.

"Me too," Julia said, as did a few others.

Maddy beamed at them. "I knew you would. I'll text out the time and date, and you can let me know if it works for you."

"That kind of goes with my news," Tessa said, and all eyes shifted to her, Robin's included. The room seemed to grow even quieter simply to match the demeanor of the person speaking.

Tessa reminded Robin of a mix between Kelli and Eloise. She had dark hair and eyes, and she thought before she spoke. But she also possessed a fierce strength swimming just below the surface.

"I took a promotion at work," she said. "You're looking at the new assistant library director."

"Oh, that's wonderful," Kristen said, her delight genuine as it slid across her face.

"I'm going to be in charge of the adult programming," Tessa said as Julia reached over and squeezed her hand. "I want to do a focus group in the next week or so, and then I'll be able to put a few things together, and...get started."

"What does 'adult programming' mean?" Alice asked. She glanced around the group like it might be something nefarious. "Like...?"

"Programs for adults," Tessa said.

"Duh," Clara added, and the two of them laughed lightly together. They'd also worked on a dilapidated inn together for a few months last year, and their smiles made Robin happy.

"Our new library director wants more adult programming," Clara said. "For those in their twenties, thirties, and beyond."

"Like...knitting classes?" Kelli asked.

"Sure," Tessa said. "I was thinking of crafting as something we could do. We already have the Cove Crocheters use our multi-purpose room on Thursdays. It's kind of that idea, but it's more like an eight-week program that focuses on something. It starts and stops. Then we have something else come up."

"So like, similar to the rec center," El said.

"Yeah," Tessa said. "But specific to books. To reading. To reading more books." She smiled, and her eyes landed on Robin. "I have some ideas I'd love to run by specific groups of people. So Bonnie—she's the director—and I have been setting up focus groups to come into the library next week and provide some feedback."

"I'd love to do that too," Robin said, knowing that sometimes people wanted someone else to speak up before they would. Not everyone wanted to be first, or out in the spotlight.

"I'd love that too," AJ said as she came forward. "I'd especially love to see something for moms."

"We have programming for children," Tessa said. "That's what you'd bring Asher to." She glanced over to Robin and Jamie, and then El and her girls. "And lots of stuff for teens."

"But that's a day for Asher," AJ said. "I'm talking something for moms—like how to choose books for your kids, or what kinds of books to read to them."

Tessa focused on her again. "I'd love it if you came to the focus group for that." She pulled out her phone. "Bonnie is running the one for parents of teens and children. I think that would be the best one for you."

AJ said nothing, but her jaw jumped a little.

"You can come to any of the adult ones too." Tessa flashed her a smile. "I'm running three next week. One for men and women in their twenties."

"I'm out," Aaron said, and a few people chuckled or laughed.

"Thirty to forty-five," Tessa said next. "And then anyone older than that."

As Robin looked around the room, the only people who wouldn't be in the "anyone older than that" category would be Laurel and Paul. Maybe Jean, though Reuben had definitely turned forty-five already.

Tessa looked at Mandie. "And I'd love it if you'd come to the single young adult one. Bonnie and I are running it together."

"If I can, I will," Mandie said.

"What are you thinking?" Robin asked, still watching Tessa. The woman had secrets, and she kept them *close*.

"I'm in charge of all the Book Clubs," Tessa said. "And I'd love to see our younger population working with our older one."

"You know what we need?" El asked. "A small library branch on all the islands."

Tessa swung her attention to her. "That's one of our ideas." She swallowed as she took in the tall, dark, Chief of Police next to Eloise—her husband. "It might require some additional funding and permits, though, so Bonnie hasn't done much with it...yet."

"Programs for dads might be good," Paul said, to which Aaron nodded.

Tessa started thumbing into her phone, her face turning more and more crimson by the moment.

"Research skills," Alice said. "You would not believe what people can't do."

Robin's stomach growled, and she decided that was the perfect impetus to get Tessa out of this situation she'd somehow fallen into. "All right," she said as she stepped in front of the poor woman. "She's having focus group meetings, you guys. This isn't the time to fire all of your suggestions at her."

She gave Alice a pointed look, but her friend only smiled. She surveyed the small area where they'd all crammed. "Okay, let's get this house livable."

"Be sure to RSVP to our beach bonfire," El called. "You can just do it on the group text, with how many to expect."

"We can all bring something," Jean said, but El shook her head.

"This one is on us. Our start-to-the-summer beach day." She looked so pleased about it, and Robin would gladly show up with her favorite drinks, sunscreen, and a chair to sit in and let someone else do all the work. She had no problem with that.

"Let me know about the tasting," Maddy said. "Group text is fine too."

"And I'll text out the dates for the focus groups," Tessa said, her eyes still glued to her phone.

"Perfect," Robin said. "Now, Clara. Scott." She

looked at both of them." Boss us around and put us to work."

* * *

Yay! More Five Island Cove friend-ships! Another summer in the cove, with beaches and sunshine and BOOKS!

I can't wait to see what happens with everyone in the next volume in the Five Island Cove romantic women's fiction series, THE BICYCLE BOOK CLUB.

You can preorder the ebook now from my Book Shop for an exclusive, early release date of March 1, 2024! Just scan this code with your phone to preorder now.

Books in the Five Island Cove series

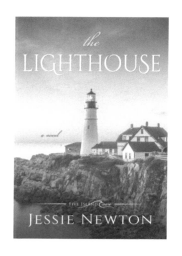

The Lighthouse, Book 1: As these 5 best friends work together to find the truth, they learn to let go of what doesn't matter and cling to what does: faith, family, and most of all, friendship.

Secrets, safety, and sisterhood...it all happens at the lighthouse on Five Island Cove.

The Summer Sand Pact, Book 2: These five best friends made a Summer Sand Pact as teens and have only kept it once or twice— until they reunite decades later and renew their agreement to meet in Five Island Cove every summer.

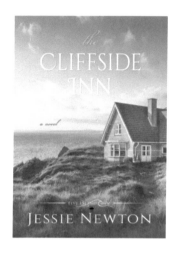

The Cliffside Inn, Book 3:
Spend another month in Five Island Cove and experience an amazing adventure between five best friends, the challenges they face, the secrets threatening to come between them, and their undying support of each other.

Christmas at the Cove, Book 4:
Secrets are never discovered during the holidays, right? That's what these five best friends are banking on as they gather once again to Five Island Cove for what they hope will be a Christmas to remember.

Books in the Five Island Cove series

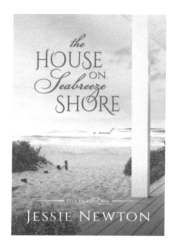

The House on Seabreeze Shore, Book 5: Your next trip to Five Island Cove...this time to face a fresh future and leave all the secrets and fears in the past. Join best friends, old and new, as they learn about themselves, strengthen their bonds of friendship, and learn what it truly means to thrive.

Four Weddings and a Baby, Book 6: When disaster strikes, whose wedding will be postponed? Whose dreams will be underwater?

And there's a baby coming too... Best friends, old and new, must learn to work together to clean up after a natural disaster that leaves bouquets and altars, bassinets and baby blankets, in a soggy heap.

Books in the Five Island Cove series

The Seafaring Girls, Book 7:
Journey to Five Island Cove for a roaring good time with friends old and new, their sons and daughters, and all their new husbands as they navigate the heartaches and celebrations of life and love.

But when someone returns to the Cove that no one ever expected to see again, old wounds open just as they'd started to heal. This group of women will be tested again, both on land and at sea, just as they once were as teens.

Rebuilding Friendship Inn, Book 8:
Clara Tanner has lost it all. Her husband is accused in one of the biggest heists on the East Coast, and she relocates her family to Five Island Cove–the hometown she hates.

Clara needs all of their help and support in order to rebuild Friendship Inn, and as all the women pitch in, there's so much more getting fixed up, put in place, and restored.

Then a single phone call changes everything.

Will these women in Five Island Cove rally around one another as they've been doing? Or will this finally be the thing that breaks them?

Books in the Five Island Cove series

The Glass Dolphin, Book 9: With new friends in Five Island Cove, has the group grown too big? Is there room for all the different personalities, their problems, and their expanding population?

The Bicycle Book Club, Book 10: Summer is upon Five Island Cove, and that means beach days with friends and family, an explosion of tourism, and summer reading programs! When Tessa decides to look into the past to help shape the future, what she finds in the Five Island Cove library archives could bring them closer together...or splinter them forever.

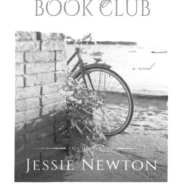

Books in the Nantucket Point series

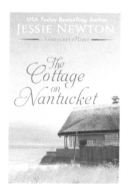

The Cottage on Nantucket, Book 1: When two sisters arrive at the cottage on Nantucket after their mother's death, they begin down a road filled with the ghosts of their past. And when Tessa finds a final letter addressed only to her in a locked desk drawer, the two sisters will uncover secret after secret that exposes them to danger at their Nantucket cottage.

The Lighthouse Inn, Book 2: The Nantucket Historical Society pairs two women together to begin running a defunct inn, not knowing that they're bitter enemies. When they come face-to-face, Julia and Madelynne are horrified and dumbstruck—and bound together by their future commitment and their obstacles in their pasts...

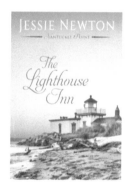

Books in the Nantucket Point series

The Seashell Promise, Book 3: When two sisters arrive at the cottage on Nantucket after their mother's death, they begin down a road filled with the ghosts of their past. And when Tessa finds a final letter addressed only to her in a locked desk drawer, the two sisters will uncover secret after secret that exposes them to danger at their Nantucket cottage.

About Jessie

Jessie Newton is a saleswoman during the day and escapes into romance and women's fiction in the evening, usually with a cat and a cup of tea nearby. She is a Top 30 KU All-Star Author and a USA Today Bestselling Author. She also writes as Elana Johnson and Liz Isaacson as well, with almost 200 books to all of her names. Find out more at www.feelgoodfictionbooks.com.

Made in United States
Troutdale, OR
05/19/2024

19977783R00257